C000059796

Vegetables from Small Gardens

by the same author

SALADS THE YEAR ROUND
(Hamlyn)

THE VEGETABLE GARDEN DISPLAYED
(1981 revision) (Royal Horticultural Society)

SAINSBURY'S HOMEBASE GUIDE TO VEGETABLE
GARDENING
(Sainsbury)

THE OBSERVER GOOD GARDENING GUIDE
(Vegetable section) (Webb & Bower)

THE SALAD GARDEN
(Frances Lincoln/Windward)

VEGETABLES FROM SMALL GARDENS

A Guide to Intensive Cultivation

JOY LARKCOM
with illustrations by Elizabeth Winson

faber and faber

LONDON · BOSTON

First published in 1976
by Faber and Faber Limited
3 Queen Square London WC1N 3AU
Second edition 1986

Filmset by Wilmaset
Birkenhead Merseyside
Printed in Great Britain by
Redwood Burn Limited
Trowbridge Wiltshire
All rights reserved

British Library Cataloguing in Publication Data

Larkcom, Joy
Vegetables from small gardens
1. Vegetable gardening
I. Title
635   SB322
ISBN 0–571–13664–8

Library of Congress Cataloging in Publication Data

Larkcom, Joy
Vegetables from small gardens
1. Vegetable gardening.   2. Vegetable gardening—
Great Britain.   I. Title.
SB322.L29   1986   635′.0941   85–20433
ISBN 0–571–13664–8 (pbk.)

To Brendan and Kirsten

On the merits of small gardens . . .
'As for quantity of Plot of ground to make a Suitable Garden . . .
let me caution all, not to undertake more than can be well looked
after with hands enough for the well management of things in their
proper season; for a small Plot of ground well ordered, turns to
greater advantage than a large one neglected . . . for if the weeds
get the mastery for want of hands to rid them, it will not be easie
to root them out . . . Also watering a large garden in droughty
weather requires much Time and Pains . . .'

Leonard Meager, *The New Art of Gardening*, 1697

Contents

Illustrations

Metrication: Measures are given in metric, with approximate English measurements in brackets. (Where conversions are not strictly consistent, they will be found accurate enough for all practical purposes.)

Acknowledgements

A great many people have helped, one way or another, with the writing of this book. On the technical side, I would particularly like to thank the staff of the National Institute of Agricultural Botany, who spent much time discussing modern methods of vegetable production; the Camland Advisory Service and the Soil Association, for advice on soil; Mary Alexander, for allowing me to pick her brains on herbs, and J. L. H. Chase for permission to use his suggestions for strip cropping, originally published in his book *Cloche Gardening*.

I would also like to thank the following seed firms who generously sent me samples of vegetable seed: Samuel Dobie & Son, S. E. Marshall & Co., Suttons Seeds Ltd, Thompson & Morgan (Ipswich) Ltd, and W. J. Unwin. I am especially grateful to Mr Angus Barber, Chairman of Dobies, and Mr S. E. Marshall, for many helpful ideas on the most suitable cultivars and techniques for small gardens.

A number of firms allowed me to try out their products, and I would like to record my thanks to the following: A & D Radio (windmill bird scarer), Alexpeat (compost bags), Crittall-Hope (Luminair garden frame), Fisons (Gro-bags and fertilisers), Flexipane (cloches), Grebon (Alginure compost activator), ICI (Novolux cloches and polythene tunnels), LBS Polythene (giant polythene tunnel), Lindsey & Kesteven (Arthur Bowers compost), Marmax (cloches), Maxicrop (fertiliser), Ken Muir (tower pots), North Star Manufacturing (Window-Box cloche), pBi (Baby Bio composts), Permoid (collapsible frame), Phostrogen (fertiliser), PRM Horticultural (Fertile fertiliser), Robinsons (cloches), W. Rumsey (Rumsey clips), and Tyler Boat Company (glass fibre cloches).

In the course of writing the book I visited many small gardens in various parts of the country, and I would like to convey my warmest thanks to the many people involved in these trips. I was very touched by the trouble taken by complete strangers to show me around, to find interesting gardens in their areas, and to share their ideas and experience. My apologies to those who, on my behalf, were drenched with rain, had their Sunday lunches at tea time or missed them altogether, were overtaken by nightfall and were late for their own parties! Their enthusiasm and helpfulness were much appreciated. It is impossible to mention everybody by name, but my particular thanks to Mr J. Bennett, Mandy and Roger Brown, Mrs Cynthia Broughton-Legh, Mr E. Cooper, Mrs Merrie Cave, Mr H. F. Ellis, Mr Trevor Jones, Mr J. Parkhurst, Mrs Vivien Quick, Mr N. Wainwright and Michael Winson.

I would also like to thank the late Alfred Gower, a wise and skilful gardener of the 'old school' for the knowledge he passed on to me and the kindness he and his wife showed me when I was a young student in his charge. If he is now in charge of the heavenly kitchen garden, they are eating well up there!

And now a few domestic thank-yous. Writing a book with a young family has its problems, and without friends who looked after the children or had the family to stay for weekends so that I could have precious hours of uninterrupted peace, the deadline would never have been met. My special thanks to Kim and Tony Edwards, Ann Lally, and Joanna Jellinek. But most of all, thanks to my husband Don, for doing so much more than his share of the domestic chores, for looking after the children whenever he could, and for being so understanding and patient.

Finally, thank you to the magazine *Garden News*, for help in several ways; to my parents and to Margaret Hewitt, Tony Gaskin, Ann Bonar, Mary Dymond and many others for helpful suggestions; to Nancy Tripp, for typing the manuscript with such willingness; to Elizabeth Winson, for the infinite trouble she took to make the illustrations clear and accurate; to Allan Jackson, for reading through the manuscript, gently suggesting improvements, and for giving me so much advice and encouragement and to the publishers, for all their work behind the scenes.

For the revised edition, thank you to Frances Lincoln Ltd. for permission to use material on potato barrels from *The Contained Garden*, to Alan Titchmarsh for allowing me to add his patented 'spoon tool' for cleaning spades, to 'Economy Tips', and to George Beaven of Hurst Seeds for invaluable help in updating the text and the seed varieties.

Montrose Farm   Joy Larkcom
Hepworth
Diss
Norfolk

Introduction to the Revised Edition

It seems odd to some people that a vegetable book can need to be updated. But in the twentieth century not even the staid world of vegetables is immune from change. There are three main reasons for updating this book. First, in the ten years since it was written there has been a great deal of research into commercial vegetable growing, often with a bearing on amateur gardening. A lot of the guesswork and hunches have been removed. We now *know* precisely how spacing can be varied to get the size of vegetable we want, the stage in a plant's growth when it really pays to water and so on. Much of this work has been brought together in two books written by staff of the National Vegetable Research Station: *Know and Grow Vegetables, 1* and *2*. I highly recommend them to all enthusiastic gardeners, and have made full use of them in this revision.

Second, new varieties (or cultivars as we must now call all varieties raised in cultivation) have been introduced – thanks to the plant breeders. Some old varieties are no longer available through the normal commercial channels – partly because of EEC legislation. We may rue the disappearance of some old favourites, but it's a fact of gardening life, best offset by taking advantage of the undeniable merits of many of the new cultivars.

Third, authors grow older, and perhaps wiser. I have learnt a great deal in the last ten years, much of it stemming from the year my family spent travelling around Europe in a caravan, studying old and new methods of vegetable growing. We visited eight West European countries, travelling in a southward arc from Holland to Hungary. Not only did we 'discover' new plants, such as summer purslane, claytonia (or winter purslane), iceplant, salad rocket and the many beautiful red chicories, but we saw at first hand intensive methods of vegetable growing, such as the use of seedlings, cut-and-come-again techniques, and closely-spaced narrow beds, all making optimum use of available ground. When we returned we experimented with these new plants and methods in the small organic market garden we then established, and found much of what we had learnt particularly relevant to the needs of small gardens. So some of these new ideas have been incorporated into this revision.

Our own garden is now run entirely on organic lines. We use no inorganic artificial fertilisers, weedkillers, or pesticides, other than the handful of approved chemicals that break down rapidly and do minimum damage to other forms of life. There may well be valid economic arguments for using chemicals in large-scale operations, but in small gardens I feel they are quite unnecessary. The joys of eating fresh produce that you know is untainted far outweigh the inconvenience of the odd caterpillar-carved hole.

I hope this revised edition will prove useful to a new generation of gardeners. I am always interested in readers' experiences in different parts of the country, and in their comments on how this book could be improved.

Introduction to the First Edition

Seven or eight years ago I went to see the editor of a gardening magazine. I wanted to know if he would be interested in articles on vegetables. 'Vegetables,' he exclaimed, 'my dear, nobody's interested in vegetables these days.'

But that was seven or eight years ago, and the 1970s have seen a remarkable 'revival' in vegetable growing.

Probably one of the most important reasons for this change is economic. Vegetables are no longer cheap. And ironically enough, unless you live in a big city, the choice is often very restricted. Then there is the question of flavour. The vegetables you buy in shops – pre-packed, graded and scrubbed though they may be, have inevitably lost the subtle flavour of fresh vegetables in the long journey from field to shop.

The widespread use of toxic chemicals by commercial growers is another factor. Many people are becoming extremely wary of the effects of eating vegetables which have probably been treated with chemicals, not just when growing, but often in the storing and processing which follow. And last, but by no means least, we are rediscovering the simple primitive satisfaction of producing something for ourselves.

Whatever the reason, packets of vegetable seed have not sold so well since the 'Dig for Victory' campaign in World War II.

The conditions under which most of us garden today are very different from those of twenty, thirty or forty years ago. Classical books on vegetable growing talk about open sites, good well-drained loam and three- or four-year rotation schemes. They advocated techniques – and marvellous techniques many of them were – which depended on ample supplies of farmyard manure and plenty of space. But manure and space are scarce commodities today.

The modern vegetable grower is more than likely struggling to get a quart out of a pint pot. His garden may be overshadowed by his neighbour's house or a tower block of flats. Wind may funnel across his plot through the gap between his house and the next. The garden he finds himself with, far from being good deep loam, could be a waterlogged patch of raw-looking clay, or little more than a pile of rubble the builders left behind – certainly not ideal conditions. You cannot practise much rotation on a pocket handkerchief.

On the other hand, there are now many products to ease the gardener's task: commercially prepared seed and potting composts; pre-mixed fertilisers; many types of cloche; plastic films for mulching, and so on.

With small gardens there are always competing demands. You need somewhere for the children to play, to hang out the washing, or put out a picnic table in the summer. Most people want some flowers and possibly fruit trees or soft fruit. And what about a shed? A place to keep the tools and deck chairs and hang the onions is essential. All this takes space, and it is lack of space which is the main problem bedevilling would-be vegetable growers.

It is no good pretending that vegetables will grow anywhere. The old standbys of the kitchen garden – Brussels sprouts, cauliflowers, leeks, and cabbages, for example – need good conditions and there is no getting away from it. But even the most unpromising sites can be brought to heel – with hard work, it is true. And in the meantime small areas can be made fertile enough to grow less fussy or fast growing crops such as radishes, turnips, or salad seedlings, or a start can be made with tomatoes in pots, or lettuces and herbs in a window box, tub, or one of the modern compost-filled 'growing bags'.

The vegetable grower with a small garden wants, and can get, value for space. Provided the soil is fertile, vegetables can be grown far closer than they used to be. Plant breeders have developed dwarfer, faster maturing and high yielding cultivars. Space can be saved by 'catch cropping', ie growing a fast maturing crop between rows of a slower one, such as early carrots between dwarf beans. Ground space can be saved by making use of a trellis, tripods of long canes, or the garden fence for climbing runner or French beans or outdoor Japanese cucumbers. New cultivation techniques are being developed to enable us to get quicker returns from our vegetables.

Every family wants something different from its vegetable plot. It is probably impossible to keep an average family in vegetables from a very small garden. But it is quite feasible, in a plot that is say 10 yards square, to have something worthwhile from the garden all the year round. Some people prefer to concentrate on the sort of vegetables which are difficult or expensive to buy such as kohl rabi, celeriac or sweet peppers. Others concentrate on those which lose most in the journey from field to shop to consumer – salad crops, peas, young carrots. The flavour of fresh picked peas or young carrots is a world apart from anything you can buy. Whatever your objective, a small space can be put to excellent use.

The newcomer to vegetable growing is sometimes at a loss as to how to start. He may be bombarded with conflicting advice. This is hardly surprising: gardening is a very inexact science, and there are few wrong or right answers. What works one year may well fail the next; what is suitable for a mild coastal area would be most inappropriate in a hilly area inland. The real gardener is inevitably an experimenter – constantly trying out different ideas until he discovers what is best for him, his conditions, and his requirements.

Then there is the weather to consider. One of the first lessons we have to learn is the role played by our climate. A gardener is not quite his own boss! The 'master plan' is pre-ordained by the seasons. A farmer once advised me to 'co-operate with the weather', and it was very sound advice. Even if your book tells you to sow parsnips in February, there is no point in trying to sow them on sticky wet soil. Better to wait until it has dried out. If there is a sunny spell in August when the onions are ready for harvesting, do not procrastinate for a moment. The weather might turn nasty on you, your onions will start to sprout or rot and your crop will be wasted.

It probably takes a newcomer to gardening three or four years to get the 'feel' of how the annual pattern of gardening operations fits into the overall pattern of the seasons. When the ground first becomes workable in spring, the shallots and onion sets can be planted; when the March east wind has dried out the surface, the seed bed can be raked to a tilth for the early sowings. When the danger of frosts is over the tender crops such as tomatoes and cucumbers can be planted out. When frost threatens again in the autumn, some crops will need harvesting, others protection. These are the landmarks to which an experienced gardener reacts instinctively. Everything else fits neatly in between.

For anyone new to gardening, or new to an area, it is worth investigating what established gardeners in the locality are doing. What they grow, how and when, provides many a clue to success. It is always best to start with what does well naturally – the 'difficult' vegetables can be tackled later.

I would also advise anyone growing vegetables to keep records. It is always useful to know what cultivars proved successful in previous seasons, how many rows you found you needed, where there were gaps in the household supply which could be remedied. Records of sowing dates, quantities of seeds or plants needed, cultural details, and pests encountered prove immensely valuable. You may be inundated with advice from experts, but your personal garden diary will be the only source of information about the unique conditions which constitute your garden.

And finally, a word of encouragement for complete beginners. I often come across people who, although they had never before grown anything, in their first season had results anyone would be proud of. They simply 'followed the instructions on the packet'. That could be beginners' luck, green fingers, or plain common sense. Get a feel for the sort of conditions plants like, and from then on gardening is very largely common sense.

Newcomers to gardening who want to reinforce beginners' luck will find the advice given in gardening magazines, on radio, on television and in seed catalogues (almost always free), most valuable. They should also consider joining a local gardening club or society, where they will pick up hints from more experienced gardeners, and from the lectures and demonstrations. Many gardening societies are able to obtain seeds and gardening supplies at discounts – a useful service for their members.

Part One

GENERAL PRINCIPLES

CHAPTER ONE
Soil Fertility

I have based this book on two assumptions. First, that most people reading it have only a small garden, or small part of a garden, to devote to vegetable growing. Second, that they want the maximum returns from that area, however small. In other words, they want to cultivate the vegetable plot as intensively as possible.

This means that every inch of space should be in use. Vegetables should be planted as close together as is reasonable, and as soon as one crop is finished another can be sown or planted in its place. Space between rows can be intercropped, cloches can be used to extend the growing season, and even concrete corners and paths can be made productive with the use of boxes or compost-filled plastic bags. With careful planning, it is astonishing how much can be produced from a tiny but intensively worked garden.

However, to get the best results, the garden needs to be reasonably sheltered, well watered and, above all, fertile.

Shelter and water are fairly easily provided. Fertility can pose more of a problem. Some soils are naturally fertile, but in most cases steps have to be taken to increase, and then maintain, soil fertility. Once the soil is fertile, crops grow fast and vigorously, stand a better chance of over-coming pests and disease, and yield heavily. To borrow a commercial term, turnover is greatly increased.

Soil fertility then, is the key to getting the most out of a small vegetable garden. So I make no apology for devoting a whole chapter to the subject.

What is soil fertility? To answer that question we must take a look at what soil is, how it functions, and what it does for the plant.

The nature of soil

Although soil looks solid, in an average garden soil slightly less than half consists of solid matter. This is mainly made up of mineral particles of sand, silt and clay which have been formed over the centuries by the breakdown of rocks. About 5 per cent, an extremely important 5 per cent, is organic matter. This is a mixture of the remains of plants and animals, decomposing vegetation and humus, and the tiny creatures living in the soil known as micro-organisms, many of which play a vital role in breaking down all this material. The rest of what we call the soil, about half of it, consists of air and water, which fill the spaces or pores between the crumbs of soil.

What does soil do for plants? It supplies an anchorage, and a medium through which the roots can penetrate. It supplies air for the roots to breathe. It supplies water, which is essential for all living things, and this again is absorbed through the roots. And it also supplies most of the nutrients, or foods, required by plants.

Sources of nutrients

A plant gets its nutrients from two sources. Through its leaves it takes in carbon dioxide from the air, which together with water absorbed through the roots is converted in the presence of light into sugars and starches in the 'factories' of the leaves during the process known as photosynthesis. All of the rest of the nutrients which are necessary for healthy plant growth are obtained from the soil, absorbed into the plant's system in dilute solution through the roots. Of these nutrients, the plant requires nitrogen, phosphorus and potassium (usually called potash) in large quantities, calcium, sulphur and magnesium in moderate quantities, and in really minute quantities the so-called 'trace elements', such as iron, manganese, zinc, boron and a number of others.

Some of these nutrients are found in the mineral particles of the soil, particularly in clays. But they occur mainly, in highly complex forms, in the organic matter in the soil. Nitrogen comes mainly from decaying organic matter (plant remains) in the soil, but also from atmospheric nitrogen in the soil, which is 'fixed' and converted into forms plants can use by bacteria which live in soil organic matter. Nitrogen, the most important nutrient for plants, is easily washed or leached out of the soil, especially during the rainy winter months, and on the whole plants respond faster to applications of nitrogen than to any other fertiliser.

The most important process at work in the soil is the breaking down of organic matter by minute micro-organisms, mainly types of bacteria, to release nutrients in simple forms which can be taken up by plants or – as the jargon has it – making them 'available'. This can only take place provided conditions are 'right' for the micro-organisms, ie provided they have enough oxygen and moisture, the soil is not too acid or alkaline for them, and of course, provided that they have an adequate supply of organic matter to work on.

Fertility can be summed up as creating the best conditions for soil micro-organisms to go about their work of breaking down organic matter into humus. (Humus is organic matter in a very advanced state of decay, and it is from humus that plant nutrients are released.) Good soil structure is an important factor in creating these conditions.

Types of soil

It is useful to understand what types of soil there are, how a soil develops its structure, and what can be done to improve it and hence its fertility.

The mineral element in soils is made up of particles of varying size, classified, according to their size, as sands, silts and clays. The particles of sand are the largest – the individual grains are visible to the naked eye; then come silt particles, which are infinitely smaller and cannot be distinguished by the naked eye; the smallest of all are clay particles.

Most soils in Britain are loams, a mixture of one or more types. But because sands and clays, to take the extremes, have very different characteristics, the proportion of these predominating in any particular soil largely determines the characteristics of the soil, such as its structure and how rich it is in nutrients.

Sandy soils have large particles, which are most reluctant to stick together naturally to form crumbs. (See Soil structure below.) The spaces between the particles are also large, so water drains away easily and the soil contains plenty of air. Sandy soils warm up quickly in spring, but dry out in summer. They are usually poor in nutrients, because nutrients are washed out of the soil in the drainage water. Sandy loams, however, are richer in nutrients than pure sands and hold water better.

A clay soil, on the contrary, consists of microscopic particles which have a great tendency, because of their chemical nature, to stick together. A pure clay is extremely sticky, there are few spaces for air, and water cannot drain through it easily. When it does dry it is apt to dry into hard, impenetrable lumps. A clay soil, however, is very rich in nutrients, and when organic matter is worked into it can develop an excellent crumb structure.

Silts have some characteristics in common with clay, in that they retain moisture well but can dry into hard clods. They are often very fertile, and like clay, respond well to the incorporation of organic matter.

Sandy soils are generally considered 'light', clay soils 'heavy', and silts intermediate.

Other distinct types of soil are peats and chalk soils. The Fenland peats are rich fertile soils, but the high, boggy moorland peats are usually too acid to grow vegetables. Chalky soils can cause problems by becoming very sticky when wet and drying into steely lumps. The remedy lies in frequent additions of organic matter, which decompose rapidly on chalk soils. Vegetables can be grown successfully on the deeper chalky soils, though it is harder to do so on thin chalk soils.

The ideal soil, the loam that gardeners dream about, is a balanced mixture of sand, silt and clay. The sandy elements make for good drainage and aeration, the clay elements for richness, retention of water in summer, and the cohesiveness which is essential for the formation of crumbs. Even soils such as these are dependent on fresh organic matter being added continually so that they can develop a good crumb structure.

Assessing your soil type

It is useful to be able to tell what type of soil you have – although this is not easy for an inexperienced gardener. But you can get some indication by what is called 'finger analysis'. Hold some soil in the palm of your hand, and rub a little between your fingers. If the predominate feeling is of grittiness, it is basically a sandy soil. If it feels silky, it is a silty soil; if it feels sticky and can almost be 'polished' under pressure from the fingers, it is a clay soil. If it doesn't really feel either gritty, silky or sticky it is a loam.

After cultivating a soil for a few years, you acquire a 'feel' for the type of soil you have and how to cater for its particular characteristics.

Soil structure

In all except very sandy or silty soils, the mineral and organic particles in the soil join together to form small lumps, or crumbs, of varying sizes. The crumbs can easily be seen if you crush a small clod of garden soil in your hand. You can break it down so far, but after that only the crumbs are left, and to break them down into dust-size fragments is a much harder business.

In a good soil the crumbs, which vary in size, are very stable. Around them and between them a network of spaces or pores is built up, and it is this combination of crumbs and spaces which makes up the soil structure. The channels made by the spaces between the crumbs are the aeration and drainage system of the soil. When rain falls on the soil, the surplus water drains off through the channels, preventing it from becoming waterlogged. Water remains in the smallest pores, forming a moisture reservoir for the roots and soil organisms. The large spaces are filled with air, supplying the oxygen which is necessary for the plant roots and the various living organisms in the soil.

A soil with a good structure is one in which the crumbs remain stable even when wet.

Tilth

The soil structure has a direct bearing on what gardeners call 'tilth'. This is the physical condition of the surface of the soil where the seeds are sown. Soil with a good structure can be broken down, often simply by raking in the spring, to a 'mellow' tilth where the individual soil crumbs are roughly the size of breadcrumbs. This is ideal for sowing seeds. It is very difficult to get a good tilth either on soils which dry out so much that the surface virtually becomes dust, or on those which are so sticky when wet that they dry into solid, almost unbreakable clods. In both these cases the fault of the soil orginates in poor structure.

Soil structure test

If you have a loamy soil, as most people have, you can do a simple test to see if your soil has a good, stable, crumb structure. It is worth comparing samples from different parts of the garden, ideally taking them from different depths, anything down to 45cm (18in) deep. For each sample take half a trowel of soil, dry it overnight on a saucer, then sieve it through a household sieve to remove very light material. Then take a teaspoon of the soil, put it in a glass, cover it with water and shake. Poor soil disintegrates rapidly making the water cloudy, but the crumbs of a well-structured soil will remain intact however long you shake. Soils of intermediate quality come between these extremes. You'll find the best samples come from ground that has been mulched, from beneath a compost heap, or from worm casts. Aim to bring your poorer soils up to the quality of these.

The part humus plays in soil structure

Apart from the size of the soil particles, several other factors have an important influence on the development of a good soil structure. And here we get back to humus. Apart from being a storehouse of plant nutrients, certain elements in humus have the ability to 'coat' particles of sand and silt together in crumbs. In heavy clay soils, humus helps in the process of breaking down the large clods into smaller clods, which in turn break down into crumbs. So humus has a vital effect on the physical condition of soil.

Another important feature of humus, especially on sandy soils, is that it has a great capacity for holding water. Apart from making sandy soils more resistant to drought conditions, this also prevents the nutrients from being washed out so rapidly.

The part earthworms play in soil structure

Earthworms, especially the burrowing and casting species, play a most important part in creating a good soil structure. Their burrows, some of which are permanent with 'cemented' sides, open up the soil and create aeration and drainage channels. They work and plough through enormous quantities of earth, literally eating their way through the soil. They take in soil and organic matter, mix it intimately together and treat it with gums and lime as it passes through their stomach. This is the first vital stage in the breakdown of organic matter. With several types of worm the result is the familiar coil-like casts which are deposited both on the surface and within the soil, and these bestow enormous benefits.

The casts are remarkably rich, containing more micro-organisms, more inorganic minerals, and more organic matter than the soil from which they were derived; moreover the nutrients are converted into forms plants can use immediately. Of equal importance, the casts are remarkably stable even when wet, and perform a key role in the formation of stable crumbs in the soil.

Worms feed on fresh organic matter. Their preference is for animal manure; semi-rotted compost is second choice. The fastest way of increasing the worm population is to add organic matter to the surface of the soil. The traditional method of improving soil structure was the use of grass leys, grassing down for several years. (Soil structure in old pasture land is excellent.) It is now thought that this is effective primarily because the decaying grass roots provide a constant source of food for worms; subsequently the grass roots reinforce the casts so making stable 'aggregates' of soil crumbs.

Finally, when worms die their protein-rich bodies decay and nitrogen is returned to the soil. This could amount to the equivalent of 100lb of nitrogen fertiliser per acre per annum!

How to improve soils

In practice, the structure of almost any soil can be improved by adding organic matter, which will eventually be converted into humus. Organic matter is anything with animal or vegetable origins – manure, compost, straw, seaweed, for example (see Chapter 2).

With heavy soils, cultivation itself, letting in air so that earthworms, bacteria and other micro-organisms can get to work, results in an improvement of soil structure. It is also remarkable how the action of frost, alternately freezing and thawing the soil, will break down the clods of a clay soil to produce a crumb structure. This is why clay soils should be 'dug over rough' in autumn, by the end of November, exposing the clods to the frost. My own garden is laid out in narrow beds about 1m (1yd) wide, and in autumn I like to spade the sides of the bed into the middle to form a single ridge before covering them with manure. The ridges ensure good drainage and maximum exposure of the soil to the frost.

Sharp sand, coarse grit, or weathered ashes can be worked into the surface of a heavy soil to improve drainage and help it to warm up in spring. As for fresh organic matter, which, as mentioned earlier, is food for worms, this should be added to the surface leaving the worms to work it in. If it is *dug* in there will initially be a loss of nitrogen as the bacteria break it down. Well-rotted manure or compost, however, should be dug in.

The structure of light sandy soils is easily destroyed, so they are often left uncultivated until the spring, though they can be mulched in autumn with, say, straw, bracken or compost, or even left weedy, to protect the surface from the elements. In spring dig in well-rotted manure or compost as a source of nutrients – feeding earthworms is far less important in well-drained, well-aerated soils. Peat can also be dug in to make these light soils more moisture retentive.

Soil conditioners

Various artificial soil conditioners are now on the market, which help in the formation of crumbs or tilth on sandy or clay soils. They are generally raked into the surface. The extravagant claims made for some of these products should be taken with a pinch of salt. However, if properly used they can certainly help in the formation of tilth under bad conditions, for example where most of the topsoil has been removed in building operations. If cost is a limiting factor, confine their use to special areas such as a seed bed. It seems that some of the seaweed based products are among the most effective.

Soil acidity and liming

The acidity of a soil is another factor which influences soil fertility. Acidity is measured on a scale known as the pH scale, which ranges from 0 to 14. A neutral soil has a pH value of 7.0, an acid soil a pH below 7.0 and an alkaline soil one above 7.0. The change from one pH level to the next indicates a soil that is ten times as acid (or alkaline) as the one below it.

Broadly speaking, the acidity of a soil reflects the amount of calcium, ie chalk or lime, in it. In our humid climate, rain water is continually washing calcium out of the soil, so there is a tendency for soil to become more acid all the time. This process is most marked in

parts of the country with a very high rainfall, in cities and industrial-
ised areas where acids in the atmosphere wash the calcium out even
faster, and on light sandy soils. Heavy soils such as clays are less
likely to become seriously acid, and may have enough reserves of
calcium to last for many years.

The ideal pH for a soil is 6.5, which is slightly acid. In fact most
British soils tend to be slightly acid.

Why does pH matter?

First, because plants only grow well within a certain pH range,
varying from plant to plant. Most vegetables do best on a slightly acid
soil. This is mainly because the pH value has an effect on the
availability of the soil nutrients which plants need. At pH 5.0 most
nutrients are 'available'. However, phosphate, one of the key
nutrients, gets 'locked up' if the soil becomes too acid and the pH
falls below 5.0. Calcium, potassium and magnesium may be washed
out of the soil altogether under very acid conditions. At a low pH
other nutrients may be present in such large quantities that they
become phytotoxic, ie poisonous to the plant.

When the pH rises above 7.5, ie if the soil becomes too alkaline,
most of the trace elements, which are essential for healthy plant
growth, become locked up and unavailable to plants. In other words,
if the pH is seriously wrong, plants will be starved, or poisoned.

Secondly, micro-organisms such as bacteria, which break down the
organic matter into humus, get progressively less active as the soil
becomes more acid. When the pH falls to 4.5, they cease to function
altogether. This means that not only are no more nutrients released
into the soil, but that the soil structure starts to deteriorate through
lack of humus.

Most earthworms cannot tolerate very acid conditions and will
move out of very acid soils, which should be limed as the first step
towards encouraging their return.

Finally, certain plant diseases are worse in notably acid or alkaline
conditions. Clubroot in cabbage is most serious in acid soils; potato
scab in alkaline soils.

Putting the pH right

The most common pH problem in this country is over-acidity, which
is corrected by liming. However, overliming can be very harmful, so
only lime your soil if it is really necessary. If plants seem to be doing
well and there is a large worm population (particularly if your soil is
on the heavy side) assume everything is all right.

Indications that a soil is too acid and needs liming are a 'sour look', ie moss growing on the surface, certain weeds such as sorrel and docks, and vegetation on the surface which is not rotting.

A chemical test is the only certain way of finding out what the pH is and if lime is needed. Soil testing kits are available for the amateur, or tests can be carried out by advisory services. The kits give an accurate indication of the acidity of the soil, but they cannot tell you precisely how much lime you require, as this varies with the type of soil. Lighter dressings of lime will be required for a sandy soil, heavier for a silt, the heaviest of all for a clay. Consult an expert otherwise, if in doubt, err on the light side. Sandy soils in particular are easily overlimed.

As a general rule, if you have a soil which tends to become too acid (this is most likely to happen in an industrial area), apply lime dressings every third or fourth year at the most. Lime takes a while to take effect, but further dressings can be made later if necessary. Liming is best done in the autumn, and although lime is traditionally spread on the surface of the soil, with medium and heavy soils it is far better to work it thoroughly into the top spit of soil when digging.

Never apply lime at the same time as fertilisers, farmyard manure, compost, etc., as undesirable chemical reactions occur. Allow about a month to elapse. The easiest forms of lime to handle, and the cheapest, are ground chalk, ground limestone and magnesium limestone.

Recommended dressings of ground limestone for a moderately acid soil (pH 6) are as follows: sandy soil 270g/m^2 ($\frac{1}{2}$lb/sq yd); loamy soil 550g/m^2 (1lb/sq yd); clay or humus-rich soil 800g/m^2 (1$\frac{1}{2}$lb/sq yd). The lime content of the soil can also be increased if lime is used in making compost (see Chapter 2).

Correcting soils which are too alkaline, for example soils with a great deal of chalk in them, is more difficult. Working in organic matter will help; dressings of ammonium sulphate will also have an acidifying effect. Foliar sprays often prove the quickest method of correcting deficiencies which arise on alkaline soils.

Topsoil and subsoil

Soil fertility is usually concerned with the dark layer of soil we cultivate known as the topsoil. This varies in depth from only a few inches to several feet thick, and it generally lies over a lighter coloured, poorer layer of subsoil. The main difference between the two layers is that the topsoil contains organic matter, which has given it a relatively good structure, while the subsoil has no organic matter and is solid, lifeless, of poor structure and often badly drained as a result. Roots cannot penetrate it easily.

From a gardener's point of view, the deeper the topsoil the better. The easiest way of increasing the topsoil is by the gradual addition of more organic matter to the surface, and indeed by the mere process of cultivation. On the whole subsoil is best left alone, and should never be brought to the surface. Over the years cultivation of the topsoil will gradually lead to an improvement in the subsoil through the infiltration of roots, worms, and so on from the topsoil.

Thin topsoil

There are two exceptions to the general rule of not disturbing the subsoil. Where the topsoil is very thin, say only a few inches in depth, it is worth double-digging the soil, which would mean penetrating the subsoil, working a layer of organic matter into it, and then replacing the topsoil (see Chapter 3 for double digging). This will improve the fertility of the subsoil, and it will gradually assume the character of topsoil.

Hard pan

The other case in which interference is justified is where an extremely hard layer, known as a hard pan, is found in the subsoil. This can be caused by a layer of mineral salts, possibly a foot or so down; it may be the result of extreme compaction due to heavy machinery having worked on the soil – a situation which could arise on new housing estates. A hard pan can be so impenetrable that it prevents all natural drainage, thus making the topsoil waterlogged.

You may suspect the presence of a hard pan when you dig the soil. At a certain depth the fork or spade seems to encounter far greater resistance. The only answer is to break up the hard pan by physical means. A spade will usually do the job; or plunge the tines of a fork in at an angle and wriggle them about. Failing that, use a pickaxe.

Drainage

This brings us to the question of drainage, which has an important bearing on soil fertility. A waterlogged soil is one in which surplus water cannot drain away. As a result all the spaces between the soil crumbs are filled with water and air is driven out. The roots are unable to breathe and bacteria cease to function, which in turn means that the level of nutrients in the soil falls and its structure deteriorates. A waterlogged soil can never be fertile. A badly drained soil is also a cold soil, and plants never do well in such soils. The best way to raise a soil's temperature is by drainage.

Often it is obvious that a soil needs drainage. If water lies on the surface for several days after a heavy rain, or if water is encountered when you dig a foot or so deep (this is what is meant by a high water table) drainage is necessary. Less obvious indications of a badly drained soil are poor vegetation, plants with a mass of small shallow roots rather than deep roots, lack of worms, and often soil that is grey, bluish, black or mottled rather than brown.

Bad drainage occurs either because of the nature of the topsoil itself (as is the case with a heavy clay soil with little organic matter in it) or because the topsoil lies over a non-porous layer of subsoil or rock which does not allow water to drain away – clay or granite for example. Where the underlying layer is porous, such as gravel or sand, there will be no problem. As already mentioned, a hard pan or general soil compaction can also cause poor drainage.

If the poor drainage seems to stem from the nature of the topsoil, digging in plenty of organic matter, which encourages worm activity, will go a long way towards putting the matter right. This has certainly been the case with my present garden. During the winter we moved in, half the kitchen garden was semi-permanently under water and the rest waterlogged, making it quite unworkable until early the following summer – and hard work then. By digging in vast quantities of spent mushroom compost over the next few years we now have a reasonably well-drained and fertile soil in the kitchen garden.

Where the drainage problem is caused by the nature of the subsoil, some form of artificial drainage will be necessary.

In a small garden, drainage can often be improved sufficiently by making a few 'trench drains'. This is done by taking out a trench about 30cm (1ft) wide and 60 or 90cm (2 or 3ft) deep, and filling the bottom 30cm (1ft) with a layer of large clinkers, stones, broken bricks, and so on before replacing the soil (*Fig. 1a*). A trench like this could be made across the lower end of a slope, or at both ends of a level site. It could also be incorporated into a path; a meandering path through a small garden could easily conceal a most effective drain.

1. SIMPLE GARDEN DRAINS

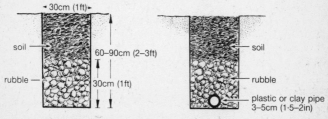

a. Trench drain filled with rubble   b. Piped drain

I've been told that in the past reasonably effective drains were made simply by filling trenches with brushwood.

In a persistently wet garden, the only solution may be to lay a proper system of drains, draining into a ditch, artificial soakaway or sump. Clay or plastic pipes can be laid in the drains (*Fig. 1b*). Both are satisfactory, but for the amateur the modern plastic pipes, 3–5cm (1½–2in) diameter, are easier to handle and lay. It is common practice to lay the pipes at the bottom of the trench and cover them with 30cm (1ft) or so of drainage material such as clinker or rubble.

Laying drains is a skilled job, so if it is necessary, it would be worth seeking expert advice on the sort of drains to use, their depth, spacing and gradient, and the most suitable layout for your particular plot.

Improving fertility: summary

A fertile soil is well drained, probably slightly acid or neutral, has a good crumbly structure and is rich in nutrients which are available to the plants.

If things are growing well in your garden, assume it is fertile. A vigorous crop of weeds in a neglected garden can be taken as a sign of fertility, even if it does mean a lot of work before you produce an equally vigorous crop of vegetables. But if either cultivated plants or weeds seem poor and sickly, something more radical is wrong. In this case, the steps in restoring fertility are:

1 Improve drainage if it is faulty. This often brings dramatic results.
2 Check acidity. Faulty pH is often at the root of failure, especially in city gardens. It can easily be corrected by liming.
3 Work in bulky organic matter such as manure, compost, seaweed, sludge or whatever is available. This will improve the soil structure and provide nutrients, and of course encourage earthworm activity. It may also be necessary in the early stages to increase the supply of nutrients with artificial fertilisers.

Maintaining fertility

Once soil has been brought into a fertile state, it pays to keep it that way. Vegetables remove considerable quantities of nutrients from the soil, and these must be replenished by regular applications of organic matter, and if necessary, additional fertilisers.

Conserving the soil structure is also most important. It can easily be destroyed by cultivating when the soil is too wet or too dry, by heavy rain on the bare surface, or by walking on the bare surface more than is necessary. The practice of keeping the surface continually mulched, ie covered with a layer of compost, peat or other form of organic matter goes a long way towards improving and conserving the soil structure. One of the great advantages of laying out a vegetable garden in narrow beds is that they can be worked from the paths, so avoiding the necessity of ever treading on the soil.

The fertility of the soil depends chiefly on the rate at which organic matter is added to it.

Special problems

The neglected garden

Neglected gardens create special problems. They are liable to be weedy, they may have a low level of fertility, and the soil is often intractable and difficult to work.

A suggested line of approach is as follows:

1 Kill off the surface weeds using a weedkiller such as paraquat and diquat mixture. This will kill the foliage, but leave the soil unharmed. (See also page 98.)
2 Dig over the ground, removing roots of all perennial weeds by hand (see Chapter 5). Do this in autumn if possible.
3 Dig in manure or some form of organic matter, or if it is very fresh, spread it over the surface. Leave the ground over the winter.
4 In spring allow the first flush of weeds to germinate (the soil will be full of weed seeds). Hoe them off before sowing or planting anything. Don't try to sow too early.
5 Apply a base dressing of general fertiliser before sowing or planting.
6 Concentrate the first year on vegetables which cover the ground well, such as potatoes (an excellent crop to start with), broad beans and dwarf French beans, New Zealand spinach, turnips or Jerusalem artichokes. These will all help to keep the weeds down. Dressings of nitrogen or a general fertiliser, or the use of a seaweed based liquid fertiliser, will help growth in the first season.
7 Mulch as much as you can to prevent weeds from germinating and to control the perennial weeds. After two years or so of cultivation weeds become less of a problem.

Do not expect marvellous crops the first year. However, by growing something and working the soil, you will see it start to improve. If crops do not seem to be doing better in the second year, it may be worth having a professional soil analysis to check on the pH and to see if there are any serious nutrient deficiencies. If you can afford it, this can always be done at the outset.

Digging up lawns and rough areas

Tackle this job in the autumn. It is best to double dig the area which is being converted into a vegetable plot (see Chapter 3 for double digging). Slice off the top 5cm (2in) of turf, and bury it grass-side down in the first trench. Chop it up before covering with soil from the next trench.

If the soil in the lawn is acid, it will probably be necessary to lime after the autumn digging.

The rubble the builders left behind

Owners of new houses are often faced with the prospect of converting a pile of rubble or raw clay into a vegetable garden. The topsoil has been removed, and the soil that remains looks impossible. Don't despair. It can be converted into a garden.

A common practice is to import topsoil, but that is very expensive, and if the soil has been stacked in a heap more than 1m (1yd) high, it will be devoid of worms. The cheaper way is to import large quantities of organic matter.

I suggest you tackle the problem as follows:

1 Remove the largest stones, bricks, brickbats, and other similar rubbish.
2 Fork over the soil, as far as is possible.
3 Cover the prospective garden with a layer, anything up to 15cm (6in) thick, of organic matter such as farmyard manure, rotted straw, sewage sludge, spent mushroom compost or seaweed. Do this in autumn if possible. By the end of the winter it will have rotted down, the earthworms will have dragged it into the top few inches, and the process of building up fertility will have begun.
4 Dig it in spring, apply a base dressing of fertiliser, and plant potatoes or sow radishes, lettuce, spinach, turnips, etc. On very poor, stony soils give plants small but frequent dressings with nitrogenous fertiliser (a mixture such as Growmore could be used) until the nutrient level has been built up.

In the early days of a raw garden, concentrate your resources. Use any spare compost or manure in one area, dig it in, and plant or sow there initially. Fertile 'pockets' can be created by making small trenches, up to 15cm (6in) deep, filling them with a commercial potting compost, and covering them with an inch or so of soil. Lettuce, spring onions, radishes, carrots, dwarf beans and so on, could be grown in these pockets.

Green manuring

This is a time-honoured method of maintaining soil fertility, by growing a crop such as mustard, rye, tares or lupins to dig into the soil as a source of nitrogen or humus. The crops occupy the grounds for fairly long periods and, in practice, green manuring is difficult to operate successfully in small gardens. Keeping the soil continually mulched with organic material is a more feasible alternative.

CHAPTER TWO

Manures, Fertilisers and Compost

'Manure' usually refers to a bulky product derived from animals, and 'fertiliser' to a concentrated powder, granulated or liquid artificial product. But there is no hard and fast rule, and the terms are loosely used. Manures and fertilisers are either organic or inorganic in origin.

Organic fertilisers

Organic manures and fertilisers come originally from plants or animals. There are two types: bulky, such as farmyard manure, sewage sludge and compost, and concentrated, such as dried blood, fish meal, hoof and horn, seaweed extracts and other proprietary fertilisers.

The nutrients in organic fertilisers are released by the action of soil bacteria. They are therefore usually available to plants slowly but over a long period. Dried blood and some seaweed extracts are exceptional in releasing nutrients fairly rapidly.

Bulky organic manures improve the soil structure and add nutrients to the soil over a long period. Concentrated organic fertilisers are mainly effective as a source of nutrients in the medium and long term.

Inorganic fertilisers

Inorganic fertilisers are often known as 'artificial' because they are either obtained through manufacturing processes or by extraction from rocks. Superphosphate, ammonium nitrate and many proprietary blends of fertilisers are inorganic. Because they are concentrated chemicals, they should always be used with care. Plants can easily be damaged by an excessive dose.

Inorganic fertilisers are valuable for adding nutrients to the soil in forms which are almost immediately available to plants. They do not improve the structure of the soil.

The organic versus inorganic controversy

An increasing number of people today are opposed to using anything but organic manures in their gardens, because of the possible harmful effects of the 'artificials'. They believe that organically grown crops taste better and have more resistance to disease. Certainly the 'soft' growth that results from the over-use of nitrogen makes plants more susceptible to pest and disease attack, and probably to the effects of bad weather. Organically grown vegetables seem to keep fresh longer once picked. But it is all hard to prove, one way or the other. Certainly excellent results can be obtained when only organic manures and fertilisers are used, and this is what I do myself. But one can also get good results from a judicious use of both organic and inorganic fertilisers, which is the more general practice. What would be extremely foolish would be to rely solely on artificial fertilisers. If the fertility of a small garden is to be maintained, bulky organic matter *must* be worked in regularly.

Bulky organic manures

It is no longer easy to find supplies of the traditional forms of bulky organic manures which are so valuable for improving soils, ie horse, cow, pig and poultry manures, mixed with straw and litter. If you have access to a supply, make the most of it.

Some modern alternatives are sewage sludge, slaughter house waste, municipal waste and spent mushroom compost, all of which are good if you can get them.

If you are close to the sea, seaweed is a valuable manure. It contains roughly the same amount of organic matter and nitrogen as farmyard manure, as well as numerous trace elements, and can be used fresh, dried or composted.

Straw is an excellent source of organic matter. It is best to compost it (see p. 47).

Tracking down organic matter calls for initiative. But it is not impossible, even in cities. I have friends in London who get free horse manure from police stables, sacks of rotting leaves and vegetable waste from markets and greengrocers, and packing straw for composting from shops. Those great piles of leaves swept up in city parks and streets and so often burnt, rot down beautifully. The boom in pony riding must mean there is a lot of muck somewhere for the asking!

As a general rule, well-rotted bulky manures are best dug into the soil, though they can be used for mulching during the growing season (see Chapter 3). Fresh manures and half-rotted compost are best spread on the surface in autumn a couple of inches thick for the worms to work in. It is inadvisable to apply fresh animal manure to growing vegetables; better to let it age first in a covered heap. Don't worry too much about the dos and don'ts: the main thing is to be working something organic into your soil, somehow!

Peat
Peat is a relatively easily obtained source of organic matter. Sedge peat and granular moss or sphagnum peat are the best forms to use for improving soil structure. They have very little nutrient value, so on light sandy soils and chalk soils in particular, it may be necessary to use additional fertilisers as well.

For a sandy soil, give a dressing of sedge peat in spring, at the rate of 2·7–4kg per sq m (6–9lb per sq yd), about 2·5cm (1in) thick, forked into the surface. Follow this with a 1–1·5kg per sq m (2–3lb per sq yd) dressing in subsequent years.

To improve clay soils, give a 2·5cm (1in) dressing of moss peat (double this on really heavy clay) either in the autumn or in spring when the frost has broken up the clods. Fork it into the top 10cm (4in) of soil and give further dressings, worked deeper into the soil, in following years.

Chalky soils also benefit from peat; it helps to correct the alkalinity of chalk and to improve the extremely sticky nature of chalky soils. A 2·5cm (1in) dressing of sedge or sphagnum peat can be given at any time of year.

Concentrated organic fertilisers

Apart from the proprietary organic fertilisers for sale today, several traditional organic fertilisers are still available, although they are a fairly expensive way of buying nutrients.

Dried blood is a good source of nitrogen, and is fast acting.

Hoof and horn contains nitrogen. Make sure it is finely ground.

Blood, fish and bonemeal supplies nitrogen and a good level of phosphate.

Bonemeal is rich in phosphorus. Make sure it has been sterilised; anthrax can be contracted through handling unsterilised bonemeal.

Fish meal is a useful source of nitrogen and phosphorus. It should be dug in to prevent it from being eaten by birds.

Seaweed meal supplies potash, some nitrogen and phosphorus, and trace elements. It also should be dug in as it may 'gel' on the surface.

Domestic organic fertilisers
Soot contains nitrogen, and is a good general stimulant. Don't use it fresh as the sulphur released can damage plants. Store it somewhere dry

for about three months, then apply it as a top dressing on young plants. It also improves the texture of clay soil, and because of its dark colour, helps to warm soils through absorption of heat. It is said to deter pests such as pea weevil, celery fly, carrot fly and slugs.

Ash from wood fires and bonfires contains potash. Slow burning hardwoods are particularly rich in potash. Either work fresh ash into the compost heap or store it in a dry place. If exposed to rain the potash is rapidly washed out. Apply it to growing crops in spring.

Liquid manure or '*Black Jack*', a valuable and cheap liquid manure, can be made by suspending a sack of well rotted animal manure in a barrel of rain water (*Fig. 2*). Grass cuttings and soot can be included in this mixture. Leave about ten days before using, and stir before use. Dilute it to the colour of weak tea before watering plants with it.

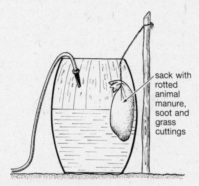

sack with rotted animal manure, soot and grass cuttings

2. 'BLACK JACK' TUB
Cheap liquid manure is made by suspending a sack of rotted manure, sometimes mixed with soot and grass cuttings, in a barrel of rain water

Comfrey liquid manure The deep-rooting perennial plant comfrey can be used to make a useful liquid fertiliser, rich in potassium (and therefore excellent for feeding tomatoes). Use either the wild plant, *Symphytum officinale*, or the very productive cultivated forms, raised either from seed or rootstocks. It is best made in a large barrel with a tap near the bottom, or a hole fitted with a hosepipe. Fill the barrel with fresh or wilted young comfrey leaves (the latter will give a stronger liquid), and fill it with water. Cover with a lid and block the holes to discourage flies, and leave it for four weeks to ferment. The liquid can then be drawn off. It can be used concentrated or diluted up to one pint in a gallon of water. Be warned: it is very smelly!

Artificial fertilisers

Artificial fertilisers are mostly used to give plants extra supplies of the main nutrients they require – nitrogen, phosphorus and potash. This is necessary either because the soil is short of one or more of these, or to give plants an extra 'boost' so that they will produce a better crop.

Nitrogen is the most likely nutrient to be in short supply, as great quantities are washed out of the soil in winter. It has an important effect on the growth of leaves and stems in particular, and most plants respond favourably to a little extra nitrogen during the growing season. Too much, however, would make plants soft and disease prone.

Most soils have considerable reserves of phosphorus and potash, and in gardens where all plant wastes are returned to the soil as compost, losses are low. The average garden's requirements for phosphorus and potash would be met with annual applications of 5.4kg/sq m manure (10lb/sq yd) or at least 2kg/sq m (5lb sq yd) of good garden compost.

Potash deficiency is most likely on chalk and light sandy soils; phosphorus deficiency on heavy soils and peaty soils.

Amateur soil testing kits give some indication of nutrient deficiencies, but have limited value. Where growth is poor and a soil problem is suspected, a professional soil analysis may be advisable (see Appendix III).

In the long run deficiencies will be corrected gradually by the addition of organic matter to the soil.

Forms of fertiliser

Fertilisers are available in dry forms as dusts, granules or pellets, or as concentrated liquid solutions. The fertiliser value is the same.

The granular forms and dusts are usually spread on the ground and worked into the surface with a hoe. If they are applied to dry soil, they must be watered in so that the fertiliser will be dissolved and washed down to the roots. Some of the dry forms can be made up into solutions and watered on to the soil. Some forms of pelleted fertiliser are placed in the soil near the plant roots.

The liquid forms of fertiliser (apart from foliar feeds) are watered on to the soil. This is best done in the evening or in dull weather. Give each plant as much as you would for an ordinary watering. Foliar feeds are watered on to the plant, using a watering can with a fine rose, or a hand spray.

Many different fertilisers are now being sold, some are all-purpose, others formulated to meet particular requirements, such as a high potash fertiliser to help tomatoes to ripen. Whatever is used, always follow the manufacturer's directions. Never add 'a little bit more' in the hope that you will get better results! The reverse is far more likely to be true.

Application of fertilisers

Vegetables vary in their specific requirements for different nutrients; and they have different requirements at different stages of growth (these will be dealt with under the individual vegetables in Part Two). They generally need to take in major nutrients in balanced amounts, so where artificial fertilisers are used, nitrogen fertilisers should usually be balanced by a source of potash and phosphorus.

Traditionally, balanced fertilisers were made up from the basic salts, using ammonium sulphate as a source of nitrogen, superphosphate as a source of phosphorus, and muriate of potash for the potash. These chemicals are bulky and awkward to store, and today amateurs tend to use balanced proprietary mixtures, of which Growmore is among the best known.

Fertilisers can be applied as 'base dressings', 'top dressings' or 'foliar feeds'.

A *base dressing* is applied to the soil two or three weeks before sowing or planting in the spring. This is to meet a plant's very high requirements for nitrogen (in particular), but also for phosphorus, during the early stages of growth in late April or May. With most crops this would see them through to maturity.

A *top dressing* is applied during growth as a booster. Its main use is on plants which have overwintered in the soil, such as spring cabbage and overwintered onions, which may need a nitrogen-rich fertiliser to compensate for the loss of nitrogen from the soil in winter.

Foliar feeds can be useful under dry conditions or to correct trace element deficiencies. As plants can only take in limited quantities of nutrients through their leaves they should only be used on a supplementary basis.

Rule of thumb manuring
The golden rule of organic gardening is 'feed the soil, not the plants'. My own manuring policy is simple. Whenever a piece of ground is cleared, I either dig in some organic manure or mulch the next crop with something organic. Particularly demanding crops like brassicas, leeks, and lettuces get a seaweed based feed during the growing season when it seems necessary.

For gardeners using artificial fertilisers the main recommendation from the NVRS is for an annual base dressing of a compound general fertiliser such as Growmore (NPK 10:10:10) at the rate of 60–90 g/sq m (2–3 oz/sq yd). This needs to be higher for 'hungry' crops, and assumes that most vegetable wastes are being returned to the soil as compost.

Trace elements

Although most soils contain sufficient quantities of the trace elements required by plants, deficiencies sometimes occur, especially on sandy soils. Plants exhibit deficiency symptoms such as poor growth and unusual leaf colouring. The most economic way of correcting these deficiencies in the short term is through specific foliar feeds designed to correct the deficiency. In the long term the best remedy for trace element deficiencies is the addition of organic matter, and taking steps to ensure that the soil pH is correct. Some crops respond surprisingly well to treatment with fertilisers containing trace elements (such as the seaweed extracts), even though no deficiencies are apparent.

Compost

Suitable forms of peat and most bulky manures cost money. Home-made compost is cheap and can be an extremely valuable source of humus. Anyone growing vegetables, in however small a garden, should make space for a compost heap. Many very successful gardeners use no fertiliser other than compost.

There are many theories about the best way to make compost with even the experts often failing to agree – at least over the details. There *is* an art to making good compost, and it is worth mastering.

A compost heap is simply a heap of vegetable and animal waste, which generates heat and is decomposed with the aid of bacteria in a naturally occurring process. When it is fully decomposed the resulting compost is blackish brown in colour, moist, crumbly and uniform in texture. There should be no half decayed stalks or vegetation that are still recognisable as such.

To bring about decomposition properly, the bacteria need moisture, air, warmth and a source of nitrogen, which is normally leafy vegetation. The key to making good compost is ensuring that these conditions are met. However small the garden, you can never make too much compost. It's extraordinary how a huge heap settles into an insignificant pile!

A simple heap

This can be made by piling up wastes as they accumulate, or better still, collecting together enough material to build it up a layer at a time. When it is about 90–120cm (3–4ft) high, cover it with 2·5cm (1in) of soil, then cover it completely with an old carpet, hessian or heavy duty plastic, and leave it to rot. This could take about a year. The drawback with this anaerobic (ie airless) method is that high temperatures are not generated, so weed seeds and disease spores may not be destroyed, and tough material may not all be broken down.

Aerobic compost heap (*Fig. 3*)

In this case air circulates through the heap and, provided it is large enough and well insulated, high temperatures are generated, weed and disease spores are therefore killed, and the rotting process is faster and more complete.

The bin: in a small garden compost is best made in a semi-permanent bin at least 90–120cm (3–4ft) high and the same width – the larger the better. It should stand on a soil base. A long narrow bin might prove feasible in some gardens, tucked alongside a fence or hedge.

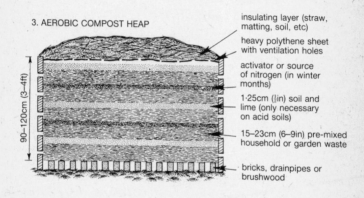

3. AEROBIC COMPOST HEAP

insulating layer (straw, matting, soil, etc)

heavy polythene sheet with ventilation holes

activator or source of nitrogen (in winter months)

1·25cm (½in) soil and lime (only necessary on acid soils)

15–23cm (6–9in) pre-mixed household or garden waste

bricks, drainpipes or brushwood

90–120cm (3–4ft)

It must be a robust construction. Three sides should be made of material with good insulation properties such as timber, bricks, breeze blocks or even hay or straw bales. The front should be designed to let in plenty of air. If the front can be erected in stages, it is easier both to put in raw materials and later, to remove the rotted compost. Two or three wire mesh panels, or poles or logs slipped between upright posts or pipes are two possibilities (*Fig. 4*). Where space allows build two bins side by side: one heap can be decomposing while the other is being built up. Provided they are reasonably strong, some of the patented bins on the market can be useful in small gardens.

Foundations: when you start to build the heap, fork the soil underneath. This improves drainage, and helps worms to move in later on. Start the heap with a 7·5cm (3in) layer of tree prunings or brushwood, or build it on a layer of drain pipes or double rows of bricks set a few inches apart. This is to improve aeration.

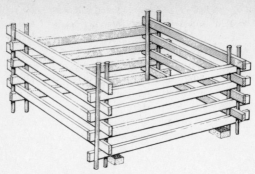

4. HOME-MADE COMPOST BIN
Here lengths of old water pipe are used for the corner
uprights. The sides, made from planks or old posts, are built
up as the heap progresses. To improve insulation two sides
and the back can be lined with cardboard, several
sheets of newspaper, or plastic sheets

What to use: almost any material of vegetable or animal origin can be used, for example:
kitchen waste such as vegetable peelings, egg shells, orange peel, tea leaves, teapot dregs, vacuum cleaner waste; garden waste such as weeds (nettles are excellent), vegetable remains, old potting soil, lawn mowings, autumn leaves (even pine needles), thin prunings, bonfire ash, straw, also green bracken gathered between May and September; animal manure such as pigeon droppings, etc.

Do not use: diseased vegetables (burn them); perennial weeds such as docks, couch grass, bindweed, ground elder, unless they have been laid out first to die off in the sun; evergreens such as holly or ivy; woody material; scrap pieces of meat which would attract rats; anything artificial, such as plastic, tin, glass, or man-made fibres, none of which would rot.

Building the heap: ideally wastes should be pre-mixed before putting them on the heap. The easiest way is to collect them in airtight plastic or rubbish sacks. Keep one for household wastes and one for weeds, and when there is enough material, make them into one layer 15–23cm (6–9in) thick.

Avoid a thick layer of any one material, such as grass cuttings, straw or leaves. This would stop the heap working.

If the heap is short of fresh green stuff (most likely in the winter months) the first and alternate layers can be sprinkled with a source of nitrogen, for example a commercial compost activator, ammonium sulphate, an organic fertiliser or a layer of animal manure.

Intervening layers can be covered with a 1cm (½in) layer of soil, sprinkled with lime if your soil tends to be acid.

Never add lime and activators to the same layer.

Moisture: the compost heap needs to be damp, but not soaking wet. Water if necessary. In areas of very high rainfall it may be necessary to protect it with a cover to prevent it from becoming waterlogged.

Completion: when the heap reaches the top of the bin cover it with a sheet of heavy polythene punctured with holes for ventilation. Make the holes about 2·5cm (1in) diameter and 30cm (12ins) apart. Then cover the whole heap with permeable insulating material, such as a thick layer of straw, matting, two inches of soil or an old carpet.

Turning: the heat generated in the heap will not reach the outer 15cm (6in), so theoretically the heap should be turned 'sides to middle' after about three weeks to give the outer edges a chance to rot. Where this is difficult, slice off the outer 7·5cm (3–6in) before the compost is used, and use them to start the next heap.

In summer a heap made this way will be ready in three or four months; in winter it will probably take at least six to eight months.

The compost can either be dug into the soil or spread on the surface, using up to a barrow load per square metre (yard).

Composting straw

If you are able to get a supply of straw, it is advisable to compost it. Either incorporate it gradually into your normal compost heap, or build it up into a heap on its own. Make it in layers about 15cm (6in) thick, water each layer until thoroughly moist, and sprinkle layers alternately with lime and a source of nitrogen. Turn in dry material on the outside and bury it in the heap. It can be made up to 1·8m (6ft) high, and should be ready in a few months.

Composting leaves

Autumn leaves are best composted on their own, as they eventually decay into wonderful leaf mould. This can be used in sowing and potting compost, or when half rotted, as drainage material in pots or for mulching. Pack the leaves into a wire-netting enclosure 60–90cm (2–3ft) high. They may take up to two years to rot down completely.

Leaves can also be gathered in black plastic sacks and left to rot.

Worm compost

A useful system for making compost in small households has been developed by American biologist Mary Appelhof, author of *Worms Eat My Garbage* (see Appendix IV). It consists of feeding domestic and garden waste to the small, red manure or fishing worms, who eventually

convert it into 'vermicompost', a pleasant peat-like substance which
can be used as ordinary compost or in making potting compost.

Use a box roughly 45cm × 60cm × 25cm deep (18 × 24 × 9in),
filled with about 3½lb of shredded newspaper which serves as 'bedding'.
This is moistened with about 4·5lit (1gal) of water, then a handful of
fishing worms are put in. The box is covered to keep it moist. The
worms are fed regularly with wastes. The squeamish need have no fear
of the worms escaping. Once the food supply is exhausted, the worms
die but before that stage is reached some can be transferred to another
box with fresh bedding to keep the system going.

CHAPTER THREE
Tools and Techniques

Basic tools and equipment

Even for a small garden, money has to be spent on basic tools and equipment. Always buy the best you can afford. Cheap tools are false economy. They make the job harder, and have a depressingly short life span. The best quality tools are made of stainless steel with ash handles, and often carry a ten-year guarantee.

When you are actually buying tools, try them out for size (particularly the handles) and weight, as it is most important that they should feel 'comfortable'.

It is worth taking care of good tools. Soil should always be scraped off before the tools are put away, and ideally they should be wiped with an oily rag. Spades and hoes need occasional sharpening with a sharpening stone. Needless to say, this does not always happen – even in the best gardening circles.

The following tools are almost essential: a spade, a digging fork, a rake, a Dutch hoe or a draw hoe, a hand fork and trowel, an onion hoe, a garden line and a watering can. A dibber is always useful. If you intend to raise plants from seed indoors, a set of miniature tools (often sold as a house-plant set or 'rockery tools') and a small dibber, are worth having. Now a few words about the use of tools (*Fig. 5*).

The spade is the traditional digging tool, and the best for thorough digging on heavy soil, for breaking up clods, and for work which involves moving soil. However, in a small garden with reasonably well worked soil, you could manage using only a fork.

Digging is hard work, so always go at it gently, taking smaller 'slices' of soil if the going is tough. Various sizes of spade are sold, the smallest, the border or ladies' spade, being the most suitable for women.

The fork is also used for digging. It is preferable to a spade on a very stony soil. It is also used for breaking up soil which has already been turned with a spade, and generally 'working' the soil. For ordinary garden use the round-pronged fork is the most popular, though some people prefer to dig with the flat-pronged fork, which is also useful for lifting potatoes and other root vegetables.

Rakes are mainly used for levelling soil, removing stones, and preparing the tilth on a seed bed. For general purposes an eight- or ten-tooth metal-headed rake is quite adequate. I am very attached to a hand-made rosehead nail-tooth rake (a wooden head fitted with iron teeth) which is perfectly balanced and wonderfully easy to use. These are worth getting if you come across them. A springbok rake comes in handy for raking up leaves and rubbish.

The **Dutch hoe**, in which the blade is pushed lightly through the soil, is for removing weeds and loosening the soil when it is not too heavy. It can also be used for drawing a drill. When hoeing with a Dutch hoe walk backwards as you work, so that no footmarks are left on the soil. In small gardens, of course, it is often possible to hoe most of the garden from the path. Always hoe with gentle movements, or it can become surprisingly tiring.

The **draw hoe** is pulled towards you, rather than pushed. It can be used for hoeing on heavier soils, and for such jobs as earthing up and drawing a shallow flat-bottomed trench for peas.

The **onion hoe** is a small swan-necked draw hoe on a 15cm (6in) handle. It is invaluable for weeding, specially in confined spaces, for thinning, drawing drills and even earthing up. If restricted to one hoe in a small garden, this would be my choice (*Fig. 6*).

Triangular, serrated-edged, and double-edged hoes are also available and recommended. It's a question of finding what suits you personally.

The **cultivator** is a tool with 3 to 5 claw-like prongs, which can be very useful for breaking up ground and for weeding between plants.

A **hand trowel** is the best planting tool, and a small **hand fork** is useful for weeding near plants and loosening the soil in small areas. I mainly use the **dibber** for planting leeks. It enables you to make a straight 20cm (8in) hole into which they can be dropped. It is also handy for planting large seeds such as broad beans.

Garden lines can be bought, or made by attaching twine to a pair of skewers or tent pegs. If your garden beds are a constant width, make your line the same width: that will save hours of ravelling and unravelling.

It is useful to have a 7 or 9lit (1½ or 2gal) watering can with a fine and a coarse rose. A small house-plant can, with a very narrow spout, is very handy for watering seedlings. Most gardeners will also find that

5. USEFUL GARDEN TOOLS

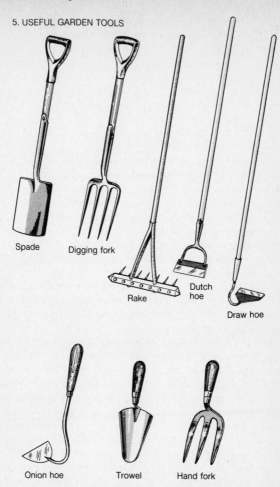

Spade   Digging fork

Rake   Dutch hoe

Draw hoe

Onion hoe   Trowel   Hand fork

they need a wheelbarrow, or at least a trug basket or pail for collecting weeds, a small sprayer, $\frac{1}{2}$lit (1pt) capacity is probably sufficient, and a hose, preferably with a fitting for adjusting the spray.

Digging

Digging is necessary for a number of reasons: to get air into the soil; to expose as much of the soil as possible in winter so that it can be 'weathered' by the elements; to break soil down so that roots can

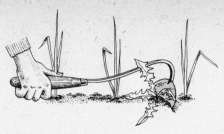

6. WEEDING WITH AN ONION HOE

penetrate, and as a means of working manure or organic matter into the soil. Unless soil has been dug properly at regular intervals, it is very difficult to get it into a suitable condition for sowing or planting.

The 'degrees' of digging, according to how much effort is involved, could be described as first forking, second plain or single digging, and third double digging, also known as bastard trenching (real trenching is a complex business, and not necessary or practicable in small gardens).

The easiest operation, **forking**, is generally done between crops. After clearing a crop of early peas, for example, fork over the ground before sowing the next crop of lettuces, beetroot or carrots. In spring, after the soil has been broken down by the frosts, it can often be forked over easily. If you are fortunate enough to have a really good loamy soil, forking may be sufficient to keep it in good condition permanently, but most soils benefit from being dug annually, with double digging at least until they are in good condition.

Single or **plain digging**. This means working the top spit of soil only – a spit being the depth of the spade, about 23 or 25 cm (9 or 10in). To allow room for manoeuvring (although it is not absolutely necessary), the traditional way of digging is to start by taking out a small trench, the depth of the spade and about 30–37cm (12–15in) wide, across the width of the area you are digging. Remove this soil to the end of the plot, where your digging will finish. Then dig the strip beside your trench, turning the soil into the first trench – and so on. If you are adding manure or organic matter, lay this in the bottom of the trench before turning in the soil from the adjacent strip. Then fork it over, so the soil and manure are mixed thoroughly together. Fill the last trench with the soil you removed from the first (*Fig. 7a*).

Double digging. Here a wider trench is made, about 60cm (2ft) wide, and the top spit is turned into the preceding trench in the same way. The bottom spit is then forked over to the depth of the fork, and manure or organic matter is worked into the broken up soil as thoroughly as possible. The top spit of soil from the next trench is then used to fill it in (*Fig. 7b*).

7. METHODS OF DIGGING

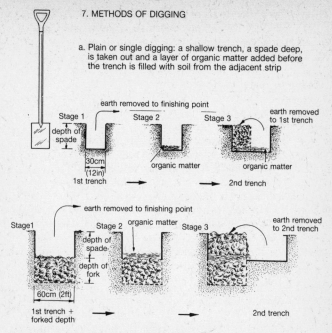

a. Plain or single digging: a shallow trench, a spade deep, is taken out and a layer of organic matter added before the trench is filled with soil from the adjacent strip

b. Double digging: a wider trench is made and the bottom spit is forked over to the depth of a spade before adding organic matter and filling the trench with soil from the adjacent strip

Although double digging is harder work, it is worth doing, especially if you are starting off with poor soil or bad conditions. It helps to improve the drainage of heavy soil and increases the moisture deeper in the soil. This encourages roots to go deeper in search of moisture. We now know that Brussels sprout roots can penetrate two or three feet deep. By using the deeper moisture reserves, moisture near the surface is conserved: and this is important because it is from the upper layers that the surface roots extract nutrients, and they can only do so when the soil is moist. Where you have a thin sandy soil, or a shallow soil over gravel or chalk, double digging helps to deepen the topsoil.

The manure or organic matter which is being dug in can either be spread evenly over the surface first, or kept 'at the ready' in small heaps or a wheelbarrow.

There are several points to make about digging.

1 Always put the spade in as vertically as possible. You get through the ground faster and penetrate deeper.

2 Always remove the roots of perennial weeds such as dock, ground elder, bindweed, dandelions, couch grass and thistles, and weeds that have gone to seed. Smaller weeds can be dug in.

3 With heavy soil, digging is easier if you use the spade to make preparatory 'slits' in the soil at right angles to the trench. The soil can then be removed cleanly.

4 Do not attempt to break up the soil finely. Just turn it over and leave it rough as frost action helps to break up the clods. Frost 'tilth' is very beneficial for soil structure. When you see it on the soil surface, leave it undisturbed for a week to get the maximum benefit.

5 Never dig when it is very wet, very dry or very frosty. However, if you keep your soil covered with a light mulch, say of bracken, the surface is protected and will remain 'diggable' in adverse conditions. The mulch itself can be dug in. On heavy soils, aim to complete the digging by Christmas, to allow plenty of time for frost to break down the clods. On light sandy soils digging is best left until January or February.

6 Where possible, allow at least six weeks for the soil to 'settle' before sowing or planting.

One of the problems with very small gardens is finding the space to double dig: there rarely seems to be a large enough vacant patch of soil. So often forking has to suffice, and opportunities to dig more thoroughly and incorporate organic matter into the soil have to be snatched as they arise. For this reason it is worth trying to plan your garden so that crops which will mature at roughly the same time are adjacent – which is not always as simple as it sounds!

Narrow beds (*Fig. 33*)

The typical modern kitchen garden is a rectangular plot with the vegetables grown in widely spaced rows. But there's a lot to be said for returning to the market gardener's traditional method of growing closely spaced vegetables in narrow beds. Beds can vary from 'a man's reach' – 1·5m (5ft) to the more ladylike metre (3ft), which I myself like. Work out something that suits you and the dimensions of your garden. The beds don't have to be straight: they can be curved.

Paths between beds can be about 30cm (1ft) wide, with an occasional wider path to allow for wide barrow loads.

Narrow beds have several advantages:

1 There is no need to tread on the soil, so the soil structure is preserved. All digging, picking, etc, can be done from the path.

2 All manure is concentrated precisely where the plants will grow.

3 No energy is wasted digging ground that will merely be trodden.

4 They lend themselves to intensive planting and equidistant spacing (see Space saving, Chapter 7). The foliage of most plants then makes a canopy over the soil which prevents weed seeds from germinating. This effect can be reinforced by mulching between the plants. Raised beds and intensive beds are variations on the narrow bed theme (see *Raised Bed Gardening the Organic Way*, Appendix IV).

Ridging narrow beds: on my heavy soil I dig and ridge my narrow beds in autumn in the following way. I first fork the soil down the centre of the bed, then fork the soil on each side, throwing it on to the centre strip to form a ridge which is covered with manure and left all winter. The ridge ensures good drainage and exposes the maximum soil area to frost. In spring it is easily broken down and the remaining manure forked in. The soil is rapidly brought into a suitable state for sowing or planting.

'No-digging'

The 'no-digging' technique is worth a mention. This is a system where digging is abolished in favour of continually mulching the soil, with cultivation more or less restricted to light forking and hoeing. A small area of mulch is scraped away when seeds are sown or planting is carried out. I have no first-hand experience of a totally 'no-digging' system, which is usually combined with narrow beds. It is probably most suited to light soils, and certainly the soil must be well drained, and brought into a high state of fertility, before it can work successfully. The more fertile your soil becomes, the closer you are to that nirvana where no digging is necessary.

Seed and sowing

Seed quality

Most garden vegetables are raised from seed, and for the majority, minimum standards of purity and germination are laid down, so the seed you buy is normally of good quality. All seed deteriorates with age, however, losing its viability, ie its ability to germinate. This process varies with the species. Parsnip seed is a particular problem: it is only good for two seasons. Deterioration is most rapid under damp or hot conditions. So seed should always be kept as cool and dry as possible, *never* in a hot kitchen or damp shed.

The best way to keep it is in an airtight tin or jar, in which there is a handful of cooked rice grains, or a bag or dish of silica gel, to absorb moisture. If possible use cobalt-treated silica gel, which is blue when dry and pink when moist. When it becomes moist dry it in a low oven, then return it to the tin.

Vegetable seed today is often packed in hermetically sealed foil packs. In these seed remains viable much longer than in paper packets, but once the foil packs are open, normal deterioration sets in.

Types of seed
Besides ordinary 'naked' seed, seed firms now offer seed in different forms and with various treatments.

Pelleted seed. Individual seeds are made into tiny balls with a protective coating that breaks down in the soil. They are very easy to handle and can be spaced out accurately, so little if any thinning is necessary. There can be germination problems, however. Sow shallowly, in watered drills (see p. 60) if conditions are dry, and water if necessary until the seed germinates. It will not do so if it dries out.

Seed tapes and sheets. Seeds are embedded into soluble tapes, or tissue-like sheets, well spaced out so that subsequent thinning is minimised. The tapes or sheets are 'sown' by laying them on the soil, or on a seed box, and covering with soil in the normal way. Although they come and go on the market, those I have used have been successful.

Chitted or pre-germinated seed. The seed has just started to germinate – a tiny root can be seen – and is despatched by a seed firm in a small sachet ready for pricking out (see Chapter 4, p. 74). It is a useful short cut for amateurs for seed, such as cucumbers, which require a high temperature to germinate, but can be grown in slightly cooler conditions once they have germinated.

Dressed seed. Seed can be dusted with fungicides to combat soil diseases that prevent germination, especially in cold, wet soil. Sweet corn and peas are often treated. Dressed seed loses its viability rapidly, so should not be kept for a second season. Wash hands after handling it.

Treated seed. Some vegetable diseases (celery leaf spot for example) are seed borne. Seed can be given hot water or chemical treatment to prevent the disease being transmitted.

F_1 hybrids. Plant breeders produce F_1 hybrid seed by crossing two parent lines that have been inbred for several generations. The resulting seed has exceptional vigour and quality. The crossing has to be made each time to produce the seed, so it is expensive but almost always worth the price. Never save F_1 seed: it will not breed true.

Saving your own seed
Amateur gardeners are generally advised against saving their own seed because of the risk of cross pollination and the difficulty in ripening seed in our climate and maintaining its quality. However, I sometimes save

seed from vegetables that seed in early summer, such as broad beans, cress, and Mediterranean rocket. Always save seed from the very best, healthiest plants and, as far as possible, let it ripen naturally on the plant, but if the weather turns wet, pull up the plants and hang them under cover. When the pods are brittle the seed can be shaken out and stored in jars or paper envelopes.

Sowing methods

Several alternative methods are used for sowing:

– *in situ*, ie directly where they are to grow;
– in short close rows in a seed bed from which they are later transplanted into their permanent positions;
– under glass or some other form of protection 'indoors'.

The first method is generally used for root vegetables such as beetroot, carrots, parsnips, radish and turnip, none of which transplant easily, and also for peas and beans.

A seed bed is favoured for brassicas (members of the cabbage family such as cauliflower, Brussels sprouts, kale, etc) mainly to save space. As these vegetables are planted out at least 60cm (2ft) apart, the space they eventually occupy can meanwhile be used for other crops.

Vegetables are raised under glass or indoors either because they are tender and cannot be planted outside until late spring or after the danger of frost is over, or else to extend the growing season and so obtain better or earlier crops (see Chapter 4 for sowing indoors).

There are no hard and fast rules about which method to adopt for any particular vegetable. It will vary according to the part of the country, the cultivar (some cultivars are bred to withstand colder temperatures), and what you are trying to achieve. Take lettuce: it can be sown under glass to provide an early outdoor planting; it can be sown in a seed bed early in spring for the early summer crop, and later sowings can be made *in situ*, when conditions are drier and transplanting more risky. These plants would be thinned out to the required distance.

In the next few pages sowing methods are described in some detail for the benefit of new gardeners. It may sound a little complicated at first, but in fact soon becomes as instinctive as driving a car.

The site for a seed bed

1 If possible make the seed bed in an open position. It is tempting to tuck it into an odd corner near a hedge, for example, but unless the seedlings are transplanted very young, they will become drawn and spindly if they have to strain towards the light, and will suffer from lack of moisture.

2 Make sure the site chosen is free of perennial weeds, as it will be difficult to weed without disturbing the seedlings.

3 Don't use last year's potato plot; tiny sprouting potatoes can be a menace amongst small seedlings.

4 There is a lot of capital locked up in a seed bed, so if plagued by cats and dogs, children, and so on, it is worth wiring it off. Single strands of strong black cotton over individual seed rows will usually deter birds.

Preparing the soil

The same principles apply to sowing in a seed bed or sowing *in situ*. The ground needs to be firm but not consolidated, with the surface free from stones and large lumps of soil, and raked to a fine tilth.

The art lies in knowing the precise point at which to start making the seed bed, ie when the soil is not too wet and not too dry. As a rough guide, if the soil sticks to your shoes as you walk on it, let it dry out for a few more days before tackling it. On the other hand, don't wait until it is completely dry and dusty. Choosing the right moment is largely a question of experience. It is particularly important on clay soils, which are apt to turn from a wet and sticky state into hard intractable clods almost overnight.

If the soil is kept mulched after the spring digging, it will be much easier to make a good seed bed when the time comes. Just rake the mulch aside before starting to work.

Assuming the soil is dug over in the winter or spring, the following are the steps in preparing a seed bed:

1 Fork the soil lightly to a depth of 5 or 7·5cm (2 or 3in) or hoe it, to allow it to dry out.

2 When it is dry enough to crumble to a tilth (possibly the same day, or maybe a few days later), break down any clods with the back of the rake, rake it level, and rake off stones and any remaining lumps of soil. Small lumps can sometimes be crumbled in your hands.

3 Rake the soil gently backwards and forwards until you have the sort of tilth you want. The finer the seeds being sown, the finer the tilth should be. But large seeds like peas and beans are best sown in a fairly coarse tilth, which helps to reduce weed germination.

In the past, treading over the soil before raking was recommended, but now that is felt to be advisable only on very light soils.

Sowing in drills

The commonest method of sowing is in drills, miniature trenches in the soil up to 2cm (¾in) deep. Once the ground has been prepared for sowing, the various stages are as follows:

1 Try and choose a day when the soil is moist, and there is not much
   wind.
2 Mark out your row with the line. Put sticks in either end. In the seed
   bed rows can be very close, say 10–12cm (4–5in) apart for lettuces or
   leeks, about 20–23cm (8–9in) for brassicas.
3 Make a straight, shallow, smooth drill along the line, no more than
   1–2cm ($\frac{1}{2}$–$\frac{3}{4}$in) deep, with the blade of the trowel or the corner of a
   draw hoe, or even a pointed stick.
4 Sow the seeds VERY THINLY. I find it easiest to put some seed from the
   packet into the palm of my left hand, taking a few seeds from there
   with the thumb and forefinger of my right hand. Before covering,
   press them gently in the ground with your hand or the back of the
   rake. In the seed bed it is often best to sow the seeds about 2·5cm
   (1in) apart. It is laborious but much better than shaking a packet at
   random along a row. If sowing *in situ* 'station sowing' is advisable, ie
   sowing a small group of three or four seeds together at intervals
   (*Figs. 8a and 8b*).

   Careful spacing and station sowing both save a great deal of time
in thinning, make weeding easier, and prevent seedlings from
becoming too 'leggy' and entangled with each other, as happens

8. METHODS OF SEED SOWING

10–12cm (4–5in)

a. 'Station sowing' economises on seed so less
   thinning is needed

2·5cm (1in)

b. Space seeds 2·5cm (1in) apart to prevent
   overcrowding

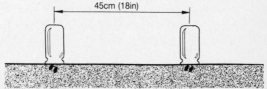

45cm (18in)

c. Large seeds such as cucumbers, marrows and sweetcorn can
   be sown under glass jars to give them an earlier start

when sown too thickly. Exceptions to spaced and station sowing are radishes, carrots and onions, where the 'thinnings' are eaten. Even so, don't sow too thickly.

5 As far as depth is concerned, most small seeds only need to be just covered with soil; larger seeds by about 1cm (½in) of soil. Exceptions are peas and beans which are sown 5–7·5cm (2–3in) deep. As a general rule sow slightly deeper on lighter soils than heavy.

6 Cover the drill by pushing the soil back gently with the fingers, the rake, your boot or the edge of the hoe. Put in a label.

7 Provided the ground is moist, put a 2·5cm (1in) layer of grass cuttings, peat, or well rotted compost between the rows as a mulch, once the seedlings are through and well established. It keeps the weeds down and helps retain the moisture in the soil.

8 If troubled by slugs, put slug pellets between the rows as well.

Sowing in adverse conditions

It is not always possible to sow in ideal conditions.

Wet conditions: if the ground is very wet, drying out can be accelerated by putting cloches over the area you want to sow several days beforehand.

If you must sow while the soil is still stickyish, put a wooden board alongside the row, and stand on it while working. This takes your weight and prevents the soil becoming consolidated.

A little peat sprinkled in the drill will provide more hospitable conditions for the seed.

Dry conditions: if it is necessary to sow when the soil is very dry, for example in one of the dry spells which occur in late spring, or for July and August sowings, either:

give the seed bed a very thorough watering the night before, so that it is moist to the depth of a couple of inches, or

make the drills, and water the *drills only*, until almost muddy (for this use a small house-plant can, or an ordinary can in which a cork with a V-shaped notch cut in it has been inserted into the spout). Sow the seeds, and cover with the *dry* soil from beside the drill, which acts like a mulch and prevents moisture from evaporating.

In dry conditions drills can be lined with moist peat to help germination.

Other methods of sowing

Peas are often sown in flat drills, about 15–20cm (6–8in) wide, 5–7·5cm (2–3in) deep. These are best made with a draw hoe. The drills can be covered with cloches a few days before sowing to allow the soil to warm up (*Fig. 9a*).

I prefer to sow peas in three parallel drills made with the onion hoe. I make the first drill about 5cm (2in) deep, sow the peas about 2·5 or 5cm (1 or 2in) apart, and cover this drill with soil from the second drill (*Fig. 9b*).

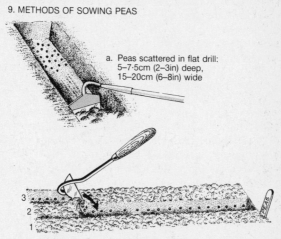

9. METHODS OF SOWING PEAS

a. Peas scattered in flat drill: 5–7·5cm (2–3in) deep, 15–20cm (6–8in) wide

b. Peas sown in three parallel drills, each 5cm (2in) deep, 2·5–5cm (1–2in) apart. Seeds in one drill are covered while making the next

Very large seeds like broad beans can be sown in holes made with the dibber. Just make sure they are not suspended in a pocket of air.

With seeds sown singly always sow a few 'spares' alongside the rows. They are useful for filling in gaps if there are casualties.

Large seeds like cucumbers, marrows and corn can be sown in pairs under jam jars to give extra protection (*Fig. 8c*). Remove the weakest seedling after germination.

Broadcasting

In this method of sowing, seeds are scattered on the surface. Afterwards the soil is usually raked over lightly to cover them. It can be used for early carrots, turnips grown for turnip tops, mustard, cress and other seedling crops (see Cut-and-come-again p. 126). Choose a weed-free piece of ground as weeding can be difficult. Or prepare the seed bed, allow the first flush of weeds to germinate and hoe them off before sowing. In hot weather cover the seed bed with polythene film to keep the surface moist, until the seeds have germinated. You may prefer to sow in very close rows, say 2·5cm (1in) apart. This is easier to weed.

A final word on outdoor sowing. Almost all vegetable seeds germinate very much faster in warm rather than cold soils. Lingering in the soil before germination is often, literally, fatal. So never be in too much of a hurry to start early in the year unless you can provide protective covering such as cloches. The precise time of sowing will depend on where you are and your type of soil. This is one case where the early bird does not catch the worm: he is more likely to catch a cold.

Thinning guidelines

1 Seedlings must never be allowed to overcrowd each other either in their permanent rows or in the seed bed. They must be thinned and surplus seedlings removed, if they are to reach their potential. Unless the thinnings are to be transplanted (as is possible with onions, leeks, lettuces, etc) the best way to thin without disturbing the remaining seedlings is to nip them off at ground level.
2 The ultimate distance to which you thin varies according to the vegetable (recommendations are given in Part Two).
3 Start thinning as soon as you can handle the seedlings, so that they never get cramped; they need room to develop without touching their neighbours.
4 Thin in successive stages to offset any losses from pests or diseases.
5 Choose a time when the soil is moist. If it is dry, water a couple of hours beforehand.
6 Make sure remaining seedlings are not unduly disturbed and firm the soil around them if necessary. Remove all thinnings as their smell can attract the plant's pests.

Planting guidelines

1 As a general rule, the earlier seedlings can be transplanted to their permanent position the better, ie lettuces when they have four leaves, brassicas when about 10cm (4in) high. Beetroot, parsnip and carrots can only be transplanted when they are very small.
2 If possible transplant in dull weather, not in the heat of the day.
3 If the soil is dry, water both the seed bed and the soil into which the plants are being moved, either overnight or several hours beforehand.
4 Handle plants by the leaves rather than the roots, to avoid damaging the delicate root hairs.

5 Use a trowel, dibber, or smaller tool to make a hole large enough to accommodate the roots without cramping them. Hold the plant in the hole as you replace the soil. If planting brassicas in dry weather, 'puddle' or water the hole first.

6 Finally firm the soil around the stem with your fingers and water, (with a rose on the can). Firm planting is essential. Give a leaf a tug when you have finished; if the plant is wobbly, replant it!

7 I like to mulch after planting, to keep moisture in and weeds out.

8 Transplanting is inevitably a shock to a plant; it can be softened by raising plants in pots or soil blocks (see Chapter 4, p. 76).

Heeling-in

If plants are bought but cannot be planted immediately, they are sometimes 'heeled-in' temporarily. Make a shallow V-shaped trench or hole, lay the plants in it close together, cover the roots and part of the stem with the soil, and water them. This technique can be used for mature crops which have to be lifted because the ground is needed – leeks, celeriac or parsnips, for example. Heeled-in plants will keep in reasonable condition for several weeks (*Fig. 44b*).

Storage

Frost-tolerant root crops, such as carrots, beetroot and swedes, can be lifted and stored, either in sand or ashes in a shed, or in small clamps outdoors. Place the roots in a pile on a layer of straw, cover with straw and a layer of soil 5 or 7cm (2 or 3in) thick. Or dig a hole 45cm (18in) deep and put them in it in layers covered with straw or soil.

Mulching

Mulching is the technique of keeping the soil covered with a layer of material, usually organic matter. Suitable materials include compost, peat, lawn mowings, bracken, rotting straw, shredded or pulverised bark, leaves, seaweed, leafmould, spent mushroom compost, spent hops and wilted comfrey. It is worth doing for a number of reasons:

1 It preserves moisture in the soil by preventing evaporation.
2 It keeps down weeds.
3 It improves the soil structure, partly by encouraging the activities of worms. It protects light soils from winter weathering and rain.
4 It has an insulation effect, keeping the soil cooler in summer and warmer in winter.

5 It prevents the soil from being compacted when walking on it.
6 When used under sprawling plants like cucumbers, marrows and
   trailing tomatoes, it keeps the crops clean and dry and helps prevent
   mould infections.
7 Mulches add organic matter and some nutrients to the soil.

All sorts of materials can be used for mulching. The point is that they
should be loose in texture so that air and water can permeate them.
Avoid the sort of material that would settle into a close solid mat. For
this reason don't apply fresh lawn mowings in very wet weather,
though they are most effective when dry (and don't use lawn mowings
that have been treated with a hormone weedkiller). On very wet, low-
lying land only mulch with a dry material such as straw. Seaweed is apt
to attract flies in summer, but they can be deterred with a thin covering
of lawn mowings or peat.

The thickness of the mulch depends on the material and the purpose
of mulching – another case of learning by experience. For keeping
down weeds and preserving moisture, I would suggest about 2cm (1in)
or so of peat, at least 5cm (2in) of lawn mowings, and 15cm (6in) of old
straw which will 'settle' to much less.

Always apply spring and early summer mulches when the soil is
moist and warm.

The remnants of a mulch can be dug in, or allowed to rot naturally
on the surface.

The following are some suggestions for mulching in the vegetable
garden.

In **autumn**, mulch overwintering crops such as celeriac, leeks,
parsnip and winter radish, to keep the soil warm, preserve soil
structure, and make lifting easier in frosty weather.

In **early spring**, mulch after digging; it keeps the soil in a beautiful
condition before making the seed bed.

In **late spring and summer**, mulch between rows in the seed bed after
seedlings have germinated, and between growing crops such as peas,
beans, onions, and carrots, to keep down weeds and preserve
moisture.

In **summer** mulch tomatoes, cucumbers and similar crops to keep
fruit clean.

Watering

In spite of our apparently wet climate, most vegetables benefit from an
increased supply of water, particularly in the drier eastern regions of
the country.

The golden rule of watering is to water gently and thoroughly. For young seedlings and small plants, use a can with a fine rose, a hose with a nozzle which can be adjusted to a fine spray, or a house-plant can with a narrow spout. 'Layflat' polythene tubing, perforated with holes about 30cm (12in) apart, is also useful. It is attached to a hose or tap, and laid on the ground between plants to water them.

A good occasional watering is far more beneficial than light intermittent waterings – which are worthless. Never just sprinkle the surface for ten minutes or so. As a working guide, aim at applying 2·5cm (1in) of water at a time, ie 20lit per sq m (4½gal per sq yd), which will soak the surface to a depth of several inches. This takes much longer than most people realise. It is salutary to poke your finger into the soil after what seems like a heavy shower; it is often remarkably dry. To minimise evaporation losses always water towards evening (but allow time for the plants to dry before nightfall). Rain water is said to be preferable to tap water, so it is good practice to collect your own water from roofs in tubs.

Vegetables need water throughout their growth – key periods being germination and transplanting. But apart from this, different types of vegetables have 'critical periods', when lack of water is most damaging. If water is scarce, confine watering to one really heavy watering during the critical period.

Leafy vegetables such as brassicas, spinach and lettuce are probably the thirstiest of all. Their critical period is 10–20 days before the plant is due for harvesting. The critical period for vegetables grown for their 'fruits' – tomatoes, cucumbers, peas, beans – is when the flowers, fruit and pods are forming. Most root vegetables need to grow steadily: overwatering can result in too much leaf at the expense of roots. So only water them if there is a danger of the soil drying out.

Windbreaks

As anyone with an exposed garden is only too aware, plants hate being buffeted by wind. It has recently been proved that by sheltering vegetables from even light winds, yields can be increased by as much as 20 or 30 per cent.

The best windbreaks are about 50 per cent solid, allowing the air to filter through, for example a well grown hedge, a lath fence, or wattle hurdles. A completely solid windbreak such as a wall can create a destructive area of turbulence on the lee side.

Where wind is a problem, it is worth erecting or growing some sort of barrier. Netting such as Rokolene or Netlon windbreak can be attached to posts with batons. Even a wire netting enclosure around a vegetable patch has a sheltering effect. Nylon netting or hessian sacks a foot or so high can be strung between rows of vegetables to provide a shelter. Such shelter is considered effective for a distance of roughly six times its height: so 60cm (2ft) high barriers would need to be about 3½m (12ft) apart.

In small gardens draughts caused by gaps between buildings are very damaging and should be remedied. Erect a windbreak extending several feet beyond the gap on each side to make sure the gap is fully protected. Winds have nasty sneaky habits!

CHAPTER FOUR

Sowing Indoors

Fortunately most of our vegetables can be sown outdoors. The few that have to be sown indoors are 'tender', and unless started off in protected conditions, would be unlikely to reach maturity in our comparatively short summer.

They are mostly foreign introductions such as tomatoes, peppers, cucumbers, marrows, sweetcorn and some herbs. Celeriac and celery are also best raised this way. Leeks, lettuces, runner and French beans and Brussels sprouts, among others, are sometimes started indoors to get earlier or superior crops.

You can either raise these plants yourself, or buy them from a nurseryman at the planting out stage. There is a good deal to be said for doing it yourself. It is intrinsically very satisfying, and it is cheaper in the long run. Once you have mastered it your plants will be better and healthier than any you buy and you will not be restricted to the very narrow selection sold for planting out. With the equipment available today, raising plants is not difficult.

Sowing 'indoors' or 'under cover' generally implies sowing in a heated or unheated greenhouse, or in your own house, perhaps in a porch or on a window sill, or in frames or under cloches outside.

For a small garden elaborate and costly facilities such as a heated greenhouse are unnecessary. A reasonably early start, with adequate results, can be obtained by using small domestic propagators, or warm cupboards or shelves above radiators; slightly later sowings can be made in cold greenhouses or cloches or frames outside.

But a word of warning. With modern sowing composts getting seeds to germinate is no problem. The skill, especially for the tender plants, lies in providing good growing conditions *after* germination, in the intervening weeks before planting out. If the temperature at this stage, particularly at night, is too low the seedlings may die off; if the light is inadequate they will become weak, spindly and pale. So make sure you have somewhere warm and light to keep plants in the interim period.

The great temptation with sowing indoors is to start too early. But the tender vegetables cannot be planted out in the open until all risk of frost is over, which in much of the country is not until the end of May or early June. If plants are ready too soon they simply hang about deteriorating. The aim should always be to maintain steady growth, which leads to sturdy healthy plants. Recommendations on sowing times will be given under the individual vegetables.

The main stages in raising plants indoors can be summarised as follows:

1 Sowing seed in soil or compost in small containers.
2 'Pricking out', ie transplanting the individual seedlings into larger containers.
3 Either 'potting on', ie transplanting the small plant into a larger pot or planting it directly outside after 'hardening off'.

Large seeds such as sweetcorn can be sown singly in 7·5cm (3in) pots, so the intermediate steps of pricking out and potting on are eliminated. They can also be avoided by using soil blocks and the various types of divided seed tray (see p. 76).

Equipment for indoor sowing

The following are the essentials:
  a container
  sowing or potting compost
  propagator or some means of creating a warm damp atmosphere.

10. RANGE OF CONTAINERS FOR SEED SOWING
Seed tray fitted with plastic dome; clay seed pan; plastic
seed tray; compressed Jiffy 7s; peat, plastic and clay pots

Containers (*Fig. 10*)

The most commonly used containers are:

clay or plastic seed pans, no more than 4cm (1½in) deep

seed trays – use the smallest available size

clay or plastic pots, 5 or 7·5cm (2 or 3in) diameter

peat pots, black polythene pots and types of paper pot. All these are 'disposable', so valuable where storage space is limited.

Cheap forms of container (*Fig. 11a & b*) are easily improvised, for example:

plastic sandwich boxes with fitting lids; these are excellent

plastic pots in which yoghurt, cottage cheese, etc, are sold, and discarded plastic beakers

plastic 'squash' cartons

strawberry punnets, plastic egg cartons

egg shells. Stand these in egg trays or cartons. Shells can be planted out direct, as roots penetrate them. Squeeze the shell gently when planting, if not already cracked.

fibre egg cartons, which can be cut into sections and planted out direct. (Sow seed in the lid and prick out into the bottom sections.)

The important point with all improvised containers is that, if the seeds are liable to be in them for some time, they must be porous or else drainage holes should be made in the base to prevent the soil or compost going 'sour'. Drainage holes can be made in plastic pots with hot knitting needles or a hot poker.

Sowing and potting composts

Compost is the general term given to the mixture into which seeds are sown, pricked out, or potted. It should not be confused with compost from the compost heap, which is usually referred to as garden compost.

If seeds (particularly small seeds) are sown indoors in ordinary garden soil the results are usually poor; a more porous medium is needed. Traditionally, sowing and potting composts were made by mixing sieved garden loam, peat and sand. This is laborious, time and space consuming, and difficult to do well, so I would recommend people with small gardens and limited shed space to use the modern peat-based (soilless) composts, which are widely sold. In some brands there are different grades for sowing and potting; with others the same compost can be used for all stages. Follow the manufacturer's instructions.

Results with these composts are excellent. They provide a well drained porous medium in which roots make good fibrous growth. They are sterile, so there are no problems with weed seeds and seedling diseases. They are light to handle and store well. The main

11. IMPROVISED CONTAINERS

a. Plastic cartons, sandwich boxes, yoghurt pots, egg shells in egg trays

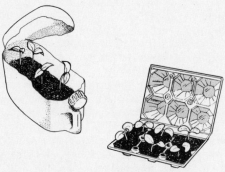

b. These, with lids, are closed in the initial stages of germination. The 2-lit (½ gal) plastic squash carton is useful for large seeds such as beans

difficulty is that once in use the composts must be kept moist or the seedlings will suffer. The peat is very difficult to re-wet once dry.

Alternative composts

John Innes composts. These are a range of soil-based composts, mixed to a formula. They are heavier to handle than peat-based composts, but less liable to dry out. The J.I. seed compost should be used for sowing small seeds like celery and celeriac, but most seeds can be sown direct into J.I. potting compost No 1. The quality of J.I. compost varies, so always buy from a reliable source.

Sieved leafmould. The top 5 or 7·5cm (2 or 3in) of soil from a hardwood forest or wood make excellent sowing compost. It is best to sieve it through a 0·5cm (⅛in) sieve.

Peat/sand mixtures. A suitable sowing compost can be made by mixing 2 parts of good quality peat with 1 part of coarse builders' sand or silver sand.

Combined containers and composts

Several commercial products which combine container and compost are now being sold. Best known are the Jiffy 7 pots, made of sphagnum peat compressed into a disc, and enclosed in a fine net. When watered Jiffy 7s swell to seven times their original size – great fun for children to watch! They are particularly useful for sowing seeds or pricking out seedlings. The roots eventually penetrate the pot, which is planted out direct with the minimum of disturbance.

Seed-raising kits with seed pre-sown in a carton of compost are also available. The container lid is used as a watering tray after germination. These are useful for seed raising on windowsills.

Creating a warm atmosphere

Most vegetable seeds will germinate satisfactorily if a temperature of 13 or 16°C (55 or 60°F) can be maintained. As soil temperature is more important than air temperature at this stage, the ideal source of heat is from below – 'bottom heat' as it is called.

The small 'plug-in' propagators operate on this principle. The heat source is either a light bulb or electric cables housed beneath a tray on which pots or a seed tray stand (*Fig. 12*). A moist atmosphere is created by a sheet of polythene or a plastic dome over the seed trays. These small propagators are economic to run. An ordinary, free-standing table hot plate can be used as a propagator base.

Without a propagator germination will probably be slower and more erratic, but can still be very satisfactory. Any warm place – near a

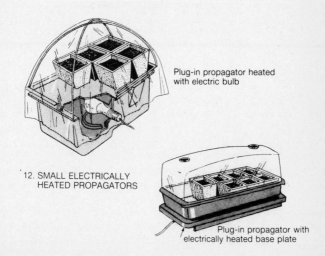

Plug-in propagator heated with electric bulb

12. SMALL ELECTRICALLY
HEATED PROPAGATORS

Plug-in propagator with electrically heated base plate

stove, in an airing cupboard, above a radiator, on a window sill (but away from direct sunlight or draughts) will do.

13. STAGES IN SEED SOWING

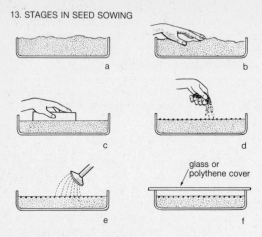

a. Fill box loosely with compost
b. Firm lightly with fingertips, making sure corners are filled
c. Firm surface using a piece of wood
d. Sow seeds thinly on surface. Cover all but tiny seeds with thin layer of compost or coarse sand. Firm surface lightly after sowing
e. Water thoroughly with a fine rose, or by soaking up water from beneath. This can either be done several hours before sowing, or after sowing
f. Cover with glass sheet or dome, or put into a plastic bag, and leave somewhere warm to germinate; or put uncovered into a propagator

Sowing in peat-based compost

1 Slightly overfill your container. Provided you leave room for 4cm (1½in) of compost you can economise on it by putting a 1 or 2cm (½ or ¾in) layer of moistened foam rubber in the bottom.

2 Firm the compost lightly with the fingertips. Make sure there are no gaps at the edges or corners. Then press it down firmly with a piece of wood or the bottom of the pot.

3 Sow the seeds very thinly on the surface. Germination is so good with peat composts, that thick sowing will result in overcrowding. If seeds are spaced carefully, they will suffer less if pricking out has to be delayed. They can even be spaced 1–2·5cm (½–1in) apart.
   Small seeds do not have to be covered, but cover larger seeds with a thin layer of compost or sand. Firm the surface lightly after sowing.

4 Water the seeds thoroughly with a fine rose, or stand the containers in a watertight vessel or sink, and allow them to soak up the water from below. This system is certainly preferable for very small seeds and for peat pots. An easy way of doing it is to line a large seed tray with polythene or tinfoil, or use a 2¼lit (½gal) plastic container (*Fig. 11b*) (the sort squash is sold in), cut in half. Some manufacturers of peat composts recommend watering their composts several hours in advance of sowing. Do not ever allow seeds to become waterlogged.

5 Put seeds into the warm, moist atmosphere of a propagator to germinate. Where there is no propagator, put into a warm place, conserving moisture by, for example:

covering the seed tray with a sheet of glass (wipe off the condensation daily);

putting seed tray or pots into a plastic bag (remove the plastic daily for a short airing);

using seed trays fitted with transparent domes, sandwich boxes with lids on, and so on.

Sowing in soil-based compost

The procedure is the same, only a layer of roughage should be put in the bottom of the container to assist drainage. Old pot crocks, stones, or granite chippings can be used, covered by a few dried leaves or dried moss. Seed trays can be lined with several layers of newspaper. Make the compost firmer than you would with a peat-based compost.

(For stages in seed sowing see *Fig. 13*).

Treatment after germination

Examine your seeds daily – things can happen very fast! Most vegetable seeds will germinate within four to ten days.

As soon as they are showing through:

1 If they were in the dark (say in a warm cupboard), bring them into the light at once, or the seedlings will become weak and drawn.

2 Remove close-fitting sandwich box lids, glass covers, etc. Propagator domes can be partly lifted to give some ventilation.

3 Keep seedlings away from bright sunlight for a few days; direct sun can massacre tiny seedlings in minutes. If you have to go out and leave them all day on a windowsill, prop up a piece of cardboard as shading.

4 From then on give seedlings airy conditions and as much full light as possible. The big danger is allowing them to stagnate. If on a windowsill turn them regularly so that they do not get drawn in one direction.

5 Keep moist, but not over-watered, either with careful overhead watering or with the soaking up method.
6 Prick out as soon as possible.

Pricking out (*Fig. 14*)
Seedlings are 'pricked out', ie moved when very small, into seed boxes or seed trays, 7·5cm (3in) deep for preference, or into small pots, usually 6 or 7·5cm (2½ or 3in) diameter, filled with potting compost.

14. STAGES IN PRICKING OUT
Celeriac seedlings being pricked out into a seed tray from the pot in which they were sown. Seedlings should always be held by the leaves

Better plants will result from pricking out into individual pots, but they of course take up more space. For celery, celeriac, leeks and herbs, seed trays or seed boxes are quite adequate. The main requirement at this stage is for space around each seedling to allow it to develop, and a good growing medium for the roots. Prick out as follows:

1 Seedlings can usually be transplanted as soon as two true leaves, as opposed to the initial 'seed leaves', have appeared; if they have plenty of space they can be left longer.
2 Only prick out healthy seedlings; duds very rarely recover sufficiently to grow into good plants.
3 Make sure the compost they are in is moist before moving them. If not water and leave to drain before pricking out.
4 Fill the new containers with potting compost, making it firm and

watering as for seed sowing (if the compost is already slightly moist, watering can be done after pricking out).

5 Remove seedlings very carefully with the minimum root disturbance. Hold them by the leaves, not by the stem or roots.

6 Make a small hole with a miniature dibber, or 7·5cm (3in) nail, just large enough for the roots.

7 Hold seedling slightly above soil level, put into hole, press the compost around it firmly but gently, so that seed leaves are almost at soil level.

8 Make sure there are no air pockets under the seedling.

9 Level off the box.

10 Water with a fine rose, unless previously watered.

11 Shade seedlings from direct sun for first two or three days.

Seedlings which are pricked out into peat pots or Jiffy 7s (*Fig. 15*) can be stood on a moist layer of peat, compost or sand to prevent them drying out. If in addition, moist peat, compost or sand is packed around and between the pots, the roots will grow into the compost, making fine sturdy plants. This is a good way of overcoming the harmful effects of 'hanging about', until it is warm enough for planting outdoors.

The pots in which plants are growing should be spaced out as they grow so that the leaves of adjacent plants are not touching. If the soil in the pots starts to look 'stagnant', and greens over, give the surface a stir with a small tool or plant label.

Potting on

Tomatoes, peppers, and similar plants which will be finally grown in large pots of 15, 20 or 25cm (6, 8 or 10in) diameter, need to be moved from their seed boxes, small peat pots or Jiffy 7s, into larger pots when about 10cm (4in) high. As it is never advisable to move plants into a much larger container at one go, it may be necessary to pot them into an intermediate-sized pot first.

Potting procedure:

1 Water plants several hours in advance and allow to drain.

2 Put a little compost in the new container, on top of drainage material if a soil compost is used.

3 Tap the pot base on a flat surface to consolidate the compost.

4 Place the plant centrally in the pot, holding it so that the lowest 'seed leaves' are just above the soil.

5 Fill with compost, leaving about 1cm ($\frac{1}{2}$in) space below rim for watering.

6 Firm around plant with fingers, tapping the pot base occasionally to consolidate and level the soil.

7 Water or spray very lightly; water more heavily after two or three days.

8 Shelter from direct sun for two or three days.

15. RAISING PLANTS IN INDIVIDUAL PEAT POTS

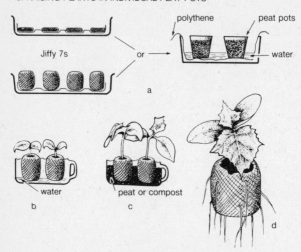

a. *(top left)*. Compressed compost-filled Jiffy 7 discs absorb water from below so that they swell to their full size before seeds are sown in them. *(top right)*. Peat pots are filled with potting compost and allowed to soak up water until thoroughly moist before seeds are sown in them

b. Compost in peat pots easily dries out, so the pots are stood in a water-tight container, with a little water in the bottom to keep them moist

c. At later stages, especially if there is a delay before planting, peat compost or sand can be packed loosely around the pots, preserving moisture. Roots will grow out of the pots into the medium, making a strong plant

d. Gherkin ready for planting out at 4-leaf stage

Soil blocks (*Fig. 16*)

Soil blocks are compact, compressed blocks of soil- or peat-based compost into which single (occasionally several) seeds are sown. When the seedlings are large enough the blocks are planted straight into the ground or, where appropriate, into large pots. Blocks vary in size and shape, the most common being cubes 4cm (1½in) deep. The use of blocks is highly recommended, for several reasons:

1 They are very economical with seed.
2 No pricking out or thinning is necessary.

3 Exceptionally strong, good quality plants can be grown, as each develops in its own block with no competition.
4 There is no root disturbance when planting. Plants that normally dislike transplanting, e.g. Chinese cabbage, can be planted in blocks.
5 There is flexibility over planting. The protection offered by the blocks means planting can take place in otherwise unfavourable conditions, such as in very wet soil. Plants can 'hang about' in blocks without too much of a set-back and 'spares' can be kept in the wings for planting into gaps or vacant ground as space becomes available.
6 A variety of plants can be raised in a small space. A seed tray of 40 blocks could have 10 each of lettuce, cabbage, sprouts and onions.

Making soil blocks

Soil blocks are easiest to make with a proprietary *blocking* compost. If it is unobtainable, use a soil- or peat-based potting compost. *Sowing* compost has insufficient nutrients to sustain seedlings until planted out. Blocks are made with hand-blocking tools (see *Fig. 16*) which leave an indentation on the top of the block into which the seed is sown.

It's important to get the compost to the right consistency. It needs to be wetter than ordinary compost, and may need to be left to soak overnight in a basin. When it is ready, pack the compost fairly firmly into the blocker, push down the lever, and release the blocks into a seed tray or on to a flat base. Pack them closely to conserve moisture.

Normally only one seed is sown per block. (If you're uncertain of the seeds' viability, test a few somewhere warm, on moist blotting paper. They should germinate in a few days.) Alternatively sow several seeds per block, nipping off all but one seedling after germination.

Large seeds are easily sown by hand. Smaller seeds are trickier. Either put them on a piece of paper and push them off singly into the blocks, or spread them on a saucer, and pick up one at a time with the moistened tip of a piece of glass. When the glass touches the block the seed falls off. I know I shouldn't recommend broken glass as a tool but personally I've found nothing touches it for efficiency. Please use it carefully! Cover the seeds with a little soil from the edge of the block. In some cases – leeks, onions, beet for example – several seeds can be sown in one block and planted out 'as one' without thinning. These will be discussed where relevant in Part Two. Pre-germinated seed can also be sown direct into blocks.

Procedure after sowing is the same as for sowing seed in trays, but take extra care not to let the blocks dry out. They are ready for planting when roots are visible on the outside of the block. Water very thoroughly *before* planting out, especially where peat-based compost is used.

16. SOIL BLOCKS AND 'CELLULAR' SEED TRAYS

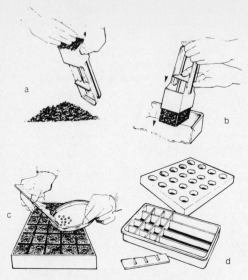

a. Packing blocking or potting compost into the
   hand blocker
b. Pushing out the block into a seed tray
c. Using a piece of glass to sow a single seed
   in the block
d. Other 'cellular' systems: polystyrene 'Propapack' *(above)*;
   seed tray with interlocking plastic dividers *(below)*

There are several types of cellular seed tray which perform much the same function as blocks (*Fig. 16d*). Best known are the moulded polystyrene 'Propapacks'. 'Cells' or holes in the trays are filled with loose compost, which settles into a compact block. Seeds are sown or seedlings transplanted into the cells, which are pushed out for planting. The trays are reusable: their main drawback is that they occupy a fair amount of space. Standard seed trays can also be divided into compartments with interlocking plastic dividers or makeshift dividers of some kind. With all these the object is to produce good plants with strong root systems. In a small garden a few productive plants are far better value than numerous poor specimens.

Hardening off
Young plants should never be subjected to shocks – such as cold water, draughts, drought, or a sudden drop in temperature. Before moving

plants outdoors permanently from the protected environment of the greenhouse or house, they should be allowed to acclimatise or 'harden off' over a ten-day to two-week period. Gradually increase their ventilation, stand them outside for a few hours each day when the weather is warm (gradually increasing the length of time outside) or move them to frames or cloches. Keep these closed at first, then open a little longer each day, until finally they are left open at night as well. By then the plants should be tough enough to be planted out in their permanent position.

Hardening off is particularly important where seeds have been raised in peat-based composts, which tend to produce rather lush, soft growth; soil-based composts produce somewhat harder growth.

CHAPTER FIVE

Pests, Diseases and Weeds

Pests, diseases, unfavourable conditions and weeds take their toll of vegetables in terms of quality and quantity. Commercial vegetable growers spend a great deal of money on insecticides, fungicides and weedkillers so that they get the highest possible yields and completely unblemished produce for marketing.

On a small scale this is unnecessary. It does not matter if there are a few holes in a cabbage leaf or the odd maggoty pea. However, it is most annoying to lose all one's carrots to carrot fly, or to find most of the brassicas have succumbed to clubroot. But there are practical, non-chemical solutions to most of these problems, which can be used successfully in small gardens. More on that subject later.

The main pests and diseases to which particular vegetables are prone will be covered later in Part Two. But here let us take an overall look at the various types of trouble.

Pests

To start with, there is the damage caused by insects and closely related species. Vegetables are mainly attacked by the caterpillars of various moths and butterflies, by the adults and grubs of some beetles, by weevils and by the maggots of tiny flies such as the onion fly and the carrot fly.

Pests which live in the soil (*Fig. 17*) include millipedes, cutworms, wireworms, chafer bugs and leatherjackets. These last three are the larval forms of the click beetle, May and June bugs, and the crane fly alias daddy-long-legs, respectively. Besides these there are eelworms, microscopic soil pests which are particularly damaging to potatoes.

Working mostly above ground, night-feeding slugs skeletonise leaves by the morning. Their cousins the snails, though less damaging, are by no means innocent. All these creatures feed on plants by biting the leaves, stems or roots.

Another group of insects, most notable among them the aphids, greenfly and blackfly, and the related whitefly, pierce leaves and other parts of the plant and suck the sap. Aphids not only cause physical damage, but often transmit virus diseases in the process. Instead of the typical holes left by biting insects, leaves attacked by sucking insects are distorted, often twisted, curled or blistered.

Fortunately there are ways and means of dealing with most of these pests.

In many gardens it is the larger pests which are the real problem: mice taking peas and broad bean seeds, moles tunnelling unmercifully

17. SOIL PESTS

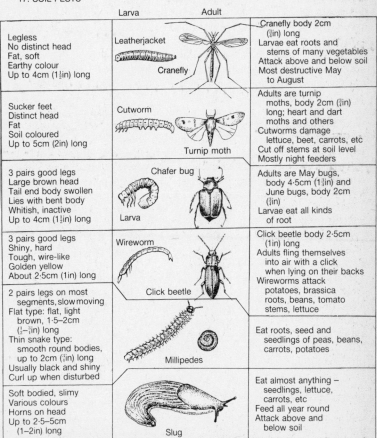

	Larva	Adult	
Legless No distinct head Fat, soft Earthy colour Up to 4cm (1½in) long	Leatherjacket Cranefly		Cranefly body 2cm (¾in) long Larvae eat roots and stems of many vegetables Attack above and below soil Most destructive May to August
Sucker feet Distinct head Fat Soil coloured Up to 5cm (2in) long	Cutworm Turnip moth		Adults are turnip moths, body 2cm (¾in) long; heart and dart moths and others Cutworms damage lettuce, beet, carrots, etc Cut off stems at soil level Mostly night feeders
3 pairs good legs Large brown head Tail end body swollen Lies with bent body Whitish, inactive Up to 4cm (1½in) long	Chafer bug Larva		Adults are May bugs, body 4·5cm (1¾in) and June bugs, body 2cm (¾in) Larvae eat all kinds of root
3 pairs good legs Shiny, hard Tough, wire-like Golden yellow About 2·5cm (1in) long	Wireworm Click beetle		Click beetle body 2·5cm (1in) long Adults fling themselves into air with a click when lying on their backs Wireworms attack potatoes, brassica roots, beans, tomato stems, lettuce
2 pairs legs on most segments, slow moving Flat type: flat, light brown, 1·5–2cm (½–¾in) long Thin snake type: smooth round bodies, up to 2cm (¾in) long Usually black and shiny Curl up when disturbed	Millipedes		Eat roots, seed and seedlings of peas, beans, carrots, potatoes
Soft bodied, slimy Various colours Horns on head Up to 2·5–5cm (1–2in) long	Slug		Eat almost anything – seedlings, lettuce, carrots, etc Feed all year round Attack above and below soil

through rows of seedlings and uprooting plants; cats and dogs scratching around as they go about their business. Last, but by no means least, are birds. The ravages of pigeons and jays on young peas, winter greens, or a seed bed of brassicas is heart-breaking. Sparrows are very serious pests in some areas. They usually attack seedlings, in particular lettuce, beetroot and spinach. With most of these pests the answer lies not so much in destroying them as in deterrents, and in physically protecting the crops. Birds, it should be added, also do much good in devouring insect pests.

Diseases

The diseases which affect vegetables can be divided into two groups. The first includes those caused by fungi, bacteria and viruses. The fungi produce threads which are visible to the naked eye, while the bacteria and viruses are microscopic; you only see the resulting damage.

Fungi and bacteria cause greyish moulds and mildews on leaves; clubroot gall in brassicas; the various rots which can ruin stored onions, and damping off diseases, which cause seedlings to droop and die shortly after they come through the soil.

Virus diseases are very strange, often fatal, and still something of an unknown quantity. One example is cucumber mosaic. The leaves of the cucumber become mottled, gradually develop a yellowish mosiac pattern, the whole plant becomes stunted and eventually dies. If you suspect a plant of having a virus disease (obviously stunted growth and mottling are fairly common symptoms), it is wisest to pull it up and burn it to prevent the spread of infection.

All these diseases are infectious, and can spread very rapidly in conditions which suit them. They are much harder to control, either with chemicals or by other means, than pests. Indeed in many cases once the disease has become obvious it is too late to do anything about it. Prevention is better – and easier – than cure.

The second group of diseases, usually dubbed 'physiological', are not infectious in the same sense. They are caused by poor conditions: for example temperatures that are too high or too low for the vegetable; lack of water or faulty watering; poor nutrition, a mineral deficiency or even an excess of a chemical salt in the soil due to using too much artificial fertiliser. Again, these troubles can be prevented. In well-grown plants they should not arise.

General preventive measures

If this catalogue of plant troubles seems unduly long, take comfort from the fact that many pests and diseases can be avoided, or their effects considerably minimised, by growing plants well. Vegetables growing in a fertile, well-drained soil with plenty of organic matter, a balanced supply of nutrients and adequate moisture are much more likely to withstand attacks by pests and diseases.

It is the seeds which are slow to germinate because the soil conditions are poor, the lingering seedlings unable to develop a good root system, and the plants which never 'get away' which are most vulnerable to pests and diseases.

In very acid soils that bane of the cabbage family, clubroot, is often prevalent. Liming is the first step here towards prevention of future attacks. In light hungry soils potato scab, a disease which gives potatoes a most unwholesome look, is often a problem. It can be remedied by digging in organic matter such as decayed leaves or grass mowings – anything up to a barrow load to 4sq metres (4sq yards).

So the first and most important step in preventing disease is to improve the soil's fertility.

Garden hygiene

The next series of preventive measures come under the general heading of garden hygiene. At some stage in their life cycle many of the common garden pests and diseases depend on rubbish, bricks, etc, that are lying about, or weeds, to provide them with protection. Remove these sources of protection and you are hitting the pest where it hurts. There are many examples.

The fungi which cause downy mildews overwinter in plant debris; aphids which attack cabbages and many other plants hide in cabbages, broccoli and Brussels sprouts in winter, and in late spring produce a winged generation which immediately flies off to infect the nearest victim. That wretched pest of young seedlings, the flea beetle, hides in convenient rubbish or patches of weeds during the winter; slugs are permanently on the look-out for sheltered spots, such as rubbish, bits of wood or rotten cabbage leaves under which to lay their eggs or shelter from bad weather.

One of the virus diseases which attacks lettuce survives the winter in weed seeds, particularly chickweed. Weeds also harbour pests such as cabbage root fly, carrot fly, the blackfly which attacks broad beans and the fungus which causes clubroot.

For these reasons rubbish should always be removed from the garden. Dead wood and diseased material of any kind should be burnt; everything else that will rot can go on the compost heap. Odd bits of slate, wood, bricks, and so on should be tidied away. Never leave the roots of vegetables in the ground when they are finished. Chop them up and put them on the compost heap if they are healthy; burn them if they are diseased. If possible, try to clear those old brassicas out of the ground by mid-May, to prevent the spring hatch of aphids. Keep weeds down, and clear out hidey-holes for pests: old dry leaves under hedges and debris in the bottom of ditches are favourite haunts.

18. COMMON PEST AND DISEASE DAMAGE

a. Clubroot: distorted root swellings on
   cabbage plant caused by clubroot fungus

b. Carrot fly: carrot root tunnelled by tiny
   maggots, about ½cm (⅛in) long, which
   cause severe damage

c. Cabbage root fly: young plant
   severely damaged by cabbage root fly
   maggot. Infected plants wilt and die

Cultural practices

By adopting certain cultural practices diseases and pests can often be avoided.

Sowing

Many seedling diseases result from seeds being sown too thickly or in a cold atmosphere. Always sow thinly, and wait until the soil has had a chance to warm up; if possible put cloches over the soil a couple of days before sowing in early spring. A firm seed bed with a good tilth is the best guarantee of quick germination, which in turn is the first step towards avoiding the pests and diseases which attack seeds and seedlings.

Rotation

Many pests and diseases which remain in the soil only attack plants of a particular family. They can be starved out if they are deprived of their favourite hosts, to use the technical term. So it is always advisable to move crops around as much as possible from year to year. For example, if a piece of ground has been used for root crops (beetroot, carrot, parsnip), grow onions, peas, beans, spinach or cabbage there the next time, and so on. Rotation is almost impossible in a very small garden; but whenever there is a chance to use a particular piece of ground for a different type of crop, take it. Long term rotation, anything up to seven years, is the only practical means of overcoming some eelworm pests. (For rotation groups see pp. 141 and 142.)

Overcrowding

Never overcrowd plants. There must be room for air to circulate around them; fungus diseases in particular spread rapidly in stagnant conditions. Where plants are too close they will compete for water and nutrients. There is no need to be as extravagant with space as our forefathers, but better results will often be obtained from a few plants given sufficient space rather than too many crowded together – another case of finding a happy medium.

Handling vegetables for storing

Always handle vegetables that are being stored very carefully. This applies particularly to onions. The rots which can destroy stored onions are most liable to infect onions which have been cut or even bruised in handling.

Timing and deterrent tactics

Some pests and diseases can be avoided by varying the sowing time.

For example, autumn and early spring sowings of broad beans escape the worst of the blackfly aphids; turnips sown in June largely escape flea beetle attacks.

If onions are grown from sets rather than seed, damage by the onion fly is avoided. In my experience, planting French marigolds between tomato and pepper plants, grown under cover, lessens whitefly attacks, perhaps on account of the strong scent of the foliage.

In a garden where both potatoes and outdoor tomatoes are being grown, plant the tomatoes as far as possible from the potatoes to cut down the risk of infection from potato blight.

Resistant varieties

Scientists have had considerable success in breeding cultivars of vegetables which are immune, or at least display considerable resistance, towards certain diseases (there is no guarantee that resistance is permanent; pests and diseases are quite capable of developing new strains which will overcome the resistance!). However, examples of useful recent introductions include Marian swede, which is highly tolerant of mildew and clubroot, Great Lakes, Avoncrisp and Avondefiance lettuce with resistance to lettuce root aphid, Avonresister parsnip with resistance to canker, and many more besides. Scientists are currently trying to breed carrots with resistance to carrot fly. I wish them luck!

Seed treatments

Seeds can sometimes be treated chemically to eliminate certain seed-borne diseases or give protection against others. Celery and celeriac seed are now regularly treated to prevent celery leaf spot. It is worth perusing seed catalogues to take advantage of any new developments along these lines. While on the subject of seed, always get the best quality seed you can. It pays.

Chemical control of pests and diseases

As we are all aware, there are now many chemicals with which pests, diseases and weeds can be controlled. I personally feel that anyone growing vegetables in a small garden should only use them as a last resort. Almost all these chemicals are poisonous to creatures besides those which they are intended to kill. Bees and other pollinating insects can be killed by insecticides, as can the natural predators of many pests and diseases. Pets can become addicted to and poisoned by some slug baits; the insecticides which kill soil pests also kill beneficial insects in the soil, and there is always the risk of children swallowing weedkiller or pesticides with tragic results. It is also easy to damage the plants themselves with overdoses of chemicals.

In the long term insects and diseases can build up resistance, so the less a chemical is used, the longer its effective 'life' will be. As for human beings, in many cases we do not know what effect the chemicals we absorb will have on us. It is better to err on the safe side. Finally, chemicals are expensive. If your main motive for growing vegetables is economic, a shelf full of chemicals will rapidly eat into your profits. Use preventive and alternative measures wherever you can.

If you do use chemicals, it is important to keep to the rules:

- Always follow the manufacturers' instructions meticulously;
- Always spray in the evening or in dull weather when pollinating insects are not flying;
- Never spray water, ditches, ponds, rain tubs, and so on, or allow spray to drift on to water;
- Never spray when it is windy, or allow spray to drift on to neighbouring gardens;
- Try to make up no more spray than is needed, as the surplus will have to be disposed of;
- Never transfer chemicals to other containers such as beer or soft drink bottles;
- Store chemicals in tightly shut containers or tins, in a cool dry place well out of the reach of pets and children;
- Wash hands and equipment very thoroughly after use.

Types of pesticide

The term pesticide covers all chemicals used for controlling pests and diseases. It includes insecticides for controlling insects, and fungicides for controlling fungus diseases. Pesticides act either as 'contact' poisons, killing the pests or diseases on the surface at the time or shortly after application, or as 'systemics', which are absorbed into the plant's system in the sap and remain effective over a longer period, killing insects which attack subsequently.

Systemic insecticides are useful for reaching aphids which are otherwise inaccessible inside curled leaves; they are less useful against caterpillars which do not ingest much sap. Systemic fungicides allow control of fungus diseases which have already established themselves within the plant's tissues.

In many cases several applications of a pesticide are necessary to control the pest or disease completely; again, follow the manufacturer's instructions.

Methods of application

Pesticides can be applied as dusts, sprays, aerosols, paste or pellets. In the case of insect pests it does not always follow that the same range of pests will be controlled by all forms of the pesticide – so study labels carefully.

On a small scale puffer packs of dusts and aerosols, in both of which the chemical is in a form ready for use, are very handy. Sprays have to be made up from the concentrated powder or solution and applied through some form of sprayer. As spray goes a long way, a half litre (one pint) capacity hand sprayer, preferably with an adjustable nozzle, is quite adequate for average use in a small garden.

Some pesticides, but not all, are compatible with others, ie they can be mixed together or applied with foliar feeds. Always check first before using a particular mixture.

The safer pesticides

There are a few pesticides that are approved for use by 'organic' gardeners and growers. These are mainly derived from plants, and compared to chemical pesticides, break down fairly rapidly into harmless products. There is therefore far less risk of harmful residues being left in the soil or on the plant, or of damage to the environment. On the whole they don't affect the beneficial insects which, if left unharmed, will see a lot of pests off the premises! The drawback is that their effectiveness against any pest is relatively short-lived, and they are not as powerful as the modern chemical pesticides. But I recommend their use in small gardens. Remember, though, even these 'safer' pesticides are poisons and should be handled with care.

Where unobtainable through normal gardening outlets, most are available from Henry Doubleday Research Association (see Appendix III).

SAFER PESTICIDES

Product	Comments	Effective against
Derris	Available as liquid or dust Harmless to bees and hoverfly larvae Harmful to fish (keep away from ponds)	(liquid form) aphids, cater- pillars, red spider (dust form) flea beetle

Product	Comments	Effective against
Pyrethrum	Available as liquid or dust Not harmful to natural predators or bees Its effectiveness against pests is increased if mixed with derris, as in 'Pydercite'	aphids caterpillars flea beetles
Nicotine	Available as 2% liquid nicotine soap Harmless to predators, but kills bees so spray in evening Poisonous to mammals; wear gloves when spraying to protect skin; don't eat sprayed plants for 48 hours Dilute 1 in 40 for aphids, 1 in 20 for other pests	aphids, mealy bugs, most caterpillars, pea and bean weevils, red spider, thrips
Home-made rhubarb spray	Chop up 3lb rhubarb leaves, boil for $\frac{1}{2}$hr in 3·5lit (6pt) water, strain off liquid and leave to cool; dissolve 28g (1oz) soapflakes in 1·2lit (2pt) water, mix with rhubarb liquid and spray Some rhubarb varieties (eg Victoria, Albert) more effective than others; Glaskins Perpetual not recommended	aphids
Bordeaux mixture	General fungicide The traditional liquid mixture was made from copper sulphate and quicklime and had to be freshly mixed; a dust form is now available	Preventive spray for potatoes and tomatoes against potato blight
Fertosan slug killer	Powder made up into a liquid Harmless to mammals, birds, earthworms, etc Keeps ground slug/snail-free for several months Must not be watered on to seedlings or leaves in dry conditions	Slugs and snails

Biological control

In some cases the natural enemies of a pest or disease can be harnessed to control it. This avoids the use of chemicals (and the problems of pests building up resistance to them), and there is no damage to beneficial insects, or the environment, or risk of poisoning humans. In practice there are difficulties in applying biological control, but a lot of research is going on, and its scope and methods are continually being improved. From a gardener's point of view, the following are now a practical proposition:

Cabbage caterpillar control with the bacterial spray thuricide, which can be used outdoors

Whitefly (in greenhouses) with the parasite *Encarsia formosa*

Red spider mite (in greenhouses) with the predator *Phytoseiulus persimilis*

These last two need fairly high temperatures, over 13°C (55°F) to operate successfully. When the pest is first noticed, write to a supplier and the predator or parasite will be sent by post. It normally arrives on leaves, which are cut into pieces and placed on infested plants. It gradually spreads and kills off the pests, dying out itself when the pest has been demolished. (For suppliers see Appendix III.)

Alternative measures for controlling pests

Insect pests

Aphids. Keep plants well watered; attacks are less frequent on turgid plants. Collect ladybirds (they feed on aphids), and move them to infested plants. Aphid colonies can sometimes be squashed by hand.

Caterpillars. Pick them off by hand.

Cabbage root fly (*Fig. 18c*). The adult fly can be prevented from laying the eggs which hatch into damaging maggots by protecting the stem of newly transplanted plants with a physical barrier. These are best made with a 15cm- (6in) diameter circular disc of carpet foam underlay. Make a small hole in the centre, then cut from the central hole to one outside edge, and use this slit to place the disc around the stem of the plant at ground level. Alternatively use a plastic yogurt pot or cottage cheese carton as a protective collar around the plant's stem. Make a hole in the bottom of the pot large enough to slip the cabbage root through from above, plant it, and bury the pot rim 1cm (½in) deep in the soil.

Carrot fly (*Fig. 18b*). The most successful preventive measure against this devastating pest is to surround the carrot bed with a barrier of heavy duty polythene, at least 45cm (18in) high, buried 5cm (2in) deep in the soil. One method of doing this is to put posts at the corner of the bed, staple wire to the top of the posts, then to fold a metre- (yard) wide sheet of polythene over the wire.

Soil pests

Slugs and snails. My advice is to hunt them down at night with a torch, and catch them feeding. Collect them in yogurt pots or buckets, depending on the scale of your problem! If you can't bear to squash them, make it an instantaneous death by pouring boiling water over them. During the day you can find them hiding under pieces of wood or board. Slug traps can be made by putting beer into a container sunk into the ground at ground level. The drawback is that you also catch beneficial beetles. Slugs can be trapped in half coconut shells with ½cm (¼in) holes cut in the shell. They apparently crawl inside if the shells are damp. Baked crushed egg shells are said to deter slugs.

Other soil pests (Fig. 17). Digging and hoeing expose many pests – millipedes, cutworms and leatherjackets in particular – to their natural enemies, birds. Destroy any you come across yourself. Many soil pests, for example wireworms, cutworms and millipedes, can be attracted to traps made from scooped-out potatoes or carrots fixed on skewers just below the soil surface. Examine the traps daily and destroy any pests that have been caught. Investigate casualties. If a lettuce plant has suddenly keeled over, dig it up. You may catch the guilty wireworm or leatherjacket red-handed, so preventing damage to adjacent plants. Cutworms, like slugs, can often be found at night, feeding on plants at ground level.

Animal pests

Mice. Their main target is peas, and traps the best remedy. Some people cover pea seeds with holly leaves or something prickly to deter mice. I don't know if it works!

Moles. They can be caught with traps set in their runs, or killed with chemical fuses. Other products on the market merely drive moles away – presumably to your neighbour's garden. Mothballs pushed into their runs, or pieces of foam rubber soaked in paraffin and set on fire, are also said to frighten them away.

Cats. Hawthorn twigs laid on the surface help to protect seeds and seedlings from cats. So do pea guards.

Birds (Fig. 19). Small birds such as sparrows, which can be very damaging, are best deterred with single strands of black cotton alongside or above seedlings, about 5cm (2in) above ground. Use strong cotton; button thread is ideal. A row of brightly coloured windmills, the sort sold to children at the seaside, are effective deterrents at ground level.

Of the larger birds, pigeons, and sometimes jays, are the most serious pests. Wire netting 60–90cm (2–3ft) high around a vegetable patch usually keeps them away, although it is a nuisance for cultivation and access. It can be made fairly mobile by anchoring it with bamboo canes. Cages, made from nylon, wire, or plastic netting are increasingly being used where bird damage is serious, 10 or 15cm (4 or 6in) square mesh will be sufficient to keep off pigeons. This sort of device, of course, also keeps out cats and dogs, but prevents birds from scavenging for pests. Better, perhaps, to give temporary protection to vulnerable crops with netting over the wire hoops used for low

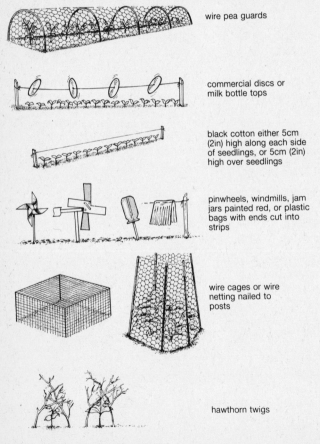

wire pea guards

commercial discs or milk bottle tops

black cotton either 5cm (2in) high along each side of seedlings, or 5cm (2in) high over seedlings

pinwheels, windmills, jam jars painted red, or plastic bags with ends cut into strips

wire cages or wire netting nailed to posts

hawthorn twigs

19. VARIOUS FORMS OF BIRD SCARER

polythene tunnels (see p. 108) The snag is that the netting is apt to catch on the wire. Smooth surfaced hoops, made from 5cm (2in) wide strips of the double layered corrugated polypropylene, anchored into the soil with steel pins inserted between the two layers, have proved a good alternative. The recently introduced 'humming wire', tape strung around a cropped area, is also recommended.

Other common deterrents include:

windmills of many types, often incorporating a jangling sound;

plastic sacks with edges cut into fringes, or rags strung in lines over the vegetables;

milk bottle tops suspended on string or wire;

upturned bottles painted red, placed over sticks, even ordinary wine bottles, stuck, necks down, into the ground;

low protective wire guards, such as pea guards;

aluminium discs cut into shapes;

hawthorn and other sharp twigs placed around growing crops.

The scope is endless, but ring the changes as much as possible. Birds become used to anything!

Birds are particularly attracted to young seedlings and newly planted greens such as lettuces. It always pays to put up your protection when sowing or transplanting. Tomorrow is often too late!

Beneficial and related creatures (*Fig. 20*)

The soil is inhabited by a number of beneficial creatures, and care should be taken not to destroy them by mistake. As a general rule, fast moving grubs and related creatures are beneficial. They need to be fast as their prey, small slugs and insects, is mobile. Plant eaters, pests from our point of view, tend to be more 'sluggish'.

Beneficial creatures living mainly in the soil include centipedes, carabid beetle and ground beetle larvae, and of course earthworms. Above ground the devil's coach horse beetle and other beetles, ladybirds, the parasitic ichneumons which lay their eggs on caterpillars, lacewings, wasps, frogs and toads are all beneficial (wasps, of course, are a pest if you have fruit trees.)

Advice

Identification of pests and diseases and advice on control can be obtained from various organisations (see Appendix III).

Weeds

Weeds are a serious problem in any garden. They compete for plant nutrients and water in the soil and for space and light above ground. The weight of a barrow load of weeds is proof of how much they take from the soil. Weeds are very vigorous, and will take over completely if unchecked. A row of vegetable seedlings can easily be smothered by weeds, which generally germinate and grow faster than cultivated

20. SOME BENEFICIAL INSECTS AND OTHER CREATURES
(Part I)

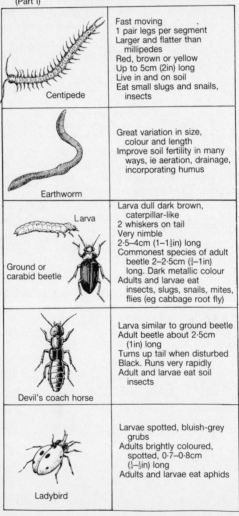

Centipede	Fast moving 1 pair legs per segment Larger and flatter than millipedes Red, brown or yellow Up to 5cm (2in) long Live in and on soil Eat small slugs and snails, insects
Earthworm	Great variation in size, colour and length Improve soil fertility in many ways, ie aeration, drainage, incorporating humus
Larva Ground or carabid beetle	Larva dull dark brown, caterpillar-like 2 whiskers on tail Very nimble 2·5–4cm (1–1½in) long Commonest species of adult beetle 2–2·5cm (¾–1in) long. Dark metallic colour Adults and larvae eat insects, slugs, snails, mites, flies (eg cabbage root fly)
Devil's coach horse	Larva similar to ground beetle Adult beetle about 2·5cm (1in) long Turns up tail when disturbed Black. Runs very rapidly Adult and larvae eat soil insects
Ladybird	Larvae spotted, bluish-grey grubs Adults brightly coloured, spotted, 0·7–0·8cm (¼–⅓in) long Adults and larvae eat aphids

plants. As already mentioned, some weeds harbour pests and diseases during the winter. So one way and another, weeds must go.

One of the advantages of a small garden is that controlling weeds is not an impossible task. The problem falls into two parts: annual weeds, which germinate, flower and die in one year, and perennials, which go

(Part II)

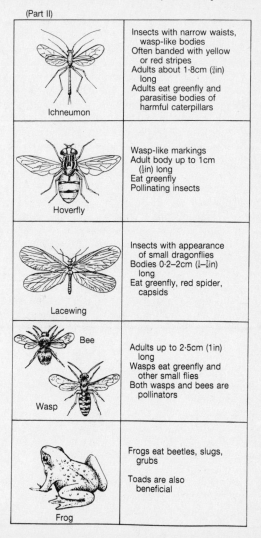

Ichneumon	Insects with narrow waists, wasp-like bodies Often banded with yellow or red stripes Adults about 1·8cm (¾in) long Adults eat greenfly and parasitise bodies of harmful caterpillars
Hoverfly	Wasp-like markings Adult body up to 1cm (½in) long Eat greenfly Pollinating insects
Lacewing	Insects with appearance of small dragonflies Bodies 0·2–2cm (⅒–¾in) long Eat greenfly, red spider, capsids
Bee **Wasp**	Adults up to 2·5cm (1in) long Wasps eat greenfly and other small flies Both wasps and bees are pollinators
Frog	Frogs eat beetles, slugs, grubs Toads are also beneficial

on from year to year and develop very vigorous, persistent root systems.

Annual weeds

The annuals, groundsel, chickweed, fat hen, and so on, are easily dealt with by hand weeding or hoeing. Start as early in the year as you can, to minimise the competition to the crops you are trying to grow. With most vegetable crops, weed competition starts to become really serious about three weeks after the seedlings have germinated. So start weeding then if you haven't already done so. Interestingly, recent research has shown that it is the weeds between rows, rather than within rows, that are the most competitive. So work on them first.

At all costs, annual weeds must be prevented from going to seed. It's a much quoted and somewhat depressing statistic, that one large fat hen plant can produce 70,000 seeds! Even small insignificant weeds can produce a fair number of seeds. Take heed of the old proverb 'one year's seed is seven years' weed'. There's a lot of truth in it.

One of the most satisfactory ways of keeping weeds under control is to abandon the idea of growing plants in rows with wide spaces between them, in favour of growing plants in blocks or patches, at equidistant spacing (*Fig. 33*). When fully grown the leaves of neighbouring plants will touch and form a blanketing canopy over the soil, which effectively prevents most weed seeds from germinating. Here again, research supports the practice: apparently the filtered light created by a canopy of leaves actually makes the weed seeds dormant! This system won't work with narrow-leaved vegetables like onions and leeks, and it will be necessary to weed or hoe between plants in the early stages – or even better, mulch with dry lawn mowings, mushroom compost, or some well-rotted organic material. Some weeds inevitably find their way through the mulch, but they are relatively easy to pull up. A snag is that the mulch itself can be a source of weeds; even so, it is worth using.

Mulches of black plastic film can be a valuable way of keeping down weeds and conserving moisture in the soil – though they are unsightly. Either plant first, then unroll the film, cutting cross-like slits in it over the plants and pull the plants through, or lay the film on the ground, cut slits in it, and plant through the slits. Use whichever method you find easier. The type of film that is white above and black beneath is useful for mulching crops like tomatoes in summer. The black side keeps down the weeds, but the white surface reflects heat and light up on to the plant and ripening fruit.

Weed seeds remain viable for many years, and ground that has not been cultivated for some time holds a huge reservoir of seed. Much of this will germinate on cultivation. In this case it is advisable to prepare the ground for sowing or planting, leave it for a week or so to allow the first flush of weeds to germinate, and hoe them off before sowing or planting. In the first season try to avoid deep cultivation, as this will only bring up more weed seeds from the lower layers. Just hoe shallowly, or pull up weeds by hand – or mulch! All annual weeds can be put on the compost heap – unless they've gone to seed.

Perennial weeds

Perennial weeds are much more of a problem. The most common are probably couch grass, with its sharp underground runners, dandelion, ground elder, docks, nettles, marestail or horsetail, and bindweed. There are others, of course, and occasionally a so-called 'cultivated' plant from a garden runs riot in a vegetable plot and becomes a weed – Japanese knotweed for example.

With most of these weeds, the answer is to learn to recognise them, both by their leaves and by their roots, and to dig them out. Use a good wild flower book to identify them (see Appendix IV). As a rule the perennials either have long deep roots (dandelions, thistles), or rambling extensive, often white roots (couch grass, ground elder, bindweed).

Annuals have shallow roots and are easily pulled up. If in doubt, pull it out!

With thistles, bindweed, ground elder, couch and dandelion, even small pieces of root can sprout, so it really is important to remove the plant as completely as possible. The best time is during winter digging. In summer try not to hoe perennials off at ground level, which may even encourage them to re-sprout, but get them out by the roots if you can. One piece of good news, docks will apparently die if you chop off the top 10cm (4in) of root – sparing your back and your conscience!

The roots of perennials should either be burnt or dried up in the sun before being put on the compost heap. Some of them have remarkable powers of recovery in second-rate compost heaps!

Perennials can be very discouraging to anyone tackling a new or neglected garden. If it is very overgrown, cut them back with a hook first, then start the job of digging them out. If you decide to use a Rotavator, rotavate several times as the first and even second rotavation may just chop the roots into pieces that will regenerate. Don't be discouraged. A few seasons' digging, and dare I say it again, mulching, works wonders!

Chemical control

On the whole, there is little scope and relatively little need to use weedkillers (or herbicides as they are called today) in small gardens.

All that was said previously about pesticides applies to weedkillers. They are poisonous substances to have around; it is often difficult to restrict them to precisely the plants you want to be rid of; chemical spray or solutions may drift or creep on to neighbouring gardens; some of them leave residues of harmful chemicals in the soil for considerable periods, and lastly, they are expensive.

If you feel it is essential to use a weedkiller, HDRA recommend Amcide (ammonium sulphamate) as being one of the safest. It kills couch grass, docks, marestail, oxalis, comfrey and many annual weeds, and sometimes bindweed. It is non-selective, so can only be used to clear ground in which no plants that are wanted are growing. And nothing can be planted until eight weeks after treatment.

On a small scale weedkillers are usually applied with a watering can, using either a fine sprinkler rose or a dribble bar. It is advisable to keep one can especially for weedkilling to avoid accidents!

CHAPTER SIX
Protection

Anyone wanting maximum returns from a small garden should invest in some kind of protection – whether it be cloches, frames, a small greenhouse, low or walk-in polythene tunnels, or the new perforated films or 'floating' cloches. With protection the growing season can be extended by at least three weeks in spring and as much again in autumn, the quality of many vegetables can be improved, especially during the winter months, by protecting them from the elements, and the more tender vegetables can be grown successfully in colder parts of the country. Any form of protection is worth its weight in gold, for the reasons given below.

Raising the temperature

Plants normally start growing when the average daytime temperature reaches about 6°C (43°F) in the spring. The date this happens varies from year to year, but can be any time from mid-February in Cornwall, to the end of March in the north of England and cold parts of Scotland. Similarly growth stops again when the temperature falls below 6°C (43°F) in the autumn. The days between these two points are considered 'growing days'. The warmest parts of England get over 300 growing days; the coldest less than 250. Quite a difference! Moreover, provided plants have moisture, the higher the temperature above 6°C (43°F) the faster they grow.

As a general rule, protection raises the temperature of the soil and air around plants, and slows down the rate at which heat is lost from the soil at night. This amounts to increasing the number of growing days. Protection is therefore particularly valuable in cold, high and exposed areas where the growing season is shortest.

When the sun shines in mid-winter, temperatures can soar under glass or polythene, allowing plants under cover to grow when those outside are still gripped in arctic conditions.

Frost protection

Some vegetables withstand frost satisfactorily, but many are killed or damaged by frost. So protection against frost is useful. Cloches and other unheated forms of protection can be relied upon to give protection only against slight frost. They will not keep out severe frost. On cold clear nights, the air temperature under cover can fall as low as the temperature outside, although the soil temperature may be warmer than the exposed soil's temperature.

Where there is protection, however, frost causes less damage, for several reasons:

- the plants are dry, and frost damage is much worse on wet plants;
- they are protected from wind, and wind greatly increases damage to plants at low temperatures;
- frost penetrates less deeply, and does not remain so long in the soil.

Incidentally, if there has been a heavy frost on unprotected plants, frost damage, which is caused by rapid thawing, can be lessened by spraying the plants with water the following morning, before the sun reaches them. This helps to thaw them more slowly.

Protection from wind and heavy rain

The benefits of protecting plants from wind are not always appreciated. It is now known that plants give much higher yields if they are protected from even light winds. The damage done by gales and the bitter easterly winds which can occur in spring is enormous. Winds dry out leaves, batter and tear them, and make it a struggle for the plant to survive, let alone grow. Even the most rudimentary protection is of value. In coastal areas it is worth protecting plants from the salt spray in the wind. Protection from heavy winter rains, which wash nutrients out of the soil, and heavy spring rain, which can wash out seed and even seedlings, is also beneficial. Cloches also, of course, give protection against bird damage.

Cloches

Cloches, because they are small and easily moved, are probably still the most popular form of protection for small gardens, though perhaps less so than they used to be. There are various types.

Glass (Fig. 21)

Traditionally cloches were made of panes of glass, held together in a wire frame. 'Tent' cloches were made of two panes, low and high 'barn' cloches of four, and the flat-topped 'tomato' or 'utility' cloches of three panes.

Glass has two important qualities. First it is a very effective heat trap. During the day the soil absorbs heat in the form of short waves, but some of this heat is subsequently lost from the soil as long-wave radiation. While glass transmits the incoming short waves, to some extent it holds back the outgoing long waves, which therefore warm up the air above the soil instead of being lost. Most plastic materials, on the contrary, transmit the long waves as well, so there is less build up of heat under the cloche, particularly at night.

Secondly, provided it is kept clean, glass transmits a great deal of light. This is extremely important in winter, where poor light is one of the major factors limiting the growth of plants.

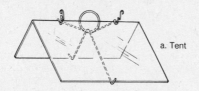

a. Tent

21. TYPES OF GLASS
    CLOCHE

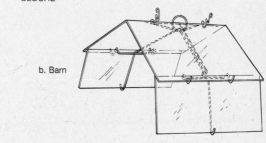

b. Barn

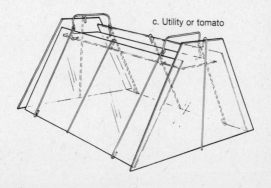

c. Utility or tomato

Glass cloches have several disadvantages. They are expensive, easily broken, heavy to handle, and many people find them awkward to erect single-handed.

Plastics (Fig. 22)

The supremacy of glass cloches is now being challenged by cloches made of plastics and related materials. Most of these are considerably cheaper than glass, give more or less the same protection against wind and rain, and are lighter and easier to handle. On the other hand they do not last as long and few conserve heat as well as glass.

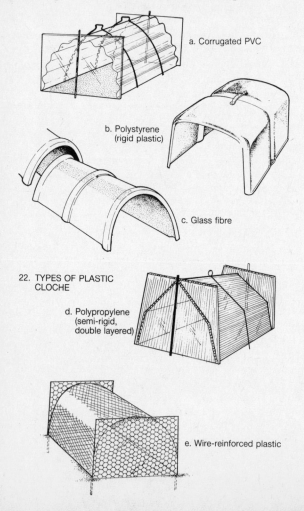

a. Corrugated PVC

b. Polystyrene (rigid plastic)

c. Glass fibre

22. TYPES OF PLASTIC CLOCHE

d. Polypropylene (semi-rigid, double layered)

e. Wire-reinforced plastic

Many of the transparent plastics transmit light as effectively as glass, and plants seem to grow surprisingly well in the diffused light created by some translucent cloches. A drawback of plastics is that they discolour with time, due to exposure to ultra-violet light. This limits the light they let in. Treatments against ultra-violet make them last longer.

Plastic cloches are often semi-circular in shape.

Improvements in the materials used for cloches, and in their design, are continually being made. The following are some of the materials in use at present.

Rigid materials
Corrugated PVC sheeting transmits plenty of light, retains heat well, is strong, and should last at least five years.

Acrylic sheeting (originally known as Perspex) is at present mostly used in frames; it has good qualities of heat retention and light transmission, and is very durable.

Glass fibre is very strong and durable, although opaque, but plants grow satisfactorily under it.

Semi-rigid materials
Polypropylene is a double-layered woven form of plastic with a corrugated appearance. It has the effect of double-glazing; the thermal insulation is higher than glass. Light transmission is considerably lower than glass, but this is a case where plant growth is good in the diffused light. The cloches last at least four or five years.

Wire reinforced plastics of several types are used to make cloches. Within limits the cloches can be bent into higher, narrower shapes or wider lower shapes as required. With care they would last three or four years.

Home-made cloches (Fig. 23)
DIY cloches can be perfectly satisfactory. Most of the materials mentioned above are now sold in suitable lengths and widths for making cloches. They can be tacked, nailed or screwed on to a wood frame. Polythene film is best fixed between two pieces of wood. A tent shape is the easiest to construct. Make the supporting frame as narrow as possible, so that maximum light is admitted.

Clips. Odd panes of glass can be converted into cloches with wire links or special clips, such as the Rumsey clips.

Plastic bags. Medium and light-weight plastic bags can be made into low cloches. Cut the bottom off the bag, bend two pieces of fairly heavy wire (coat hangers can be used) into a semi-circular or barn

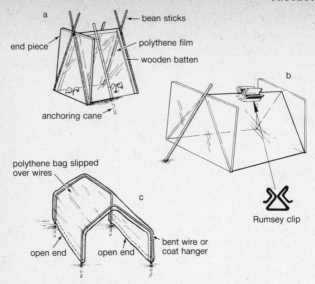

23. HOME-MADE CLOCHES
a. 'Tent cloche' protection over young bean plants, made by
   attaching polythene film to battens and securing them to the
   bean poles up which the beans later climb
b. Odd panes of glass made into cloches with Rumsey clips
c. Low cloches made from plastic bags and coat hangers;
   use glass or rigid plastic for end pieces

outline. Slip one into each side of the bag to support and anchor the
plastic. These cloches are extremely useful for protecting tender herbs
and salads in winter. They can be straddled over an insulating layer of
bracken, straw or dried leaves.

Side shelters. These, rather than roofed cloches, can be made by fixing
rigid PVC, polypropylene, wire-reinforced plastic or polythene film on
to a wooden frame. They can be supported between upright canes to
make shelters for tomatoes, leant against runner bean poles to make a
protective tent over young beans, propped against a fence as a lean-to,
or used as a 'light' on a frame (*Fig. 49*).

What to look for in cloches

The following factors are important when buying or making cloches.

Light
Cloches should let in as much light as possible, and be easy to clean. If
they are translucent, the light should be gently diffused. The light

factor is most important (a) where cloches are used during the winter to grow, rather than merely protect, vegetables, and (b) in industrial areas where smoke in the atmosphere reduces the light.

Heat

The more cloches prevent heat losses from the soil, the better. Here one has to rely on available technical information about the materials. Note that there is less heat loss from a double layer of material, although this reduces the light. Scientists are uncertain at present as to whether the value of the heat gained outweighs the light lost! An interesting point is that the layer of moisture which condenses on the underside of a clear plastic film helps to prevent heat radiation from the soil.

Strength and stability

Cloches are very vulnerable to wind. Avoid sharp angles which catch the wind. Make sure there is a secure means of anchorage, such as strong steel pins which protrude into the soil, flanges which can be pinned or weighted down, or overhead wire stays.

Ventilation

Cloches should not be completely airtight; in summer ventilation is essential. Glass cloches have gaps in the top which can be adjusted for ventilation. In some cloches roof panels can be raised for ventilation. Small ventilation holes can be made in the roof of rigid and semi-rigid plastic and glass fibre cloches. If there is no built-in ventilation, leave small gaps between the cloches when erecting them.

Draughts

The ends of a single cloche or of a row of cloches must be closed, otherwise a wind tunnel is created, with disastrous results. Ends which interlock securely over the cloche, or are self-anchoring with steel pins, are very useful. Otherwise sticks or canes have to be used to keep them in place. Glass or transparent ends are preferable to pieces of wood or slate.

Storage

Cloches which stack on top of each other or fold flat when not in use are an asset in small gardens.

Size

When choosing cloches bear in mind the main purpose for which they will be used. Larger cloches are usually more expensive. Tent cloches and low tunnels are fine for seed raising and for low crops such as lettuce. Low barns, sides 15cm (6in) high, are adequate only for the young stages of tall crops such as tomatoes, sweetcorn, peppers and peas, but high barns, sides 30cm (12in) high, and flat-topped cloches are needed for the later stages. Some cloches have side extensions to increase the height; in some utility cloches the top pane can be raised a few inches or removed to give more height. The height-width ratio of the semi-rigid cloches can be adjusted within certain limits. Several makes of cloche are sold in varying widths.

Cloche techniques (*Fig. 24*)

Soil
To make the most of cloches, always put them on the best soil. Work as much organic matter as possible into the top 15cm (6in) or so.

Anchoring
High winds are deadly. Glass cloches and brittle plastics may break, and lighter cloches be blown away in exposed positions – where of course the value of cloches is greatest. In such conditions cloches need additional anchorage by running twine through the handles and tying it

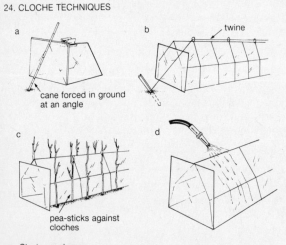

24. CLOCHE TECHNIQUES

a. Closing end pane
b and c. Methods of anchoring cloches in exposed positions
d. Watering without removing cloches

to canes or stout sticks at either end. Putting pea sticks alongside cloches is another useful trick for additional anchorage.

Use weights: with plastic cloches empty wine bottles serve the purpose well – a piece of stout string or baler twine over the ridge of the cloche, attached to the neck of a bottle on each side.

Where glass cloches are used, it pays to rub all edges with a carborundum stone when first putting them up. This cuts down breakages.

When securing the end panes of glass cloches, use a cane or stick placed at an angle, rather than upright. This is much less likely to work loose and cause friction against the cloche.

Watering

Rain water runs off the sides of cloches, and provided there is plenty of organic matter in the soil, will percolate through to the roots of plants under the cloches, which naturally grow outwards. Apart from watering small seedlings (which have not had time to develop an extensive root system), there is normally no need to remove cloches for watering; they can be watered overhead with hoses or cans. This indirect form of watering helps to conserve the tilth of the soil. Check by poking your finger into the soil in the middle of the cloche. If it feels dry an inch or so below the surface, it may be necessary to remove the cloche to water more thoroughly.

In light soils a shallow drill alongside the cloche helps the water to go straight to the roots.

25. METHODS OF RAISING CLOCHES

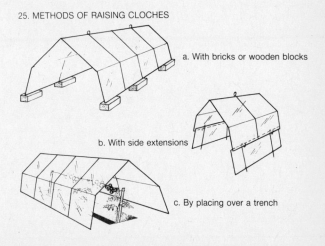

a. With bricks or wooden blocks

b. With side extensions

c. By placing over a trench

Ventilation

On hot spring days and in summer plenty of ventilation is required. When it is very hot remove every other cloche in a row to provide ventilation.

Coverage

In frosty weather glass itself can become so cold that plants touching it will be frost-bitten. Make sure the plants are not in contact with the cloche sides.

Cloches can be raised (*Fig. 25*) to cover growing crops by standing them on bricks or wooden blocks, by using side extensions where available, or by planting the crops in trenches about 15–23cm (6–9in) deep. The cloches straddle the trench. This is only practicable in light well-drained soils, otherwise the trench is apt to turn into a waterlogged ditch.

Planting distances have to be adjusted to some extent to take advantage of the width of a cloche.

Side protection

Some cloches can be stood on their side and wrapped around tall plants as a windbreak. They can be anchored by putting a cane through the handles, or with sticks placed alongside (*Fig. 27*).

Low polythene tunnels (*Fig. 26*)

Easily the cheapest form of protection is the low polythene tunnel, made from lightweight (usually 150-gauge) polythene film stretched over galvanised steel wire hoops, about 1m (1yd) apart. As the film is flimsy it generally only lasts one, or at the most two, seasons, though tears can be mended with tape. The hoops last indefinitely. The film

26. POLYTHENE FILM TUNNEL

can be bought in rolls and cut to the lengths required. Width and height can be varied: I like my tunnels to fit snugly over my 1m- (1yd) wide beds, the height at the centre being up to 45cm (18in). (Fairly heavy polythene films *can* be used for low tunnels, but are harder to manipulate than the lightweight films.)

The film is kept in place over the hoops with fine wire or strings, running over the top and hooked or tied to the base of the hoops. The ends of the film are either dug into the ground, or knotted around posts in the ground 60cm (2ft) or so beyond the end hoop. In windy situations, or in winter, it may be necessary to anchor the sides. Use clods of soil, pieces of wood, or stones, or bury one side in a slit made in the ground with a trowel. Leave the other side free for access.

For watering, ventilation and other operations, the film is simply pushed up on one side. In hot weather the combination of high temperature and humidity under the film is conducive to pests and diseases – in which case push up both sides for maximum ventilation. On the continent, where low polythene tunnels are extensively used for early outdoor tomatoes, melons and other crops, square or round 'peep holes' are cut along the lengths of the tunnels, so plants are sheltered but still get plenty of air. Low tunnels can also be made with perforated films (see p. 114), making a very well-ventilated tunnel.

Bearing in mind the limitations of their height, low polythene tunnels can be used for the same purposes as cloches, as outlined below.

All year round use of cloches

(Because temperatures vary widely from season to season and district to district, references to specific months are for guidance only.)

Spring
1 *To prepare for sowing.* Cloches can be used:
   to dry out the soil before preparing the seed bed;
   to preserve a tilth on a prepared seed bed if sowing is delayed;
   to warm up the soil before sowing, by leaving them in position several days to a week beforehand.
2 *For earlier crops of hardy vegetables* (February to April). These can be sown or planted under cloches, and grown under cloches until mature or nearly mature.

eg	broad beans	parsley
	beetroot	early and main crop peas
	carrots	early potatoes
	kale (unthinned kale; north only)	radish
		salad seedlings (see p. 126)
	lettuce	spinach/spinach beet, etc
	spring onions	turnips

3 *To raise seedlings which are better started under glass to give them a longer growing season* (February to April). They can be sown in boxes under cloches, or directly in the ground and transplanted later. (Cloches also protect seedlings against birds and cats).

eg Brussels sprouts   celery
    summer cabbage   leeks
    summer cauliflower   summer lettuce
    celeriac

4 *For early stages of half- hardy vegetables* (April and May). By using cloches sowing or planting can be done several weeks earlier. Sow in boxes or pots under cloches and transplant when large enough into permanent position under other cloches, or in the open after danger of frost is past. Alternatively sow *in situ* under cloches, removing cloches when no longer needed.

eg French beans   peppers
    runner beans   New Zealand spinach
    cucumbers   sweetcorn
    marrows   tomatoes

5 *Hardening off tender seedlings and young plants raised in heat indoors* (April and May). These can be put under cloches in boxes or pots. Harden them off by moving cloches a little further apart each day, then leaving them off during the day. Finally remove them at night unless frost threatens.

Summer

6 *Crops suitable for growing under cloches in summer*. These are usually transplanted under cloches end May/beginning June, or sown *in situ* two or three weeks earlier.

eg cucumbers   peppers
    tomatoes (bush type, or cordon types trained horizontally)

Autumn

7 *Extending the season by protecting later summer sowings in September*.

eg runner beans   endive
       (dwarf cultivars)   lettuce
    French beans   peas
    carrots   radish
    red and Sugar   salad seedlings (see p. 126)
       Loaf chicory

8 *For ripening off tomatoes and onions in September*.

Winter

9 *For autumn-sown crops which will overwinter under cloches and mature the following spring and summer*.

eg broad beans   main crop onions (in north)
    lettuce   spring onions

spring cabbages (in cold   peas
    districts)   winter spinach, spinach beet,
cauliflower (for early   Swiss chard
    summer)   Seedling Sugar Loaf chicory

10 *For hardy mature crops which will be used during the winter, but will
    benefit from additional protection.*

   eg red and Witloof chicory (earthed up Witloof matures earlier
       under cloches)
       corn salad   parsley
       hardy endives   spring onions
       land cress   winter spinach, spinach beet,
       lettuce   Swiss chard

To make the most of cloches it is advisable to draw up a simple plan
so that there is always something in the garden which will benefit from
cloche protection. The plan should be flexible enough to allow for the
vagaries of the weather (sowing dates, cultural details and recommended cultivars for cloches are given under Vegetables in Part Two).

Strip cropping

The ideal way of using cloches is 'strip cropping'. This means
cultivating two (or more) adjacent strips of ground each about a yard
wide, and planning the cropping so that the cloches are simply moved
backwards and forwards between the strips with the minimum of
effort.

The possible alternatives in strip cropping are endless. With a little
gardening experience you will be able to work out your own plans.

The basis of strip cropping is as follows:

Vegetables are divided into four groups according to the months
during which they will be under cloches, although there will inevitably
be some overlapping of groups.

The cloches are used first for a Group 1 crop during the winter
months. In late spring, when the Group 1 crop is cleared or no longer
requires cloche protection, cloches are moved on to a Group 2 crop,
sowed or planted alongside (for preference). This would be a half
hardy crop requiring cloche protection at least during the early stages
of growth.

By June, when the Group 2 crop will have outgrown the cloches, the
first strip of land will have been cleared and re-planted with a Group 3
crop, which can stay under the cloches all summer.

When this crop is finished in autumn, the cloches can be moved back
to the second strip, where a crop either maturing in late autumn or
overwintering, will have been sown or planted.

A simple strip cropping plan is given on page 119.

Group 1
Hardy spring crops under cloches January to early April. Some are cloched the previous autumn.
(a) Those which will be cleared from the ground by the end of May, allowing others to be sown or planted:
    eg spring cabbage (planted and cloched in October; usually in cold districts only)
        lettuce (sown October, January or February)
        radish (sown early spring)
        peas (sown in November)
        carrots (January sown in mild districts)
        corn salad and land cress (summer sown)
        hardy chicories, endives, Chinese mustards and Pak Choi (late summer/autumn planted)
(b) Crops which will not be cleared from the ground until June or later though cloches are removed in April:
    eg cauliflower (October planted)
        broad beans (sown November or January)
        carrots (sown February)
        peas (sown February)
        beetroot (sown March, ready June)
        spinach (autumn sown)
        peas (spring sown)
        sowings of brassicas, leeks, celery, etc., for planting out later.

Group 2
Late spring crops. These are half-hardy vegetables either sown *in situ* under cloches in April or May, or raised indoors and planted out under cloches in April or May:

eg	French beans	marrows
	runner beans	sweetcorn
	cucumbers	tomatoes

Group 3
Tender crops which can be grown under cloches all summer (*June, July, August to mid-September*):
    eg cucumbers, peppers, tomatoes (bush types, or cordon types trained horizontally)

Group 4
Autumn crops using cloches October, November, December:

eg French beans or dwarf
    runner beans   } sown July
   peas
   carrots
   corn salad
   endive
   land cress   sown August, cloched mid-
   lettuce   September, ready Christmas
   spring onion
   radish
  spring cabbage (sown August, cloched in cold districts)
  potatoes (planted August, cloched September until Christmas)
  tomatoes (covered with cloches mid-September to November
    to ripen)

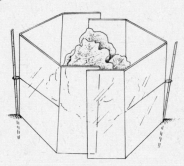

27. CLOCHES USED AS A SIDE SHIELD
    FOR TALL PLANTS

Intercropping

Often two or three crops can be sown together under cloches to make
the most of the space, for example:

1 Radishes with most crops.
2 Peas with lettuce and radish on either side.
3 Dwarf French beans either side of sweetcorn.
4 Carrots and radishes on either side of French beans.
5 Carrots, salad onions or cos lettuce intercropped with cabbage
   lettuce.
6 Turnips, lettuce, carrots or radish alongside peas.
7 Seed bed sowings of brassicas, onions, leeks, lettuce either together
   or alongside carrots.
8 Quick maturing salad seedlings such as cress, salad rape, Mediterranean rocket, alongside tomatoes, sweetcorn, French or runner
   beans.

'Floating' cloches (*Fig. 28*)

A promising new development for low-growing vegetables is the use of perforated or slitted plastic films, laid over the plants, in fact resting on their growing tips, and tucked into the soil on either side. Because of the perforations or holes the films to some extent 'grow' and expand with the crop – hence the names 'floating' cloches or 'floating' mulches. They raise the soil temperature and the air temperature around the plants, and have a sheltering, windbreak effect, which can result in crops being ready up to two weeks earlier, and sometimes giving heavier yields.

28. 'FLOATING' CLOCHES

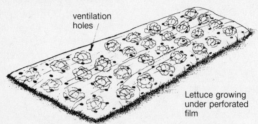

ventilation holes

Lettuce growing under perforated film

The films are put on immediately after sowing or planting. If sowing, sow in slightly sunken drills, so that the seedlings can get going before they 'hit' the film. Lay the film over the bed so that it is reasonably taut, but not over-stretched or sagging. Anchor it in slits about 5cm (2in) deep in the soil on either side of the bed, pushing the soil back against the edge of the film to keep it in place. The ground *must* be as weed free as possible, as weeds also will thrive in this cosy protected environment. Watering can be done through the film if necessary.

The trick in using floating cloches is knowing when to remove the film. This varies from crop to crop. With radishes, for example, it can stay in place until they are ready; with carrots it should be removed after about ten weeks, when they have about seven leaves. Details for different vegetables will be given in Part Two, but, as a rough guide, if the film looks as if it is restricting growth, remove it – sooner rather than later. To minimise the shock of sudden exposure, take it off on a dull day when there's no risk of frost. Water gently afterwards if the soil seems dry.

Floating cloches have been used very successfully on early crops such as early carrots, beetroot, celery, parsley, spinach, French beans, lettuce, corn salad, radish, early potatoes and outdoor bush tomatoes. It has also proved useful on overwintered corn salad and hardy endives, planted and covered in autumn. It is certainly worth trying out as a means of increasing productivity in a small garden.

It is not always easy to find supplies of the films, either the more expensive finely perforated films, or the 'holed' films. You can, however, make your own. Use ordinary lightweight film, about 200 gauge, and with a hot poker burn holes about 1cm (½in) diameter, about 4–5cm (1½–2in) apart, aiming for roughly 200 holes per square metre. Burning seals the edges so the film won't tear, as it would if the holes were cut.

Frames (*Fig. 29*)

Like cloches, cold frames are a useful means of providing extra protection. They retain heat better than cloches, are less affected by wind, but are less flexible to use. They can be portable or permanent, lean-to or free-standing, with a flat roof facing in one direction or a tent-shaped span roof.

The roof is usually sloping to catch the maximum sunlight. A shallow frame for salad crops would be about 17cm (7in) high in the front, 23cm (9in) at the back. A deeper frame for cucumbers would be about 30cm (1ft) in front, and 45cm (1½ft) at the back.

Traditionally the sides of frames were built of bricks, wood or concrete. The glass roof (known as a 'light') was held in a wooden frame. Many modern frames have steel or aluminium frames and glass to the ground on all sides. The lights may be hinged or slide backwards (bear this in mind if selecting a frame to fit into a small area). Most of the synthetic materials already discussed can be used in the construction of home-made frames.

A solid-sided frame retains heat best, especially if built against another wall. The glass-to-ground frames let in more light, an important factor where crops are being grown in winter and early spring. The scope of frames for winter and spring crops is increased enormously if they can be heated. The simplest method is with electric soil warming cables. An alternative is the old-fashioned 'hot-bed' method, using decayed manure.

Siting a frame

Frames should be in an unshaded position, facing south if single span, or in a north/south direction if double span. As with cloches, make the soil in the frame as fertile as possible. Replace the top 15cm (6in) with really good soil or compost if necessary.

Frame techniques

Ventilation. Frames are relatively airtight, so ventilation is very important to prevent a muggy atmosphere which encourages disease. Ventilate by propping up the lights or sliding them open. In summer they can be removed completely.

29. TYPES OF FRAME

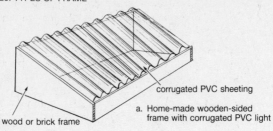

corrugated PVC sheeting

wood or brick frame

a. Home-made wooden-sided
   frame with corrugated PVC light

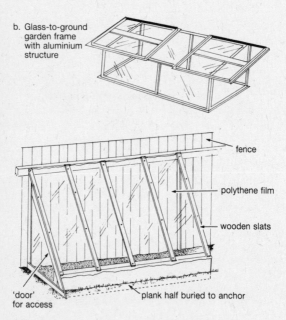

b. Glass-to-ground
   garden frame
   with aluminium
   structure

fence

polythene film

wooden slats

'door'
for access

plank half buried to anchor

c. Home-made lean-to frame, built against the garden fence, with
   polythene film fixed to wooden slats

Watering. In winter try to keep the leaves dry and water the soil only, again to prevent disease. Use warm water if possible.

Frost. In very cold weather give additional protection by covering frames with sacking, or similar material, at night.

Light. If seeds are raised in boxes in a solid-sided frame, stand them on bricks or blocks to bring them nearer the light. Otherwise they become drawn and leggy.

Uses of frames

Frames can be used for the same purposes as cloches, though the lights have to be removed for taller crops. They are particularly useful for raising seeds in boxes and pots, for hardening off seedlings, for salads such as lettuce, radish, beet and young carrots. In summer they are ideal for cucumbers, though these do better if they can be raised off the ground, for example with a horizontal trellis (*Fig. 30*). In winter, endives, chicories and dandelion can be transplanted into frames for blanching under straw; or they can be used for storing white cabbage. Mice soon track down any goodies, so set a few traps!

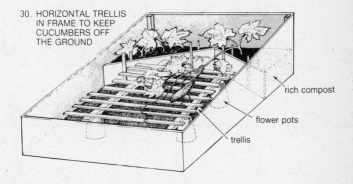

30. HORIZONTAL TRELLIS IN FRAME TO KEEP CUCUMBERS OFF THE GROUND

rich compost

flower pots

trellis

Greenhouses

A greenhouse can be used for growing tomatoes, cucumbers and peppers in summer, for raising plants in spring, and from winter to spring for growing the hardy salad vegetables suggested for winter cloches. A greenhouse glazed to soil level is the most suitable.

One of the disadvantages of a permanent greenhouse is that if tomatoes and cucumbers are grown every year in the soil there is a high risk of 'soil sickness', diseases building up in the soil making it impossible to grow further crops unless the soil is sterilised or replaced annually. The only alternative is to grow plants in fresh soil in pots, growing bags, or a soil-less system such as ring culture.

On economic grounds it is hard to justify building even an unheated greenhouse for growing vegetables – but use one if you have it! Heated greenhouses are a luxury outside the scope of this book!

Polythene structures (*Fig. 31*)

The archetypal polythene structure is the 'walk-in' tunnel, made from galvanised tube hoops, 1·5–1·8m (5–6ft) at the ridge, covered with heavy, ultra-violet inhibited film of 500 or 600 gauge. The hoops are sunk in the ground, a trench is taken out around the perimeter, and the film is buried in the trench (see *Fig. 31*).

31. 'WALK-IN' POLYTHENE TUNNEL

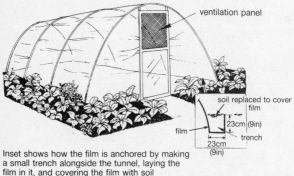

Inset shows how the film is anchored by making a small trench alongside the tunnel, laying the film in it, and covering the film with soil

It may seem absurd to suggest this sort of structure for a small garden, but *if* the space exists, they are without equal for increasing productivity at a low cost. 'Off-the-peg' tunnels – 3 × 6m (10 × 20ft) are a typical size – are a fraction of the cost of a greenhouse, but small structures can be made any shape or size by battening the film to a wooden frame, or anchoring it into the soil over a metal framework. Flowers and herbs can be grown around the edge to soften the harsh appearance.

The film lasts two to three years, when the structure can be re-covered, or moved to a fresh site, so avoiding the soil sickness problem of permanent greenhouses. Walk-in tunnels are really giant cloches without the fiddly inconvenience of cloches. They can be in use all year round, for traditional greenhouse vegetables in summer, and hardy crops suggested for winter cloches from autumn to spring. They're a wonderful haven for the winter gardener!

Hints on polythene structures

1 Film should be as tight fitting as possible. Cover frame on a hot day when the film is supple and easier to pull taut.
2 Bind any rough corners or edges on the frame with tape or cloth to prevent friction, which leads to tears and shortens the life of the film. Mend tears with adhesive tape sold for the purpose.
3 Batten the film firmly to the door frame.
4 Extra ground space can be gained at a doorless end by pulling the film out to a point (as in low tunnels) and burying it in the ground.
5 Temperatures and humidity build up rapidly even in winter, so always err on the side of over-ventilation. If possible, build a permanent ventilation panel into the door. (Heavy duty windbreak netting can be used.) If necessary cut a few dinner-plate-size ventilation 'portholes' in the film in summer. Tape them over in winter.
6 Watering must be done by hand, so keep the soil mulched to minimise evaporation.

STRIP CROPPING PLAN

Month	Strip I	Strip II
October to April	**Clocched** Winter hardy *lettuce* or *endive* planted under cloches down each side, Oct; *peas* sown down middle, Nov	
end April to May	*Peas* and *lettuce* unprotected	**Clocched** *Dwarf French beans* sown under cloches April
June to October	**Clocched** *Peppers* or *bush tomatoes* planted under cloches early June	*Dwarf French beans* unprotected
October to April		**Clocched** Winter hardy *lettuce* or *endive* planted under cloches down each side, Oct; *peas* sown down middle, Nov

CHAPTER SEVEN

Space Saving

Vertical growing

Climbing vegetables

The most obvious way of saving space is to grow plants vertically. Several vegetables are climbers by nature, and can be trained up netting, 5, 7·5 or 10cm (2, 3 or 4in) or larger squared mesh is suitable; a fruit cage; fencing or trellis work. If a small garden is enclosed with a wire netting fence, the potential area for growing vegetables is increased considerably.

Where the existing walls are brick or a plain wood surface, some additional climbing support will be needed, either right against the wall, or a foot or so away leaning towards the wall. Trellis work, or netting made of nylon, terylene, wire or plastic can be used, or a few wires strung horizontally against the wall (*Fig. 32a*).

If the wall is low, its height can be increased with a strip of trellis or roll of mesh fencing (such as Netlon or Weldmesh), along the top (*Fig. 32b*). Avoid north-facing walls which get very little sun, but don't overlook the walls of the house. Why not pick beans from a bedroom window? Grow them up strings attached to screws set in Rawlplugs.

Suitable climbers for these situations include climbing runner beans, climbing French beans, trailing marrows which make a brilliant display with their large yellow flowers, hardy Japanese cucumbers which climb over 2m (6ft) and ridge cucumbers, climbing only a few feet. Peas will also cling to supports up to 2m (5ft) high. The purple-podded peas and beans are the most decorative.

Climbing beans and trailing marrows have heavy crops and can easily reach a height of 2½m (8ft), so supporting fences or wire must be strong enough to bear their weight. Pinch out the growing point when plants reach the top of their supports. Beans need to be tied at first; cucumbers and marrows need a little tying throughout their growth.

Ground at the foot of walls dries out rapidly, so work plenty of humus into the soil, and mulch in early summer to help retain the moisture. Extra watering may be necessary in the lee of walls.

Backs to the wall

Several non-climbing vegetables do well planted against a sunny wall, basking in the extra heat. Obvious candidates are tomatoes, peppers, aubergines and sweetcorn, and sun-loving herbs like basil and rosemary. If there is room, plant sweetcorn in double rows to assist pollination.

Home-made lean-to frames and greenhouses can be built against a wall or fence, saving space and materials. Window boxes or other containers can be hung on walls or railings provided they are attached securely. They can also be stood on low walls, though if they are set into them, they will be less exposed to drying winds (*Fig. 32c*).

32. UTILISING WALLS AND FENCES

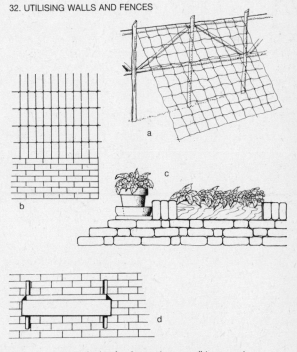

a. Netting can be attached to fencing posts or a wall to support climbing vegetables such as peas, beans and cucumbers
b. The height of low walls can be increased with wire mesh netting or trellis work
c. Low walls can be utilised by growing herbs and salad crops in pots and boxes
d. Boxes can be suspended on walls, railings and fences

Vegetables as screens

Vegetables can be used to screen off unsightly compost heaps, rubbish bins or domestic oil storage tanks, or to mark boundaries. Climbing vegetables would need some support such as a trellis or frame. Tall free-standing vegetables might need staking in exposed positions. Jerusalem artichokes, sweetcorn, or even asparagus, are good screening vegetables. Runner beans scramble happily over fences, hedges, low buildings or even up trees, and can be trained over archways or pergolas. Trailing marrows and pumpkins can completely hide a rubbishy corner. The new leafless and semi-leafless peas could be grown as low hedges. They twine together so are almost self supporting – a pale green barbed-wire 'fence'. Grow them in a band at least 30cm (12in) wide.

Tripods

A very picturesque way of supporting climbing vegetables is on tripods made with three or four bamboo canes or stakes, up to 2½m (8ft) long, pushed several inches into the soil and tied near the top in tepee fashion. Beans, marrows and cucumbers grow up them well. Extra strings can be run from top to bottom to make them suitable for peas. Bury the strings in the soil or peg them down to anchor them.

Vegetables in flower beds

Quite a few vegetables are pretty enough to be grown in flower beds if they are positioned carefully. Unless they are used as edgings, plant singly, or in small groups, or in irregular shaped patches rather than in rows. They must have enough space and light to develop, and the soil needs to be reasonably fertile – vegetables are more demanding than flowers. Here are a few suggestions.

Taller vegetables for the back of a border

Climbing beans. These make a wonderful feature growing up tripods. Runner beans were originally introduced into this country for their ornamental rather than culinary value. The old pink-and-white-flowered Painted Lady, and the purple forms of climbing beans are exceptionally pretty. Sunflowers can be used to support climbing beans by sowing beans at the base of sunflowers when they are 1m (3ft) tall.
Sweetcorn. Plant in triangles of three.
Asparagus. Plant singly. The feathery foliage makes a lovely foil to flowers. Cut it down in late autumn and give it plenty of manure. You will get a few delicious spears in spring.
Cardoons and globe artichokes. Related plants with wonderful thistle

heads and handsome blue-grey foliage, spreading 1m (3ft). Grow as single specimens. Cardoons will grown up to 1·6m (8ft) tall. The flowers of artichokes and blanched stems of young cardoons are edible.
Chicory. Sugar Loaf, Witloof and red chicories throw up magnificent spikes of sky-blue flowers. Leave a few plants at the back of a border to run to seed in early summer. They may need support.

Medium height, mid-border vegetables

Ornamental cabbage and kale. These variegated forms give brilliant autumn colour; the reddish, wavy-leaved 'Ragged Jack' kale is also pretty. These won't survive severe winters, but the pretty dwarf curly kale is hardier. Plant them all in small groups before mid-July.
Dwarf beans. Plant singly or in small groups. The purple-podded French beans are pretty, delicious and prolific.
Swiss chard. The dark green leaves and silver stems are beautiful. The red form Ruby chard has red foliage which glows brilliantly in the winter sun. So does beetroot. Sow all *in situ* in patches.
Tomatoes. Small bush types fit in well in flower borders. Pixie is a dwarf cultivar with pretty foliage.
Asparagus pea. The clover-like leaves and deep-red 'vetch' flowers are a pretty combination. As it would take several plants to provide a good picking, use them to line a path or a long narrow border. Sow *in situ*.
Chicory. The pink foliage of the cultivar Red Verona is very attractive. Sow *in situ*.
Leeks. Use the purple-leaved cultivars, such as Blue Solaise.

Low growing vegetables for front of border or edging

Carrots. The foliage is very delicate. Mix seeds of any type of carrot with seeds of annual flowers or ornamental grasses, and broadcast them together. Thin both to at least 2·5cm (1in) apart. The carrots benefit from the light shade provided by the annuals, and for some reason carrot fly seems to be deterred. My best carrots one year were grown among ornamental grasses which were dried for winter decorations.
Lettuce. Most suitable are the red-leaved cultivars, and 'Salad Bowl' types, which don't form hearts but have curly indented leaves.
Winter purslane (*Claytonia perfoliata*) with pretty heart-shaped leaves; *iceplant* (*Mesembryanthemum crystallinum*), a sprawling plant with sparkling 'dewdrops' on its fleshy leaves and stems; *curly endive*, *Mizuna mustard*, and *chop suey greens* (*Chrysanthemum coronarium*) are all pretty enough for edging, best transplanted into position. Yellow and green forms of summer purslane can be sown along an edge.

Herbs

Most herbs are quite at home in flower beds, especially the ornamental forms. Parsley, chives, chervil, marjoram and thyme make good edgings; rosemary is a pretty grey/blue shrub if kept small. The following ornamental forms can all be used in cooking: purple basil, gold marjoram, variegated apple mint, ginger mint (which is green and gold), gold lemon balm, bronze fennel, purple, gold and silver sage, silver and gold lemon thyme. Tiny prostrate herbs like caraway thyme can be grown between flagstones. The mints are invasive, so best grown in odd corners rather than in flower beds. The white-flowered garlic chive is an exceptionally pretty herb. Grow it in neat clumps.

Edible flowers

Sunflowers have edible seeds. Clary (salvia horminum) can be used in soups or sauces. The petals and leaves of the ordinary pot marigold, calendula, can be used in salad, as can the young leaves, shoots and flowers of nasturtiums. Nasturtium seeds can be pickled in the young green state as capers. Borage, anchusa, violets, pansies, roses, pelargoniums, *Bellis perennis* daisies, primroses, are all edible. You can sprinkle the flowers, or the petals of roses and daisies, over salads.

Shady difficult positions

Most vegetables like open sunny positions so shady corners, where the soil is often dry and poor, tend to be wasted. Use such corners for the compost heap, or build up their fertility and try the following vegetables, which tolerate light shade: spinach, Chinese mustard, land cress, chop suey greens, Hamburg parsley, Jerusalem artichokes, lettuces and radishes in mid-summer provided there is enough moisture; spring-sown endive, corn salad, salad seedlings (see p. 126), and sorrel. Cucumbers do not mind some shade in mid-summer, nor do summer-sown peas. Of the herbs, mints, parsley, chives, angelica, lovage and chervil all tolerate shade.

These vegetables can also be grown under the light shade of ornamental trees such as flowering cherries, or under fruit trees, early in the year before the foliage becomes dense.

Dry situations

Grow New Zealand spinach, claytonia and pickling onions in dry spots.

Moist situations

Celeriac, celery, chicory, corn salad, land cress, fennel and leeks tolerate fairly damp positions, provided they are not waterlogged.

Space saving techniques

Successional sowing

Small gardens cannot afford to waste space on gluts. Rather than sowing large quantities of any one vegetable, it is more economic to try and maintain a succession by sowing little and often. The following can be sown at fortnightly or three-week intervals for much of the year and can be eaten young to give quick returns: carrots, radish, lettuce, turnips, kohl rabi, beetroot, spinach, spring onions and for cutting as seedlings, cress, mustard, salad rape, salad rocket, Sugar Loaf chicory, curly endive and Texsel greens.

Catch cropping

The above vegetables can also be used for catch cropping, ie getting a quick crop off a piece of ground intended for a later main crop. The later crop might be tomatoes or sweetcorn, which will be planted out after the danger of frosts, or the winter brassicas, when ready to be planted out from the seed bed.

Gap filling

Sometimes gaps appear in mid-summer in the winter greens, usually due to pest damage. There is still time to transplant calabrese or kale into the gap, if any young plants remain in the seed bed. If not, sow a few seeds of kohl rabi, autumn lettuce, spinach beet or spring cabbage (wait until August in the south) in the gap, or sow a few spares in soil blocks (see p. 76) and keep them at the ready.

Mixed seed

Lettuce and radish are sometimes sold with several cultivars in one packet. Sow and thin normally. The crop matures naturally in succession – useful where there is not enough ground to sow in succession. Also useful are the salad seed mixtures, known as 'Misticanza', 'Mesclum' or 'Saladisi'. They are fun to try, containing up to a dozen different plants, germinating in turn over a twelve-month period.

Patches (Fig. 33)

Traditionally vegetables are grown in rows, because rows are easier to cultivate on a large scale. On a small scale space can be saved by growing in small patches, with the plants at equidistant spacing from each other. Sow and thin, or plant, so that plants are a little farther apart than normal in the rows, but cut down on the spacing between the rows. So if the normal spacing is 20cm (8in) apart in rows 30cm

(12in) apart, thin or plant about 26cm (10in) apart each way. The leaves of the mature plants should just overlap, so they form a canopy to prevent weeds from germinating (see p. 96). Thinning, weeding and picking are a little more awkward with patches, so limit the patch to a size you can reach comfortably from the edges. Narrow beds are ideal for working on a patch basis (see p. 54).

Almost all vegetables, except for climbers, can be grown in patches – even peas, by running wire around the outside edges as supports. Narrow-leaved onions and leeks, however, won't form a weed-suppressing canopy, so it is advisable to mulch between the rows (see p. 63).

33. SPACE SAVING SYSTEMS IN NARROW BEDS

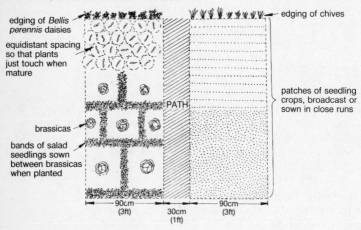

edging of *Bellis perennis* daisies

equidistant spacing so that plants just touch when mature

edging of chives

patches of seedling crops, broadcast or sown in close runs

brassicas

bands of salad seedlings sown between brassicas when planted

PATH

90cm (3ft)   30cm (1ft)   90cm (3ft)

Cut-and-come-again systems

Many of the leafy vegetables will grow again after being cut, giving two or three crops from one sowing, an intensive, productive way of using precious ground. It can be done at the seedling stage or later.

Seedlings. Seed is broadcast (see p. 61), or sown in rows 8cm (3in) apart, and the seedlings cut for use in salads when 5–8cm (2–3in) high, depending on the crop. They are very nutritious at this stage. Within about ten days it is often possible to make another cut. In some conditions up to four cuts can be made in all, but the ground must be fertile and well watered to sustain such growth. Seedling crops are most successful in spring and autumn, especially under cover. They may run to seed rapidly and become coarse in summer. When brassicas are planted out they can be 'ringed' by sowing a 5–8cm (2–3in) band of seedlings to utilise the ground between plants. Uproot the seedlings when the space is needed by the growing brassicas. For a list of suitable salad seedlings, see p. 143.

Mature cutting. Spring and summer cabbage may produce a second crop if a shallow cross is cut across the stalk when the main head is cut. In some cases four or five new cabbages will grow (see *Fig. 41* and p. 166). A spring lettuce may similarly make a second head if cut leaving a few basal leaves, rather than being pulled up. Among plants that will throw useful leaves after cutting the main head are Chinese cabbage, curly and broad-leaved endive, red and Sugar Loaf chicories, and fennel. Interestingly, these cut plants seem to survive lower winter temperatures than a whole plant. If cut in autumn they will often re-sprout early in spring, when they might have been expected to be killed off by frost. This last group, along with Salad Bowl lettuce, corn salad, Chinese Pak Choi, curly kale, Mizuna mustard and salad rocket can also be cut repeatedly at a semi-mature stage.

Double cropping in rows (*Fig. 34a*)

A slow and a fast maturing crop can often be sown in the same row. The fast-growing crop is out of the way before the slower one requires all the space. Dwarf lettuces such as Little Gem and Tom Thumb, which only reach a size of 10 or 12·5cm (4 or 5in) across, or a few carrot seeds of a short type, can be sown between station-sown root crops like parsnips, Hamburg parsley, salsify and scorzonera, or between leeks or brassicas in their early stages.

Radishes and spring onions can also be sown between stations. Alternatively they can be mixed with and sown almost on top of other seed – carrots, turnips, beetroot, parsnip, parsley and so on. Sow very thinly and pull the radishes or onions out carefully when large enough to eat to avoid disturbing the main crop. Radishes and spring onions are often sown in a row together. Leeks and spring onions can also be sown together. Start using the onions in July to allow the leeks to develop.

Intercropping between rows (*Fig. 34b*)

The principle is the same. A quick-growing crop is sown or planted very close to, or between the rows, of a slower maturing crop. The quick one is cleared before the space is required for the last stages of the main crop. Seeds of vegetables which will be transplanted can be 'intercropped' instead of being sown in a special seed bed.

Intercropping is a very useful technique in small gardens, but take care not to overdo it. Points to remember are:
both crops must have enough space, light and moisture to develop;
there must be room to cultivate and pick.

34. SPACE SAVING TECHNIQUES

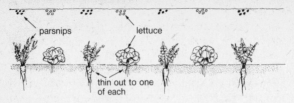

a. Double cropping in rows:
   lettuce and parsnip seed are
   station sown alternately in one
   row; each station later thinned to
   one seedling per station. The
   lettuces are cut first, leaving the
   parsnips to mature

b. Intercropping: young Brussels sprouts are planted between
   two rows of peas. The space between the sprouts is sown
   with radishes and land cress. The peas are cleared first, then
   the radishes; the land cress will continue growing in the
   shade of the mature sprouts and can be used in winter

For these reasons sow or plant the main crop rows a little farther
apart than usual. Generally speaking avoid intercropping with very tall
or sprawly vegetables, such as potatoes. Water very generously when
plants are being established, and mulch to preserve moisture and
minimise weeding.

There are many possibilities for intercropping, for example:
Between rows of shallots – carrots, Little Gem or Tom Thumb lettuce,
radishes, small turnips, alternating rows of carrots and spring onions.
Between and alongside dwarf forms of French, runner, and broad beans
– lettuce, winter brassicas, summer spinach.
Between rows of winter brassicas – carrots, small summer cabbages,
turnips, lettuce, land cress, Chinese mustard, kohl rabi.
Between peas (*preferably the more dwarf types*) – winter brassicas,
turnips, carrots, lettuce, summer spinach.
Under double rows of runner beans – forcing or Sugar Loaf chicory,
spinach, corn salad, land cress.

In addition, alternating rows of lettuce and beetroot; carrots and
onions; lettuce, carrots, and salad onions, can be planted very close

together. Land cress, radishes, and lettuce are suitable for intercropping almost anywhere, as are the salad seedling crops listed on p. 143.

The following is one example of intercropping which has proved very successful:

mid-April, two sets of peas sown about 75cm (2½ft) apart;

end April, a row of Brussels sprouts planted between them, 60cm (2ft) apart;

end April, radishes sown between half the sprouts, and land cress between the other half.

Undercropping: the long, the short and the tall

Vegetables of completely different growth habits can sometimes be grown together. Sweetcorn is a good example. It is tall, but the leaves do not spread far or make too much shade. Marrows, cucumbers and even pumpkins can trail between the corn plants; small cabbages, dwarf beans and salad crops will grow underneath. Sweetcorn can also be planted between rows of brassicas. Trailing marrows can be planted among potatoes and trained between the rows. They are vigorous enough to hold their own until the potatoes are lifted.

Dwarf cultivars

Space can often be saved by growing dwarf cultivars of vegetables, which can be planted closer than the standard forms. Dwarf peas, for example, save on space as well as on netting or pea sticks, and make intercropping easier. Bush marrows take up less space than trailing types, and yield heavily. Many examples are given in Part Two.

Saving path space

In very small vegetable gardens paths can be eliminated. Instead place occasional stepping stones here and there, to give a solid working point for cultivating and picking in wet weather. Seed trays can be used to mould neat little concrete blocks for this purpose.

Wide topped mounds

Increasing the surface area is one method of making more 'growing space' in small gardens. A system developed in Germany and Switzerland was to build up beds as rectangular mounds, with a flat top and sloping sides, planting vegetables on the sides and along the top.

Pots, boxes and containers

A considerable proportion of the space in small gardens may be taken up by concrete paths, or paved areas around the house, shed or garage.

These, along with window sills, patios, balconies, flat roofs and low walls can be made productive by growing vegetables in pots, boxes or other containers. Useful supplementary crops can be grown this way, although it is hard work and fairly expensive to do so on a large scale.

Types of container

Almost anything can be used: traditional clay and plastic flower pots, wooden, plastic, polystyrene or concrete window boxes, plain wooden boxes, barrels – whole or cut in half – coal scuttles, bottomless buckets, picturesque old wheelbarrows, cattle troughs, rubber tyres cut in half and suspended from a balcony, 9-lit (2-gal) plastic cans with the tops cut off . . . the scope is endless.

Makeshift boxes can be made by boarding up an area with a piece of wood, using the existing foundation as a base. A shallow border against a wall can be 'built up' with soil if a wooden or brick edge is made. I have seen a beautiful crop of runner beans growing on a concrete path against a house. The box they were in was made from two wooden drawers with the bottoms knocked out, standing on top of each other. Around them a loose wall had been built of rounded bricks, washed up on a nearby beach. They kept the boxes in place and added a decorative touch.

A board can be fitted across a window sill and plants grown in pots behind it, to give the impression of a window box.

Whatever the container, it must be strong enough to withstand the weight of damp soil, the effects of watering, and the weight of a crop. If it is to stand on a balcony or roof top, it must be fairly lightweight.

Size

For vegetable growing *the bigger the container the better*. A minimum soil depth and width would be 15cm (6in); a depth and width of 20–25cm (8–10in) would give far more scope. Herbs can be grown in smaller 10 or 12cm (4 or 5in) pots.

Drainage

Good drainage is essential in any type of container. Wooden boxes can have holes drilled in the bottom, or burnt with a poker. They should be at least 1cm ($\frac{1}{2}$in) in diameter, preferably sloped at an angle. Containers should be raised off the ground on bricks, blocks or small pieces of wood to allow water to drain away. Or drill drainage holes in the *side* of the container, an inch or so above the base. Window boxes on sloping sills can be made level with wooden wedges.

Containers on balconies or windowsills should have some sort of drip tray underneath to prevent water dripping down walls or on to people below.

Fill the bottom layer of a box or pot with at least 1cm (½in) of broken crocks, pieces of brick, small stones, charcoal, or ashes as drainage. If there are no drainage holes, increase this to an inch. This layer can be covered with an inch or so of dry leaves, or pieces of moss or turf (face downwards) before putting in the soil – again to help drainage (*Fig. 35a*).

The soil

The soil should be as 'open', ie as porous as possible. Prepared peat-based compost or the John Innes soil based composts (No 2 or No 3) are the easiest to use, although they cost money. Otherwise use the best garden soil available, mixed with generous quantities of well-rotted compost, peat and sand. Never use fresh manure.

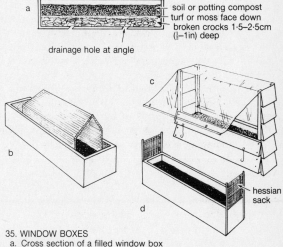

35. WINDOW BOXES
   a. Cross section of a filled window box
   b. Small cloches can be used to bring on seeds and protect young seedlings
   c. The 'window box' cloche
   d. Windbreaks at either end of exposed window boxes provide essential protection

Peat and horticultural vermiculite can be mixed in a 3:2 ratio for a general-purpose potting mixture. There are no nutrients, so plants will need supplementary feeding with some kind of fertiliser.

If you are within easy reach of seaweed, a mixture of a third part each (by volume) of seaweed, straw and compost makes an excellent growing medium. Put it in the boxes two or three months before planting and leave it to rot down.

Maintaining fertility

Soil in containers becomes stale and should be changed every two or three years. Pep it up from time to time with a top dressing of well-rotted manure or compost. Greedy vegetables, such as tomatoes, peppers or beans, need fresh soil every year.

Most vegetables in containers require occasional feeding. Use organic fertilisers or artificial fertilisers at diluted strengths. Phostrogen is particularly useful for pots and window boxes.

Herbs grown in window boxes need a light, not particularly rich soil, and should never be fed with artificial fertilisers.

Contrary to popular belief, earthworms in pots or boxes are beneficial, but they will only stay there if the soil is moist.

Preventing moisture loss

The biggest problem with all containers is preventing them from drying out. If they are against a wall they may effectively be shielded from rain. A lot of moisture is lost through evaporation from the sides and the soil surface. To offset this, containers can be lined with heavy-duty polythene with drainage holes punched in the bottom, and the surface covered with as much as 5cm (2in) of fine stones or gravel chippings. Stand pots in dishes or trays of gravel, and water through the gravel. A useful tip I was once given was to put narrow strips of cloth in the bottom of the pot, coming out through the drainage hole into the gravel. They act as wicks, making it easier for moisture to be taken up. One pot can be stood inside a larger container, filling the gap between them with soil or pebbles to minimise evaporation. Be prepared to water all containers twice a day in really hot weather.

Protection

Plants in window boxes in exposed positions, for example on high buildings or balconies, can be torn to shreds by wind. Rig up small windshields across the ends with hessian, netting, matting or even twigs; this will break the force of the wind (*Fig. 35d*).

To give extra protection in early spring or late autumn, low cloches can be fitted over window boxes or long containers (*Fig. 35b*). Or a polythene film cover can be attached as in the 'Window box' cloche (*Fig. 35c*). Inverted jam jars can be used as mini cloches over seeds.

Purpose built containers (*Fig. 36*)

The parsley pot is a clay pot with several holes in the side. It is filled with soil or potting compost, and parsley seedlings are planted in the holes. It is often used for winter parsley indoors.

Tower pots are a modern development. A series of interlocking plastic

pots make a pillar in the air, again designed so that plants grow out of
the sides. Primarily intended for flowers or strawberries, they can be
used for herbs and salads such as small lettuce, land cress, corn salad,
radish and spring onions.

Vertical polytube container system. Invented and patented by Mr
Maurice Howgill, polythene tubes of one metre (one yard) high and
about 30cm (12in) in diameter, are supported on a frame. The tubes
are filled with compost. There are holes or 'pockets' all round the tubes
and in these almost any vegetables can be grown. From the equivalent
of a square yard of ground space Mr Howgill has produced 100 leeks,
100 sticks of celery, 10 Brussels sprouts, 9kg (20lb) tomatoes, etc. The
container has not yet been commercially manufactured, but it
illustrates the principle that growing plants by vertical methods is a
means of increasing the productivity of small gardens.

Compost-filled bags. Various types of heavy duty plastic bags, filled
with prepared compost, are now on the market. Vegetables are
planted directly into the bag. They are extremely useful where space
and soil are in short supply, as they are simply laid flat on a path,
balcony or patio, or against a wall, allowing cucumbers and beans to
climb upwards. The average size is about 1m (3ft) long, 30cm (1ft)
wide and 15cm (6in) high. The compost can generally be used twice,
first for a demanding crop like tomatoes, then for a less demanding
salad crop. The spent compost can be used as a garden mulch. Old
plastic peat or fertiliser bags can be filled with good soil or potting
compost and used this way. If possible open them initially down the
middle rather than at an end. Gro-bags, as compost-filled bags are
popularly known, dry out rapidly. For this reason it is best to plant
through small holes cut in the top, to minimise evaporation (*Fig. 36d*).

Vegetables suitable for containers

By no means all vegetables grow well in the relatively confined
conditions of pots and boxes. Taking the cost of the containers and
compost into account, it is only an economic proposition in a few cases,
although it is always fun to cull a lettuce or a few radishes from the
window box.

Tomatoes are easily the most suitable and worthwhile crop, followed
by peppers, cucumbers, dwarf French and dwarf runner beans, and
salad crops such as lettuce, endive, spring onions, corn salad, land
cress and radishes – though make sure there is plenty of humus or they
may run to seed. Courgettes can be grown in large boxes or troughs;
carrots in deep boxes; early potatoes in boxes or tubs.

Colour can always be added by planting flowers among the
vegetables – for example: trailing lobelia, hanging petunias and

36. PURPOSE BUILT CONTAINERS

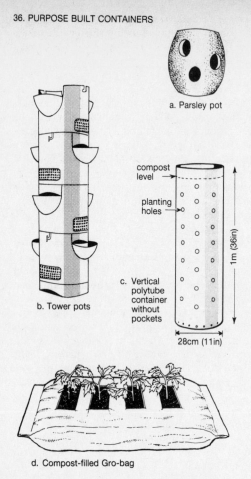

a. Parsley pot

b. Tower pots

compost level

planting holes

c. Vertical polytube container without pockets

1m (36in)

28cm (11in)

d. Compost-filled Gro-bag

begonias, and climbing nasturtiums, either hanging down or trailing up strong threads.

When short of ground space, use deep boxes standing on paths to raise brassica seedlings.

Many herbs thrive in containers. Rosemary and bay can be grown in tubs. Parsley, chives, thyme, marjoram, sorrel, young sage plants, basil, summer and winter savory and fennel grow well in pots and boxes. Mint needs to be restricted to a pot or it would take over a window box. Some herbs naturally become restricted when grown in a confined space; others need to be picked constantly to keep them small. Many herbs will grow happily on sunny windowsills indoors.

Vegetables in the house

Windowsill seedlings
An extension of the idea of growing mustard and cress on blotting paper on a saucer (see p. 197), seedlings can be grown in seed trays of sowing or potting compost on a windowsill. They will grow bigger, last longer, and may give two cuts grown this way. Mustard, cress, salad rape, coriander and salad rocket are all suitable subjects.

Sprouting seeds (*Fig. 37*)
Many seeds can be sprouted indoors. The 'sprouts', which are the first tiny shoots, are eaten anything from 5–40mm ($\frac{1}{4}$–$1\frac{1}{2}$in) long, when they are both tasty and nutritious. The most popular are mung beans, the bean sprouts of Chinese cookery (see p. 161), but many other seeds can be sprouted. A list is given on page 143.

Most of the seeds can be germinated either in the dark (for white shoots) or in the light (for green shoots). They can either be grown on a base of something like cotton wool or flannel, as with mustard and cress, or simply in a jar with muslin or netting over the top, secured with a rubber band, or in a lidded, plastic box. A shallow, ice cream box is ideal. Various manufactured seed sprouters are also available. Mung beans and lentils grow well on a base, but most other seeds can be grown satisfactorily in a jar or shallow container without any base.

37. METHODS OF SPROUTING SEEDS INDOORS

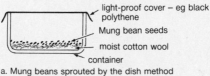

a. Mung beans sprouted by the dish method

b. Alfalfa seed sprouted by the jar method

The secret of successful sprouting is to keep the seeds cool and clean by rinsing them twice a day. Either tip them into a strainer, run water through, drain and return to the container, or run water into the container and tip it out again, so the seeds are moist but not left lying in water. Depending on the seed and the temperature, they will be ready for eating within four to ten days. Cut them if grown on a base; pull them out in tufts from a jar.

Always purchase seeds that are intended for sprouting. Many seeds today are treated with chemicals, and it would be exceedingly dangerous to use them for sprouting and eat them.

Forcing indoors

Chicory and endive can be lifted from the garden, planted in pots and forced or blanched indoors. Mushrooms can be grown indoors in commercially prepared packs.

A spare mature rhubarb plant can also be forced indoors. Lift the plant in late November, expose it to the frost, then plant it in any soil in an ashcan, covered with an inverted ashcan or black polythene over a wire frame, to keep the light out. Leave it in a warm room, watering occasionally. In late January or February it will throw beautiful fresh pink stalks, which taste superb and look marvellous against the yellow deeply-crinkled young leaves. After forcing a plant needs two seasons' 'resting' in the garden without being pulled. Seakale can be forced in much the same way. A cellar, of course, is the ideal place for this sort of indoor gardening.

CHAPTER EIGHT

Planning

In a small garden it is worth drawing up a plan each year with the aim of making the best use of all available space. It should be a very flexible plan and treated as such. All sorts of unforeseen factors – early seasons, late seasons, bumper crops, failures – will drive a coach and horses through a rigid plan.

The main questions to sort out are what to grow, and where.

What to grow

A number of factors have to be weighed up:

1 *Family preferences*. In many gardens vegetables are wasted because it turns out that the family does not like them. Whoever grows the vegetables either has to convert the family to wider tastes (the best course), or alter his or her plans.

2 *Setting priorities*. It is rarely possible to keep an average family in vegetables from a small garden, so decide on your priorities and plan accordingly. The main purpose could be:

to save money (an 'Economic' garden);

to have something fresh from the garden all year round (an 'All Year Round' garden);

to grow unusual 'gourmet' vegetables, or unusual cultivars of ordinary ones which are difficult or expensive to buy, or vegetables which are far better when picked straight from the garden (a 'Speciality' garden);

or a combination of all these.

Suggested plans for a basic 'All Year Round' garden and a 'Speciality' garden are given at the end of this chapter.

The plans are for a strip of ground about 96sq m (1/50th of an acre) in size. This was based on the assumption that the 'average' garden is about 300sq m (1/16th of an acre), and that the 'average' gardener would only want to devote approximately one-third of this to vegetables.

The plans are for fairly intensive use of a plot, and in all probability factors beyond one's control, such as the weather, will mean that some alterations will have to be made during the course of the season. The point to remember in making an All Year Round plan is that most of the vegetables we grow mature naturally between early summer and mid-winter. Between February and May there is the 'Hungry Gap', which is only filled with careful planning. Remember also that the use of protected cover will increase the output and extend the season enormously.

In making a plan for an Economic garden, root crops (except possibly young carrots), onions, Brussels sprouts, and cabbage, would probably be cut out, and one would concentrate on salad crops, peas and beans, which are nearly always expensive to buy. The Value for Space Ratings, see Planning Information Table (p. 148), help to evaluate which vegetables give the best returns for the space they occupy.

3 *Getting a balance*. Other factors being equal, aim for a balance between the main types of vegetables – brassicas (cabbage family), legumes (peas and beans), roots, salads and onions.

4 *Climatic factors*. Do not waste space on vegetables which are not happy in your area. In cold parts of the country outdoor tomatoes and cucumbers, sweetcorn, even runner beans are risky. Grow extra salads, roots or summer cabbage instead.

5 *Freezer*. If you have a freezer modify your plan accordingly. It may be worth growing more peas, beans or calabrese, to give a greater variety during the winter months.

6 *Storage space*. Most root vegetables can be stored outside, either in the ground or in clamps. But onions need to be under cover by September, so only grow them if you have space to store or hang them.

Where to grow

It is best to set aside part of the garden just for vegetables. The vegetable patch can be separated off with a low ornamental hedge, a trellis supporting climbing roses, clematis, etc, or a mixed flower border. The ideal vegetable garden is an unshaded square or rectangular plot, but small gardens often consist of odd-shaped pieces of ground, parts of which are shaded.

Here are a few planning guidelines.

1 *Permanent or semi-permanent features* such as greenhouses, frames,

compost heaps, water butts. Choose a place for these first. Greenhouses and frames should be placed to catch the maximum sun, preferably facing south. Compost heaps can utilise awkward or heavily-shaded areas. A rain butt which catches water off a roof near the vegetable garden is a boon in dry summers.

2 *Direction*. Where there is a choice, arrange rows to run north and south, so they do not shade each other. This applies particularly to a row of runner beans on poles. In steeply-sloping gardens it is easiest to cultivate across a slope, and helps to prevent soil erosion.

3 *Walls*. Use walls, fences, trellises, fruit cages for climbing vegetables. Fences are preferable to hedges in vegetable gardens as they do not compete for moisture or soil nutrients, or harbour pests.

4 *Wet, shady, dry areas*. Select suitable vegetables for these positions.

5 *Flower beds, paths, etc.* Decide what vegetables can be grown in flower beds, or in pots or boxes on paths, patios and so on.

6 *Access*. Have herbs as near the house as you can, or along edges. Where possible, put winter crops where they can be reached easily without treading over too much ground.

7 *Intercropping, catch cropping, intersowing*. Use these techniques as much as possible (see Chapter 7).

8 *Proximity planting*. Intercropping apart, where possible grow in proximity crops which are likely to:

   mature at about the same time;

   be sown or planted at about the same time.

This makes it easier to clear a patch of ground from time to time and dig it over thoroughly. Suitable crops to group are:

   spring sown salad crops such as spring onions, young carrots, early lettuce, salad seedlings;

   crops which overwinter in the soil such as leeks, celeriac, kohl rabi, Brussels sprouts;

   half-hardy summer vegetables such as tomatoes, sweetcorn, peppers.

9 *Rotation*. Crops of the same botanical family or group should not be grown continuously in the same piece of ground; this can lead to a build up of pests or diseases. The most important groups are legumes, brassicas, root crops and the onion family.

If you have enough space divide your garden into three more or less equal plots, and rotate vegetables between these annually, as shown below:

	Plot A	Plot B	Plot C
Year 1	Legumes	Brassicas	Roots
Year 2	Brassicas	Roots	Legumes
Year 3	Roots	Legumes	Brassicas

Fit in the onion family and other vegetables such as the salads and celeriac wherever you can. Legumes and onions often work in well together; so do salads and brassicas.

In the simple rotation suggested above, the legumes will enrich the soil for the brassicas with nitrogen from their root nodules.

Plots about to be planted with legumes or brassicas can be manured, but try to avoid using fresh manure on the root plot.

Where regular rotation is impracticable because of lack of space avoid planting the same crop in the same piece of ground twice running (moving it even a few yards either way will help).

Note: where a garden is divided into a number of narrow beds, there is far more flexibility in working out rotation systems.

10 *Spacing*. Vegetable rows can often be closer than traditional or recommended spacing, especially if used in their early stages. This saves space, but it does make cultivating and picking more awkward. As a guiding rule, the leaves of vegetables in adjacent rows should only touch, not overlap, when full grown. The same is more or less true of plants in a row, though some can stand being more crowded than others.

The Planning Information Table (p. 148) summarises basic planning information about different vegetables, ie weeks to maturity, spread of plant, value for space rating, season of use, whether the season can be extended with cloches, and whether the vegetable can be stored. The lists which follow indicate the different purposes for which vegetables can be grown, and are intended as supplementary aids to planning.

QUICK MATURING VEGETABLES

Under 8 weeks

Chop suey greens   Salad seedlings (see p. 143)
Land cress   Texsel greens
Radish   Turnips

Under 12 weeks

Asparagus pea   Fennel
Beetroot (young)   Iceplant
Carrots (short)   Kohl rabi
Cabbage (Chinese)   Lettuce (summer)
Cauliflower (mini)   Mizuna mustard
Chinese celery mustard   Onions (spring)
Claytonia   Peas (early)

Corn salad   Radish (Chinese)
Courgettes   Spinach (summer)
Endive   Sweetcorn

CROPS IN GROUND ALL WINTER (very cold areas excepted)

Brassicas: Salsify
  Broccoli, purple sprouting   Scorzonera
  Brussels sprouts   Swedes
  Cabbage, spring   Turnips
  Cabbage, winter   Others:
  Hardy Chinese mustards   Beans, broad (autumn sown)
  Kale   Celeriac
  Turnips for tops   Leeks
Roots: Onions (Welsh)
  Artichoke, Jerusalem   Onions (autumn sown)
  Hamburg parsley   Peas (autumn sown)
  Kohl rabi   Spinach (overwintering types)
  Parsnips   Salads: see Winter Salad Crops

WINTER AND EARLY SPRING SALAD CROPS

Success outdoors depends upon the severity of the winter, choice of the
hardiest cultivars, and use of protection where possible.
Celeriac   Onion (Welsh)
Chicory, red and Sugar   Radish (Chinese)
  Loaf (cloched)   Salad rape
Celery, leaf   Salad rocket (cloched)
Chinese leaf and celery   Texsel greens (cloched)
  mustards (hardy cultivars)   Indoors:
Corn salad   Sprouted seeds, eg bean sprouts
Endive   Seedlings, eg mustard, cress, salad
Land cress   rape, salad rocket, coriander
Lettuce (cloched)

IMPORTANT GROUPS FOR ROTATION PURPOSES

Brassicas:
  Brussels sprouts   Cauliflower
  Broccoli, purple sprouting   Chinese mustards
  Cabbage (all kinds)   Kale
  Calabrese   Kohl rabi

Legumes:
  Beans, broad
  Beans, French
  Beans, runner
  Peas
  Radish
  Swedes
  Texsel greens
  Turnips

Onion family:
  Garlic
  Leeks
  Onions
  Shallots

For vegetables suitable for intercropping, intersowing, see Chapter 7
For vegetables suitable for intercropping under cloches, see Chapter 6

VEGETABLES SUITABLE FOR FREEZING

Beans (all types)
Beetroot (very young)
Broccoli, purple sprouting
Brussels sprouts
Calabrese
Cauliflower (mini)
Kale, curly

Peas
Peppers
Spinach (certain cultivars)
Sweetcorn
Texsel greens
Tomatoes

(Consult seed catalogues for the most suitable cultivars for freezing)

FRESH VEGETABLES FOR THE 'HUNGRY GAP' (FEB TO MAY)

Artichoke, Jerusalem
Broccoli, purple sprouting
Brussels sprouts
Cabbage, savoy
Cabbage, spring
Carrots (short, cloched)
Celeriac
Chicories
Chinese mustards
Claytonia
Corn salad
Endive

Hamburg parsley
Kale, curly
Leeks
Lettuce (cloched)
Parsnip
Radish
Salad rocket
Salad seedlings (see p. 195)
Spinach (overwintering types)
Texsel greens
Turnips
Turnip tops

VEGETABLES FOR PARTICULAR SITUATIONS

Lightly shaded
Artichoke, Jerusalem
Chicories, red and Sugar Loaf
Chinese mustards

Chop suey greens
Claytonia
Endive (spring sown)

Fennel
Hamburg parsley
Herbs (some)
Kohl rabi (if well drained)
Land cress
Lettuce ⎱ (in mid-summer
Radish ⎰ provided moist)
Salad rocket
Spinach beet
Dry
Claytonia
Onions, pickling
Spinach (New Zealand)

Damp
Celeriac
Celery
Corn salad
Land cress
Leeks
Climbers
Beans, runner (some cultivars)
Beans, French (some cultivars)
Cucumbers (Japanese cultivars)
Marrows (some cultivars)
Peas (to some extent)

VEGETABLES SUITABLE FOR FLOWER BEDS

Artichoke, globe
Asparagus
Asparagus pea
Beans, climbing, and dwarf,
   French and runner
Beetroot
Cabbage ornamental
Carrots
Chicory (red forms)
Chop suey greens
Claytonia

Fennel
Herbs (some)
Iceplant
Kale, ornamental
Lettuce (pink and frilly types)
Mizuna mustard
Purslane
Sweetcorn
Swiss chard and Ruby chard
Tomatoes (some)

SALAD SEEDLINGS

(*Cut-and-come-again*)
Chinese mustards
Claytonia
Coriander
Corn salad
Cress
Endive
Lettuce ('cutting' types)
Mustard

Purslane
Salad rape
Salad rocket
Spinach
Sugar Loaf chicory
Texsel greens
Turnip

SEEDS FOR SPROUTING

Alfalfa (lucerne)
Azuki beans
Fenugreek
Lentils

Mung beans
Mustard
Radish
Rye

BASIC ALL YEAR ROUND PLAN
17 × 6 metres (17 × 6 yards), 1 metre (1 yard) strips

Position of crops in YEAR 1		Position of crops in YEAR 2
	30cm (1ft) edging of PARSLEY, CHIVES, WELSH ONIONS, etc.	
A	SEED BED	E
B	3 rows ONIONS, SHALLOTS and GARLIC, sown and planted February and March (followed by KOHL RABI, CHINESE RADISH, CHINESE CABBAGE, CHINESE MUSTARDS or ENDIVE sown late August/September)	F
C	2 rows EARLY POTATOES planted late March/early April (followed by 1 row CELERIAC and 1 row SPINACH BEET as potatoes lifted)	G
D	3 rows PARSNIPS and/or HAMBURG PARSLEY sown March/April intersown and/or intercropped with LETTUCE, RADISH, SALAD SEEDLINGS	H
E	1 row SHORT CARROTS sown March 1 row SALAD BEETROOT sown April 1 row SPRING ONIONS sown March/April (followed by LEEKS planted June/July, intercropped with LETTUCE, etc.)	J
F	Double row BROAD BEANS sown March TURNIPS sown alongside (followed by WINTER CABBAGE and/or RED CHICORY planted July)	K
G	1 wide drill EARLY PEAS sown March/April (followed by PURPLE SPROUTING BROCCOLI planted out between peas and beans July or maincrop CARROTS sown July after peas cleared)	L
H	2-rows FRENCH BEANS intercropped with LETTUCE followed by: (½ rows: CHINESE CABBAGE BLANCHING CHICORY ------- (CURLY KALE)	M

Winter brassicas can be intercropped with CHINESE MUSTARD CORN SALAD CHOP SUEY LAND CRESS SPRING ONIONS

	LETTUCE RADISH, SALAD SEEDLINGS	N
J	1 wide drill PEAS sown June (followed by BRUSSELS SPROUTS planted out between beans and peas)	
K	Double row RUNNER BEANS sown May followed by: (SPRING CABBAGE patch : (TURNIP TOPS patch : (CORN SALAD patch planted September/October) : sown end September/October) : sown September)	O
L	1 row TOMATOES planted out under cloches May, recloched to ripen September (followed by autumn sown BROAD BEANS cloched after Christmas)	P
	cloches alternate between these two rows	
M	CUCUMBERS planted out under cloches June (followed by intercropped AUTUMN LETTUCE and CARROTS or SALAD SEEDLINGS cloched October, ready Christmas)	A
N	SELF-BLANCHING CELERY planted June	PEPPERS planted June	SWEETCORN block planted June, intercropped with SUMMER LETTUCE, RADISH, CORN SALAD, etc.	B
O	SUMMER CABBAGE planted May/June	COURGETTES 4, planted June		C
P	2 rows FRENCH BEANS sown July intercropped with AUTUMN LETTUCE (followed by hardy CHINESE MUSTARDS and overwintered LETTUCE)	CALABRESE planted July	D
	60 cm (2ft) path to give access to compost heaps and frame	
	COMPOST HEAPS	FRAME

NOTE: The garden is planned in strips of 1 metre (1 yard) widths, each of which have been lettered (see left-hand column). The right-hand column shows the new position of the crops the following year. This ensures that some rotation is carried out. Main crops are given first; successional crops are given in brackets. See also note on following plan.

SPECIALITY ALL YEAR ROUND PLAN
17 × 6 metres (17 × 6 yards), 1 metre (1 yard) strips

Position of crops in YEAR 1		Crop	Position of crops in YEAR 2
Permanent beds		ASPARAGUS BED	
		JERUSALEM ARTICHOKES	
		Alternate every three years	
	4 GLOBE ARTICHOKES		
A		SEED BED	G
B		2 rows ONION sets, 1 row SHALLOTS and GARLIC planted February/March (followed by KOHL RABI, CHINESE RADISH, CHINESE CABBAGE and/or ENDIVE sown late August)	H
C		2 rows EARLY POTATOES planted late March/early April followed by (RED CHICORY) (SPINACH BEET) (as potatoes lifted) (LEEKS)	J
D		1 row PARSNIPS and/or HAMBURG PARSLEY sown March/April intercropped or intersown in rows with LETTUCE, RADISH, etc. 1 row SALSIFY and/or SCORZONERA	K
E		SHORT CARROTS broadcast in February under cloches or March in open (followed by BEETROOT sown June/July or ICEPLANT) — SALAD SEEDLINGS early spring under cloches (followed by 2 rows CELERIAC planted late May/June)	L
F		double row DWARF BROAD BEANS sown March/April TURNIPS and SPRING ONIONS sown alongside (followed by RED CABBAGE and SAVOYS)	M
G		Triple row EARLY PEAS sown April (followed by PURPLE SPROUTING BROCCOLI planted July/August intersown with SALAD SEEDLINGS)	N

A	2 rows FRENCH BEANS sown July intercropped with SUGAR LOAF CHICORY
B	MAIN CROP PEAS plus some ASPARAGUS PEAS (followed by early maturing BRUSSELS SPROUTS planted alongside and/or hardy CHINESE MUSTARDS planted August/September)
C	double row RUNNER BEANS sown May followed by (TURNIP TOPS patch sown end September/October) (CORN SALAD patch sown October)
D	EARLY LETTUCE and/or SALAD SEEDLINGS followed by (CALABRESE planted June intercropped with LETTUCE and/or MINI CAULIFLOWER)
E	SWEETCORN planted June interplanted with COURGETTES
F	

H	2 rows FRENCH BEANS sown May intercropped with FORCING CHICORY
J	(SPRING CABBAGE patch planted October)
K	(12 BUSH TOMATOES 45cm (1½ft) apart planted late May/June)
L	4 JAPANESE CUCUMBERS on tripods planted May/June underplanted with LETTUCE
M	FLORENCE FENNEL planted June
N	SELF-BLANCHING CELERY planted June PEPPERS planted June (followed by autumn sown BROAD BEANS)

Permanent 30cm (1ft) edging of HERBS or WELSH ONIONS

60cm (2ft) path for access to composts heaps and frame

COMPOST HEAPS   FRAME

NOTE: These plans can be converted to a garden laid out in narrow beds. In this case each strip would be treated as a bed, though planting would be at equidistant spacing across the bed rather than in rows. Less intersowing would be possible, but the intersown vegetables could instead be grown in patches across the beds. See also note on previous plan.

PLANNING INFORMATION TABLE – ANNUAL VEGETABLES

	JAN	FEB	MAR	APR	MAY	JUN	JUL	AUG	SEP	OCT	NOV	DEC	Average months from sowing to maturity*	Average 'spread' of plants cm (in)	Value for Space Rating (VSR)
						AVERAGE SEASON OF USE									
ARTICHOKE, JERUSALEM													7–8	30 (12)	*
ASPARAGUS PEA													2½–3	45–60 (18–24)	*
†BEAN, BROAD (autumn sown)													7–8	38–45 (15–18)	*
†BEAN, BROAD (spring sown)													3–4	38–45 (15–18)	**
†BEAN, FRENCH													3	30 (12)	***
†BEAN, RUNNER													3–4	30 (12)	***
BEAN SPROUTS													few days	—	****
†BEETROOT (salad)													3	15 (6)	**
BEETROOT (for storage)													4	23–30 (9–12)	**
BROCCOLI, PURPLE SPROUTING													10	68 (27)	*
BRUSSELS SPROUTS													7–9	61 (24)	*
†CABBAGE, SPRING													8–9	30 (12)	*
CABBAGE, SUMMER													6+	45 (18)	*
CABBAGE, WINTER													7	45–50 (18–20)	*
CALABRESE													4–5	28 (11)	**
†CARROTS (short)													2½–3	5–8 (2–3)	****
CARROTS (intermediate)													5–6	23 (9)	***
CAULIFLOWER, MINI													3	15(6)	*
†CELERIAC													7	38–50 (15–20)	*
†CELERY (self-blanching)													4½	30 (12)	**
CHICORY (forcing)													6	25 (10)	*
CHICORY, RED													4–4½	15–25 (6–10)	**
CHICORY, SUGAR LOAF (head)													4–4½	15–23 (6–9)	***
CHICORY, SUGAR LOAF (seedlings)													1½–2	dense	****
CHINESE CABBAGE													2½	30–38 (12–15)	**
CHINESE CELERY MUSTARD													3	18–23 (7–9)	***
CHINESE LEAFY MUSTARD/MIZUNA													2–3	30 (12)	****
CHOP SUEY GREENS													2	15–20 (6–8)	***
CLAYTONIA													3–4	10–13 (4–5)	****
†CORN SALAD													3	10 (4)	

Vegetable	Time to maturity	Months available (chart)	Spacing cm (in)	Space Rating
†COURGETTES		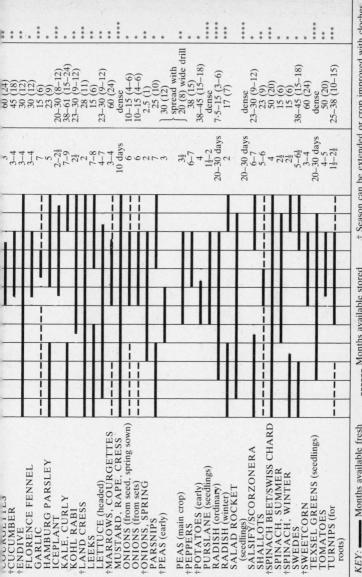	60 (24)	**
†CUCUMBER	3		45 (18)	**
†ENDIVE	3–4		30 (12)	***
FLORENCE FENNEL	3–4		30 (12)	**
GARLIC	7		15 (6)	*
HAMBURG PARSLEY	5		23 (9)	***
ICEPLANT	2–2½		20–30 (8–12)	*
KALE, CURLY	7–9		38–61 (15–24)	***
KOHL RABI	2½		23–30 (9–12)	***
†LAND CRESS	2		28 (11)	***
LEEKS	7–8		15 (6)	**
LETTUCE (headed)	4–7		23–30 (9–12)	***
†MARROWS, COURGETTES	3–4		60 (24)	*
MUSTARD, RAPE, CRESS	10 days		dense	***
ONIONS (from seed, spring sown)	6		10–15 (4–6)	.
ONIONS (from sets)	6		10–15 (4–6)	.
†ONIONS, SPRING	2		2.5 (1)	**
PARSNIPS	7		25 (10)	*
†PEAS (early)	3		30 (12)	***
PEAS (main crop)	3½		spread with 20 (8) wide drill	**
†PEPPERS	6–7		38 (15)	****
†POTATOES (early)	4		38–45 (15–18)	****
PURSLANE (seedlings)	1½–2		dense	***
RADISH (ordinary)	20–30 days		7.5–15 (3–6)	*
RADISH (winter)	2		17 (7)	...
SALAD ROCKET			dense	...
SALSIFY/SCORZONERA (seedlings)	20–30 days		23–30 (9–12)	****
SHALLOTS	5–6		23 (9)	**
†SPINACH BEET/SWISS CHARD	4		50 (20)	***
SPINACH, SUMMER	2½		15 (6)	*
†SPINACH, WINTER	2½		15 (6)	...
SWEDES	5–6½		38–45 (15–18)	...
†SWEETCORN	3–4		60 (24)	***
TEXSEL GREENS (seedlings)	20–30 days		dense	**
TOMATOES	4–5		50 (20)	***
TURNIPS (for roots)	1½–2½		25–38 (10–15)	***

KEY: —— Months available fresh   ----- Months available stored   † Season can be extended or crop improved with cloches
Value for Space Rating, see p. 154   * Variations due to different production systems

Part Two

VEGETABLES
Annual, Perennial, Herbs

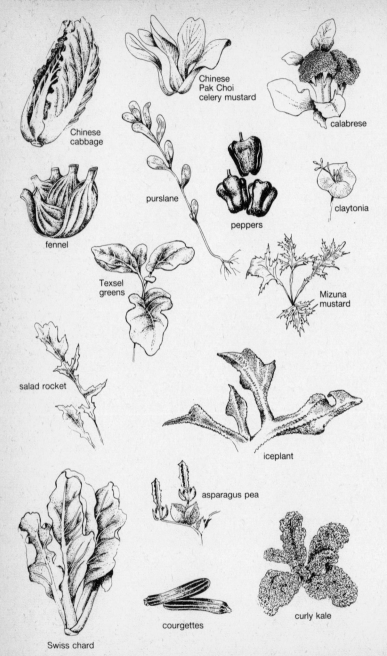

Chinese
cabbage

Chinese
Pak Choi
celery mustard

calabrese

purslane

peppers

claytonia

fennel

Texsel
greens

Mizuna
mustard

salad rocket

iceplant

asparagus pea

Swiss chard

courgettes

curly kale

Annual Vegetables

The second part of this book deals with the cultivation of individual vegetables. It is largely in note form, which I hope will make reference easy. For the benefit of those who are new to gardening, each vegetable is covered in detail, and sometimes alternative methods are suggested. Select whichever suits your needs best. Throughout, the aim is to grow vegetables for ordinary household consumption, not to produce perfect, enormous specimens for exhibition. That is another story altogether.

Most of the vegetables here are well known, but a number of less common ones are included, because they are particularly suitable for small gardens and easy to grow. Corn salad, land cress, Chinese Pak Choi, summer and winter purslane, salad rocket and the newly introduced Texsel greens are some of these. They are well worth trying.

Vegetables which occupy a good deal of space are only included where they have particular merit. For example, the tall Jerusalem artichokes can be effective screens or windbreaks, and will grow in rough pieces of ground. Purple sprouting broccoli takes up quite a lot of room but a few plants can produce an extraordinary number of 'helpings' at a time of year when vegetables are scarce and expensive.

All sowing dates, planting dates, and so on, in these notes should be treated as approximations. There is a world of difference, gardening wise, between Aberdeen and Cornwall (and between one year and the next), and it is impossible to be dogmatic. I have tried to indicate the variations as far as possible. Be guided by practice in your own locality.

Similarly planting distances, pot sizes and other measurements need not be followed slavishly. They are there as guidelines. Where the term manure is used, this includes compost and other substitutes for animal manure.

Choosing between the many cultivars of any vegetable is no easy task for the amateur. Those suggested here have been selected primarily because they are reliable, but also, bearing small gardens in mind, because they are fast maturing, dwarf in habit, and reputed to be of good flavour – always a controversial subject. As far as possible, they are cultivars I have grown successfully myself. But there are certainly others which are equally good, and new, improved cultivars are continually becoming available. Watch out for them in seed catalogues.

In the past the same cultivars were often sold under different names by different seedsmen. Naming is now being standardised, so there should be less confusion in future. Names in brackets in the text are old names still in common use, cultivars are abbreviated to cvs.

It is often difficult to buy seeds of the more unusual vegetables in shops or garden centres, but they can be obtained direct from the mail order seed firms listed in Appendix V. When buying seed, the smallest quantity sold is normally sufficient for small gardens.

Value for Space Rating (VSR)

The yields one can expect from any particular vegetable vary tremendously according to the district one is in, the season, the fertility of the soil and the cultivar – to name but a few of the variables. So instead of quoting yields which in practice are often meaningless, I have worked out a 'value for space rating' for each vegetable. This is an attempt to evaluate which vegetables will give the best returns in a small garden. In calculating the index the two principal factors considered were:

the length of time the vegetable is in the soil before it can be eaten or harvested; the number of helpings yielded per square metre (sq yd) under average conditions.

Quick growing, high yielding vegetables scored most points; slower growing, lower yielding vegetables fewer points and so on.

Additional points were also given for:

1 vegetables which are available fresh, in winter and times of scarcity
2 vegetables which are of far better quality when home grown
3 vegetables which are normally difficult or very expensive to buy.

Guide to the VSR

* worth growing in most cases provided they can be intercropped at some stage
** worth growing if you have space
*** very good value
**** best returns of all.

AMERICAN CRESS (see Land cress)

ARTICHOKE, JERUSALEM

Very hardy plant with nutritious sweet-flavoured non-starchy tubers.
Can grow 3m (10ft) tall.

Soil/Site
Open or shady site; tolerates most soils unless waterlogged or very
acid.
Useful for breaking in rough ground.
In small gardens use as screen, windbreak or in odd corners.

Cultivation
Plant tubers from February to April, 10–15cm (4–6in) deep, 30cm (12in)
apart (or wider spacing for heavier crops), rows 90cm (3ft) apart.
Egg-sized tubers best; cut very large tubers so each section has three
'eyes' or buds.
Earth up stems when 30cm (1ft) high.
Pinch out tops (flower buds) in mid-summer to keep height down to
1·5–2m (5–6ft).
In late summer advisable to stake plants or stake corners and run a
string around: yields lower if plants damaged by autumn gales.
Cut stems down to few cm (in) when leaves wither.
Leave tubers in soil during winter, lifting as required, or clamp them.
Remove *all* tubers eventually; any tiny tubers remaining will spread
uncontrollably leading to deterioration in quality.
Save some good tubers for replanting.

Harvesting
Tubers are ready when foliage is withered, from October to March.
Can be boiled, steamed, fried, baked, etc. Make excellent soup.
Very knobbly so scrub, then boil or steam in skins (20–25 minutes) and
peel just before serving.

Cultivars
Old named cvs such as Fuseau, Silver Skinned, Boston rarely
available. Dwarfer growing cvs may become available in future.

VSR*

ASPARAGUS PEA (*Fig. 38*)

Ornamental, somewhat bushy plant, with delicate foliage, pretty
scarlet-brown flowers, odd-shaped, triangular, winged, pods. Grows
up to 45cm (18in) tall with up to 60cm (2ft) spread.

Soil/Site
Open sunny site, rich light soil. Effective lining paths.

Cultivation
Sow outside *in situ* mid-April to mid-May.
Thin so that plants 30–38cm (12–15in) apart.
Or start indoors in boxes early April, transplanting outside when 2·5cm (1in) high.
Give some support with twigs; protect against pigeons.

Harvesting
Ready June to August.
Must pick pods when 2·5cm (2in) long or they become tough. Not a heavy bearer, but keep picking to encourage further growth. Boil pods in minimum water; serve with sauce or butter. Or eat cooked and cold in salads. Interesting unusual flavour.

VSR*

BEAN, BROAD

Very hardy bean; most types over 90cm (3ft) high, but for small gardens use 30–37cm (12–15in) high dwarf varieties, which require no support.

Soil/Site
Well-dug soil, preferably manured previous winter.

Cultivation
Sow: 1 Outdoors from late October to December in fairly sheltered position (in south only).
  2 Outdoors from February to April.
  3 In boxes under glass or in cold frame from December to January, planting out in March. Useful method for early crops in cold districts, or where overwintered beans attacked by soil pests.
Sow 5cm (2in) deep, 23–25cm (9–10in) apart, rows 37–45cm (15–18in) apart; or in blocks with plants 30cm (1ft) apart each way. Sow some 'spares' to fill gaps.
Can be protected with cloches from November until March.
Pull soil around stems of autumn sown beans for extra protection.
Pinch out tops when in full flower to help pods swell and prevent infestations of blackfly.
After picking put plants on compost heap; or cut off stems at ground level and dig in roots (nodules on roots return nitrogen to the soil).

Pests
Blackfly: young shoots often covered with masses of black aphids. Pinch out tops, or spray with liquid derris. Burn infested shoots.

Harvesting
Small immature pods can be eaten whole, boiled or sliced.
Young green tops also edible.
Beans are ready from early June to August, depending on sowing date.
Eat when *young and tender*. Pick frequently.
Mature beans can be dried for winter use.

Cultivars
The Sutton, Bonny Lad – dwarf.
Feligreen – semi-dwarf.
Aquadulce Claudia Express – recommended for autumn sowing.
Red Epicure – reddish beans, good flavour.

VSR** Spring sown.
        * Autumn sown.

BEAN, FRENCH (Kidney)

Tender annual. Many types of pod. Rounded pods tend to be stringless, flat pods more stringy; golden waxpods succulent and well flavoured. Most types dwarf, about 45cm (1½ft) high and 30cm (1ft) across; some forms climbing.
Excellent value in small gardens; decorative in flower borders.

Soil/Site
Open unshaded site, well dug, slightly acid, moisture retentive, well-manured soil.

Cultivation
Never sow or plant in cold, wet soil or beans will rot or succumb to pests and disease. Seed dressing useful for early sowings.
Minimum soil temperature of 10°C (50°F) needed for germination; warm soil beforehand with cloches if necessary.
Sow: 1 Mid-March//April under cloches for early crop in June. Give plenty of ventilation; remove cloches during day mid-May, completely end May.
        2 Outdoors May to July.
Sow 5–7·5cm (2–3in) deep; for highest yields space plants 15cm (6in) apart each way; thin when plant has 3 leaves.
To give early plantings a good start, put beans on moist newspaper until they swell, then sow in small pots or boxes of loose potting compost, hardening off well before planting out.

In small gardens two small sowings, three weeks apart, ensure a long season.

Mulch when well established; water heavily when flowering starts if ground is dry.

Can be propped up with brushwood and small sticks to prevent flopping over and getting muddy.

Prolong cropping of later sowings by covering with cloches in September.

Harvesting
Ready from 60 to 70 days after sowing.
Keep picking young beans to get heavy crops; otherwise beans go stringy and cease cropping.
Whole pods can be eaten when very small; whole beans when full-grown; half-ripe beans as flageolets; ripe beans dried. Some cultivars more suited to one purpose than others.

Cultivars
The Prince, Masterpiece, Stringless early, heavy croppers.
Phoenix Claudia – very early, stringless, good on sandy soil.
Tendergreen, Pros Gitana – early, tasty, good for freezing.
Loch Ness – for colder areas.
Kinghorn Wax, Wachs Goldperle – yellow waxpods.
Chevrier Vert, Dutch Brown – for drying.
Marcello, Rodolfo – excellent disease resistance.
Royal Burgundy – foliage, flowers and pods purple; very tasty.
Purple Podded (Blue Coco) – climbing French bean; very handsome purple pods and flowers; excellent flavour; treat like runner beans.
Blue Lake – outstanding climbing green bean.

VSR***

BEAN, RUNNER

Vigorous prolific bean, most types climbing – up to 3–3·5m (10–12ft); some dwarf types.
Used to be grown for ornamental flowers; useful for screening.
Beans long, flattish; more pronounced flavour than French beans.

Soil/Site
Likes well-cultivated, rich light soil, with plenty of organic matter; not too acid.
Sheltered position best, sun or partial shade.
Must be able to root deeply – needs at least 37cm (15in) topsoil.

39. METHODS OF SUPPORTING CLIMBING BEANS

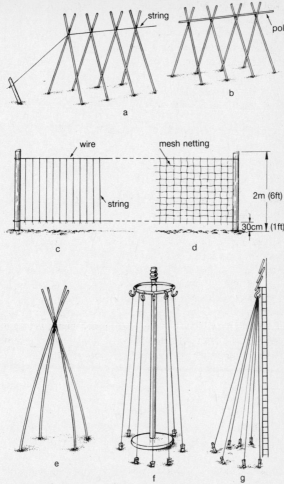

a. and b. Criss-crossed 2–2½m (6–8ft) canes or poles, secured with
string or horizontal canes or poles
c. and d. Strings 15cm (6in) apart, or mesh netting 10–12·5cm
(4–5in) square, attached to horizontal wires, secured to upright
poles
e. Tripods of 2–2½m (6–8ft) canes or poles
f. Making use of an old hat stand; the strings are anchored to
pegs in the ground
g. Method of growing beans against a house wall

Cultivation
Prepare ground previous autumn if possible. Dig trench one spit deep, 37–45cm (15–18in) wide; put in layer of strawy manure, compost, etc, before replacing topsoil.
Allow ground to settle thoroughly before sowing.
Work in general fertiliser few weeks before sowing.
Never sow in cold wet soil.
Sow: 1 For main crop outside end April (warm areas), mid-May (cold areas) until end May.
     2 For later crop cloched in late September, sow dwarf cultivar end June.
Sow seeds 5–7·5cm (2–3in) deep, 15cm (6in) apart; highest yields from two plants per sq ft (30cm sq).
Can be grown in double rows, 30–37cm (12–15in) apart; or 30cm (1ft) apart in wigwams; or on either side of garden path, etc.
Erect strong supports when sowing, eg well secured 2–2·5m (6–8ft) criss-crossed poles, bamboo canes, strings, or 10–12cm (4–5in) square netting (*Fig. 39*).
Will grow up trees, up a house, on a strong trellis or fence.
If growing near a wall, make sure roots in fertile soil with plenty of moisture.
If by hedge, slope canes towards hedge to minimise competition for moisture, etc.
Young growths may need twisting or tying around supports initially.
Water copiously in dry weather as roots should never be allowed to dry out; mulching with well-rotted manure or compost valuable.
Water well when flower buds first showing if weather dry.
Pinch out leading shoots when top of supports reached.
Flowers must be pollinated by bees (early crops sometimes fail to set if weather is cold and bees not flying); encourage bees by growing borage or helenium nearby; no convincing evidence that overhead spraying with water, as sometimes advised, helps pollination.
Note: to get earlier beans, nip out climbing tops when they start 'running away'. May need to repeat several times. Makes plants dwarf.

Pests
Slugs: sometimes attack young plants – take anti-slug measures.

Harvesting
Ready from July to October.
Keep picking young beans to ensure continuous production of best quality beans.

Cultivars
Achievement, Prizewinner, Streamline, Enorma – tall, heavy yielding.

Sunset, Painted Lady – tall, lovely pink, and pink-and-white flowers.
Kelvedon Marvel – good, prolific, early, medium height.
Mergoles, Red Knight – stringless.
Hammonds Dwarf Scarlet – dwarf, about 40cm (16in) high, good for
small gardens; can be grown under cloches.

VSR***

BEAN SPROUTS (*Figs 37 & 43*)

Germinating seedlings of Mung beans; widely used in Chinese
cookery.
Very nutritious and tasty, rich in protein and Vitamin C.

Cultivation
Can grow indoors throughout the year; but most useful in winter.
Only sprout a few at a time, 56g (2oz) is enough for three to four
people.
For quick crops of short sprouts, up to 2·5cm (1in) long, grow in a jar
or lidded dish such as an ice-cream box.
For longer sprouts, up to 5cm (2in) long, line the dish with a base such
as cotton wool, flannel, or tissues into which seeds will root. Seeds
sprout best at temperatures of 13–24°C (55–75°F).
Wash beans carefully, soak overnight in cold water until they swell.
Growing on a base: strain seed after soaking so just moist, cover base
with seed, put on lid, or slip into plastic bag to retain moisture. Put
somewhere dark, or cover container with tinfoil to exclude light. Rinse
seeds twice a day by pouring fresh water in and out again.
Without a base: as above but put seeds in container in layers up to
0·5cm ($\frac{1}{4}$in) deep. As seeds won't root, rinse by turning them into a
strainer, run water through, drain and return to container.

Harvesting
Ready within 3 to 9 days, depending on temperature.
Eat sprouts when 3·5–5cm (1$\frac{1}{2}$–2in) long (flavour and nutritious value
lost when any larger).
Cut off close to flannel or turn out of container.
Green seed coats will float to surface if sprouts are soaked in water.
Use raw in salads, in Chinese recipes, stir-fried for a minute, or boiled
for no more than 2 minutes.
Cut sprouts will keep for 2 days in cold water.

VSR****

BEETROOT

Round, obelisk or cylindrically-shaped roots; red, white or yellow in colour.
Leaves normally reddish, quite pretty in flower bed.

Soil/Site
Open, shade-free site.
Prefers light, sandy soil, though grows in any well-worked soil; lime soil if acid.

Cultivation
On poor soil apply tomato fertiliser (high in potash) 10 days before sowing.
Small beet ready 11 to 13 weeks after sowing; useful catch crop.
Good for intercropping.
Beet 'seeds' are a cluster of seed, so several seedlings liable to germinate close together; pelleted and 'monogerm' seed are single, therefore require less thinning; worth getting if available.
Only very young beetroot seedlings can be transplanted.
Early beetroot liable to 'bolt', ie run to seed, if sown early in cold conditions; use bolt-resistant cultivars.
Make several sowings for continuous supply, eg
Sow: 1 Bolt-resistant round cultivar late February/early March in cloches or frames, for small beet ready end May/early June. Remove glass April. Space seed 2·5cm (1in) apart, rows 20cm (8in) apart; or sow in patches, spacing seeds 5cm (2in) apart either way, or in 18–23cm (7–9in) wide flat drills as for peas (see *Fig. 9a*). Yields from early sowings can be doubled by sowing under perforated film, removing film after 4 to 5 weeks (see p. 114). Early sowings require little thinning. Pull roots very young.
   2 Bolt-resistant round cultivar outside late March/early April for small beet early summer, spacing as above, thin to 7·5–10cm (3–4in) apart.
     Optimum spacing for pickling beet 20 plants per sq ft (30cm sq).
   3 Round or long cultivars, May or June outside, for main summer supply and winter storage.
     'Station sow' 7·5cm (3in) apart, rows 20cm (8in) apart.
     Lift remaining beet August or it becomes tough.
     Twist off stems, gently rub off adhering soil, store in dry shed in ashes, peat, sand or lightly covered with soil – or outside in clamps.

4 Round cultivars, outside late June/July, to leave in soil for pulling during winter in mild areas. Thin to 7·5–10cm (3–4in) apart; protect with thick layer of bracken or straw.

Note: beet can be multi-seeded in soil blocks. Sow 3 seeds per block, planting 'as one' 20–23cm (8–9in) apart each way (see p. 76).

Pests
Sparrows: deadly to small seedlings; put up pea guards after sowing, or protect with black cotton.

Harvesting
Main crop July to September and then stored.
For salad from May to October.
Roots sometimes eaten raw; cooked roots eaten hot or cold.
Young leaves edible – cook like spinach.
Small beet can be pickled.

Cultivars
Detroit Regala, Boltardy, Avonearly – bolt-resistant, round type.
Crimson Globe, Detroit Improved, Little Ball – round, maincrop.
Cylindra, Cheltenham Green Top – long.
Burpee's Golden – yellow, doesn't bleed, edible foliage.
Albina – white.
Monodet, Cheltenham Mono – monogerm.

VSR**

For Leaf beet, Spinach beet, see Spinach

BROCCOLI, PURPLE SPROUTING

Fairly hardy brassica, up to 90cm (3ft) high, metre (yard) spread in rich soil; flowering sideshoots eaten in spring.

Cultivation
Sow early April to mid-May thinly in seed bed; thin to 7·5cm (3in).
Plant out firmly June to mid-July, 60cm (2ft) apart each way (planting details: see Brussels sprouts).
In exposed areas earth up stems and stake.

Soil/Site
See cabbage; manure soil previous autumn or spring.

Pests/Diseases
See cabbage.

Harvesting
Season from mid-February to May. Pick shoots when 10cm (4in) long; will re-sprout over 2 months if picked every few days; never strip one plant; freezes well.

Cultivars
Purple forms hardiest, high yielding. White forms less prolific, excellent flavour.
Early Purple – ready from January to February.
Late Purple – ready from March to May.

VSR*

BRUSSELS SPROUTS

Very hardy winter brassica, 45–105cm ($1\frac{1}{2}$–$3\frac{1}{2}$ft) high.

Soil/Site
See cabbage; manure soil previous autumn or early spring.

Cultivation
Firm ground and long growing season keys to success.
Sow: 1 Under cloches or frames February/early March; thin to 7·5cm (3in) apart; plant out April/early May; excellent method.
2 In seed bed in open March/early April; thin to 7·5cm (3in) apart; plant out May/June.
3 If space available sow 2 or 3 seeds or pellets *in situ* March/April; remove superfluous seedlings.
Sow early maturing cvs first, followed by later maturing cvs.
Planting: see cabbage (general cultivation); can be planted straight into ground vacated by peas, beans, etc, without digging over first.
Plant dwarf types 60–75cm (2–$2\frac{1}{2}$ft) apart, tall types 90cm (3ft) apart.
Plant between other crops, provided plenty of light.
Draw soil around stems month after planting.
Keep weed-free.
Stake tall sprouts (and dwarfs in exposed areas) during summer to prevent 'rocking'; two ties often necessary (*Fig. 40*).
If not growing well in mid-July top dress with general fertiliser.
Remove yellowing leaves to improve air circulation and prevent sprouts rotting.
Old practice of removing top sprout in late summer leads to earlier maturity but lower yields.

Pests/Diseases
See cabbage.

40. STAKING A
BRUSSELS SPROUT
PLANT FIRMLY
TO PREVENT
ROCKING IN
WINTER

Harvesting
Ready late September to March/April; most crop for 2 to 3 months.
Pick lowest sprouts first; eat sprout tops, which are delicious, last;
some weigh up to nearly 2kg (4lb)! Pull out stumps when finished.

Cultivars
Dwarf strains convenient for small gardens and exposed sites; tend to
be earlier; tall strains give heavier yields per square metre (yard).
F_1 Early Half Tall, F_1 Peer Gynt – semi-dwarf, early.
Bedford Masters Special, F_1 Mallard, F_1 Perfect Line – mid-season.
F_1 Achilles, F_1 Rampart – very hardy, late.
Red Rubine – red sprouts, excellent flavour, decorative.
Noisette – small sprouts, good nutty flavour, French.

VSR*

CABBAGE

Different types can be grown to produce cabbage all year round;
solid-headed types commonest; loose-headed used as 'spring greens'.

Soil/Site
Open, unshaded site; rich, moisture-retentive soil, well worked but
firm, limed if at all acid. Best manured for previous crop. Avoid
planting in ground vacated by crop from same family.

General cultivation (*all types*)
Sow in seed bed; thin or prick out seedlings to 7·5cm (3in) apart.
Transplant to permanent positions when 3 or 4 leaves formed.
Alternatively sow in soil blocks and plant out.

Spring cabbage can be sown *in situ*.

Plant only sturdy, straight-stemmed plants.

Tread ground if at all loose; plant firmly, with lowest leaves just above ground level.

Hoe or mulch to keep weed-free; remove dead, rotten leaves.

With spring and summer cabbage, after cutting heads, cut 0·5cm ($\frac{1}{4}$in) deep cross in stalk left in ground; several small cabbages should sprout from cut (*Fig. 41*), if ground moist and fertile.

Top dressing of fertiliser when re-sprouted growths 2·5cm (1in) high stimulates growth.

Spring cabbage (for use April onwards)

Sow end July in north, first two weeks August in south.

Plant mid-September to mid-October.

(For succession sow in cold frame or cloches in September, planting out in spring.)

Plant in shallow drills, 30cm (12in) apart each way.

Or space plants 10cm (4in) apart, rows 30cm (12in) apart. Leave one plant in three to heart up; use others young as spring greens.

Pull soil around stems few weeks after planting to give extra protection. In very cold areas protect with cloches until March/April.

When growth starts in spring hoe round plants, give general fertiliser.

Cultivars

First Early Market 218, Pixie, F_1 Prospera, F_1 Spring Hero – autumn sowing; April, Greyhound, Harbinger, F_1 Hispi – for spring sowing.

Summer cabbage (for use July to late autumn)

Sow: 1 February/March in cold frame, plant out late April/May.

2 March to May in open, plant out May/June/July.

3 For quick returns in small area, in spring or summer, sow few seeds, 10cm (4in) apart each way, in block. Use *spring* cultivar. Thin to one seedling at each 'station'. Within 8 weeks leaves are 10–12·5cm (4–5in) high. Chop off leaves at stem level to use as 'greens'. Either (a) leave all stalks to re-sprout, or (b) leave a few to make solid hearts, or (c) pull up all stalks and use ground for another crop.

Plant summer cabbage 35–45cm (14–18in) apart. (Wider spacing gives larger heads.)

Cultivars

F_1 Hispi, Golden Acre, Progress, F_1 Quickstep, Greyhound – earliest.

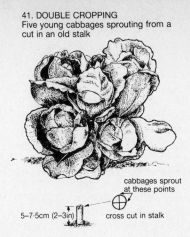

41. DOUBLE CROPPING
Five young cabbages sprouting from a
cut in an old stalk

cabbages sprout
at these points

5–7·5cm (2–3in)   cross cut in stalk

F_1 Summer Monarch, Wiam, Derby Day, Marner Allfruh, F_1 Minicole
– for succession.
Babyhead, F_1 Stonehead, F_1 Minicole – compact for intercropping.

Winter cabbage (for use late autumn to March/April)

Sow April/May.
Plant in very firm ground by mid-July/early August, 37·5–45cm (15–
18in) apart, according to cultivar.
Earth up stems, remove any rotting leaves.

Cultivars
F_1 Autumn Monarch, F_1 Winter Monarch, Christmas Drumhead – for
early winter.
Rearguard, January King, F_1 Ice Queen savoy – for late winter (savoys
have pale-green crinkly leaves, mild flavour; very hardy, succeed on
poorer soils than other cabbages).
F_1 Celtic Cross – new late winter cultivar.
Dutch Winter White – lift before heavy frosts in November. Store
hanging in frost-free shed or cellar, or on slats in frame, covered with
straw. Use for coleslaw.

Red cabbage

Sow March, plant 30cm (1ft) apart; or sow August for very early crop,
planting following March.
Use fresh, or lift and store for winter as Dutch Winter White.

Excellent cooked in minimum water with chopped onion and apple.

Cultivars
Red Drumhead, Niggerhead, Norma, F_1 Ruby Ball.

Ornamental cabbage

Beautiful variegated foliage during winter.
Plant in flower border.
Edible.

Pests/Diseases (Applicable to most brassicas).
Flea beetle: eats holes in very young seedlings. Dust with derris or pyrethrum. In dry weather spraying with water in evening helpful.
Greenfly: blue-green mealy aphids. Feed on under-side of leaves, inside sprouts. Leaves develop bleached areas and become crumpled. Worst damage August to October in dry seasons. Can kill plants. Keep an eye on plants. Catch aphids young by spraying with derris and pyrethrum, nicotine or rhubarb spray, or transfer ladybirds to plants. Aphids overwinter on brassicas. Pull out and burn old stumps by mid-May.
Caterpillars: watch for first attacks in June; most severe attacks in August and September. Pick off caterpillars by hand, or spray with derris and/or pyrethrum, or use thuricide.
Cabbage root fly: main attacks on young plants of cabbages and cauliflower shortly after planting. Small white maggots eat roots and penetrate stem. Plants wilt and die. Dig up and burn infected roots (see *Fig. 18c*). Preventive measures, see p. 90.
Clubroot (finger and toe) (*Fig. 18a*): Very serious disease in some soils. Roots develop swellings, and look like dahlia tubers. Lift diseased roots very carefully and burn. (*Never* compost them.) Difficult to eradicate because spores survive up to 20 years in soil. Liming, drainage, and possibly keeping soil heavily mulched help control disease. In infected gardens raise brassicas in 15cm (6in) pots and transplant; or dip transplants into calomel paste. To make: dissolve a little cellulose wallpaper paste in 500ml (1pt) hot water, stir thoroughly, add 50cm (2oz) pure calomel. Swirl roots in mixture before planting.
Birds: can devastate greens. Kale relatively immune. Protect young seedlings with black cotton; older plants with bird scarers. Netting, cages and 'humming wire' best answer, but expensive (*Fig. 19*).

VSR*

CALABRESE 169

CALABRESE (Italian broccoli, Green sprouting broccoli) (*Fig. 38*)

Forms green cauliflower head first and, after cutting, broccoli-like side-shoots. Not very hardy, but very useful brassica for small gardens because normally matures in about four months, and can be closely spaced. Delicious, undervalued vegetable.

Soil/Site
See cabbage, but tolerates poorer soil.

Cultivation
Dislikes transplanting. Where possible sow *in situ* (3 seeds per station thinning to one after germination), or sow in soil blocks and plant out. Space plants 25–30cm (10–12in) apart.
Sow: 1 From end March/early April until early July for succession.
     2 Late August/early September, planting in cold greenhouse for very early crop. Use an early cv. Plants may be killed in severe winter, but worth a gamble.
Calabrese must grow steadily: water well in dry weather.
Can give light top dressing of fertiliser July or August after cutting central head to stimulate growth.

Pests/Diseases
See cabbage.

Harvesting
Main season end June until frost, depending on cultivar.
Pick main head first just before flower buds open, then sideshoots develop.
Pick constantly to encourage more shoots to develop.
If attacked by caterpillars, soak in salted water before cooking.
Boil or steam heads until just tender.
Thick shoots can be peeled, then boiled or steamed.
Freezes well.

Cultivars
Dandy Early, F_1 Green Comet, F_1 Mercedes – early.
Premium Crop, F_1 Corvet – later.
Romanesco – delicious lime-green heads, best sown in May.

VSR**

CAPSICUM, see Peppers

CARROTS

Types
Short – used for continuous supply of small young carrots; mature in 10 to 12 weeks. (Mainly Amsterdam and Nantes types.)
Intermediate – larger, longer carrots for storing or lifting during winter; mature in 20 to 24 weeks (Chanteney, Autumn King and Berlicum types).

Soil
Prefer light, rich, stone-free soil; sandy loam ideal. Never sow on freshly-manured land or roots split.

Cultivation
Short types
Sow: 1 In frames or under cloches, February to March, for early crop in mid-May. Put glass in position beforehand to warm soil. Sow very thinly, either broadcast or in drills 2·5–5cm (1–2in) apart. Ideally space seeds 1cm ($\frac{1}{2}$in) apart, thinning to 5cm (2in) apart. Water in dry weather. Remove cloches April/May.

2 To advance crop by 10 days, sow outdoors January/early February light soils, end February/March heavy soils, covering with perforated film (see p. 114). Remove film after 10 weeks or when plants have 7 or 8 leaves. Use F_1 hybrids of Nantes type.

3 In open, March to July for summer supply. Drills 15cm (6in) apart. Thin in stages to 3·5–5cm ($1\frac{1}{2}$–2in) apart. Can also mix seed with annual flower seed and broadcast in flower beds.

4 In open, August (north), September (south), for young carrots November/December. Cover with cloches September or October. Drills 15cm (6in) apart.

Intermediate type
Sow late April to early June, drills 15cm (6in) apart.
Thin in stages to 4cm ($1\frac{1}{2}$in) for medium-size carrots, 5cm (2in) for larger carrots. Eat thinnings.
Can also be sown in 15cm (6in) wide bands; thin to approximately 30 per 30cm sq (1sq ft) if smallish carrots required, 10 per 30cm sq (1sq ft) for large carrots.
Keep weed-free by hoeing or mulching.
Water carrots in dry weather or they are liable to split.

Pests
Carrot fly (*Fig. 18b*): often serious. Foliage reddens, roots tunnelled by tiny maggots, plants die. Several generations may hatch annually. Egg-

laying female attracted by carrot foliage smell, especially during thinning. No completely safe control at present, but try using physical barrier (see p. 90) or grow carrots raised off ground, eg in deep boxes filled with soil, as carrot fly tends to fly low. Early sowings and cloche-covered sowings usually escape attack.

Always sow thinly to minimise need for thinning.

Thin on still dull evenings, drawing a little soil around stems, watering and firming after thinning. Bury thinnings in compost heap.

Harvesting
Short carrots. Pull as required from mid-May onwards; if ground dry water beforehand.
Intermediate. August to October use fresh. If undamaged by carrot fly can be left in ground all winter, especially in light soil, protected by 20cm (8in) layer of straw or bracken, covered with polythene. Best method for flavour. Alternatively lift in October, trim foliage 1cm (½in) above crown, store (undamaged carrots only) in sand or ashes in shed. Inspect during winter and remove any rotting carrots.

Cultivars
Short – Amsterdam Forcing, Redca, Nantes Tip Top, F_1 Nandor – Nantes types.
Intermediate – Autumn King, Vita Longa, Chantenay Red Cored, Berlicum Berjo, St Valery.

VSR**** Short carrots.
       *** Intermediate.

CAULIFLOWER, MINI

Normal cauliflower occupies too much space, for too long, to be justified in small gardens. NVRS technique for growing 'mini-cauliflower' with 4–9cm (1½–3½in) diameter curds, recommended instead. Depends on using early summer cvs, sown in situ at close spacing.

Soil/Site
Reasonably fertile, slightly acid soil (pH6); lime if very acid. Avoid freshly-manured soil; excessive nitrogen makes growth too leafy. Beds of 90–120 cm (3–4ft) width ideal for mini-cauliflowers.

Cultivation
Can fork in general fertiliser (N:P:K:7:7:7) before sowing. Rake soil. Grow plants 15 × 15cm (6 × 6in) or 18 × 13cm (7 × 5in) apart.

Make drills accordingly; water drills if weather dry to ensure rapid, even germination.

Sow 2 seeds per station, thinning to one after germination.

Keep weed free in early stages; water only if soil becoming dry.

Curds tend to mature together, so make several small sowings from late March to early July for supplies from late June to late October.

Harvesting

Curds grow rapidly; cut when no larger than 9cm (3½in) diameter.

Cut with 2 or 3 leaves beneath curd.

Cook curds whole – ideal size for single portions or freezing.

Cultivars

Snowball, F_1 Snow Crown, Dominant, Garant.

VSR*

CELERIAC (Turnip-rooted celery) (*Fig. 48*)

Bushy plant, 45cm (1½ft) high, 30cm (1ft) across, celery-like leaves, swollen base of stem edible; good substitute for celery; hardier, less prone to disease.

Soil/Site

Open site. Fertile soil, rich in organic matter.

Cultivation

Likes long growing season and plenty of moisture all the time.

Sow February/early March in heated propagator; late March on indoor windowsill; early April in cold greenhouse or under cloches.

Sow indoors; transplant 6cm (2½in) apart into boxes, preferably 7·5cm (3in) deep, when large enough to handle. Or sow in soil blocks.

Don't start hardening off outside until weather warm. Plant end May/early June. Plant 30–7cm (12–15in) apart, base of stem at ground level.

Water thoroughly in dry weather, keep plants mulched.

Weekly liquid manure from early June onwards very beneficial.

Remove lower ageing leaves as season progresses to expose 'bulb'.

Can leave in soil in winter if well protected with bracken, straw, etc.

Lift remaining plants in spring and heel in if ground required.

In very cold districts lift at the end of October and store in damp sand for winter.

Harvesting

Ready from late September until May.

Swollen stem can be grated raw in salads, puréed, boiled, used in soups, served with cheese sauce, etc; use fresh leaves sparingly in salads; dry leaves for celery flavour.

Rough outer skin harbours dirt and is a chore to clean.

Cultivars
Balder, Tellus, Marble Ball.

VSR*

CELERY

Types
Tall – requires trenching and earthing up to blanch stems; fairly hardy, unsuitable for small gardens.

Self-blanching – medium height, 30–45cm (1–1½ft) tall; requires less blanching, not hardy. American Green cvs are eaten green.

Leaf or cutting celery – finer-stemmed, smaller, leafy plants used mainly for flavouring. Very hardy; invaluable in colder months.

Soil/Site
Open site, very rich soil, plenty of organic matter.

Cultivation
Sow as for celeriac, sowing on the surface as seed needs light to germinate, or buy plants late May/early June.

Do not sow too early; if temperature falls below 10°C (50°F) for more than 12 hours, plants liable to 'bolt', ie run to seed.

Don't put outside to start hardening off until weather is warm.

Plant end May/June in block formation at equidistant spacing to get a blanched effect. Space plants 15cm (6in) to 28cm (11in) apart. The wider the spacing the heavier the plants and thicker the stems.

Do not plant too deeply.

Take precautions against slugs.

Tuck straw around plants in mid-July to increase blanching.

Water generously or plants liable to bolt or become stringy.

Feed weekly with liquid manure from June onwards.

Leaf celery

Sow late spring to summer in seed boxes, planting outside (or under cover in autumn) 13cm (5in) apart. Can also sow 8 seeds in one soil block, planting as 'clump' 20cm (8in) apart.

Can cut frequently, starting about 4 weeks after planting.

If left to run to seed in second season, plants often 'sow themselves'.

Harvesting
Self-blanching ready late July; American Green early autumn until frost.
Discard outer leaves. Eat raw, braised, in soups, in cheese dishes, etc. Dry leaves for flavouring.

Pests
Celery fly: leaves blistered and tunnelled; can be very serious. Pick off and burn infected leaves. Dusting leaves regularly with old soot may help prevent attacks; spray with derris or pyrethrum. Burn infected leaves.
Celery leaf spot: serious seed-borne disease; buy treated seed.

Cultivars
Golden Self-blanching, Avonpearl, Lathom; Self-blanching, Jason – yellow stemmed cvs.
American Green, Celebrity, Greensnap, Tendercrisp – American Green type.

VSR*** Leaf celery.
     ** Self-blanching celery.

THE CHICORIES

Of the many chicory types, red, Sugar Loaf, and Witloof are the most suitable for small gardens. Main season autumn to following early summer. Characteristic slightly bitter flavour accounts for lack of popularity. By shredding leaves, using seedlings, and blanching techniques they become very palatable. Used mainly in salads.
All chicories can be grown in wide range of soils and situations.

VSR ** Red.
    *** Sugar Loaf head; **** Sugar Loaf seedlings.
      * Witloof.

Red chicory

In summer green, loose-leaved plants; with cold weather foliage becomes deep red or variegated, many cvs, forming dense compact hearts.

Cultivation
1 Broadcast *in situ* outdoors May to early July in weed-free soil. If plants overcrowded in late summer thin to 10–13cm (4–5in) apart.

2 Sow in seed bed or seed boxes May to early July. Plant small plants outside 15cm (6in) apart.

3 Sow in seed bed, seed boxes or soil blocks in July for planting under cover September, 15cm (6in) apart for main winter supply.

Season of outdoor crop can be extended by covering in autumn with cloches, low tunnels or straw – though straw may attract mice and rats. Red Verona cultivars can be lifted in November and forced in the dark like Witloof (q.v.) to get beautiful white and pale-pink leaves.

Harvesting
Main season for outdoor crop late summer/early winter, though may survive into spring. Plants under cover used winter to spring. Tend to be larger and better quality.
Cut whole heads or pick individual leaves. Leave stumps to re-sprout.

Cultivars
Red Verona, Red Verona Scarla – red.
Sottomarina, Castelfranco, Variegated Chioggia – variegated.

Sugar Loaf chicory (*Fig. 43*)

Green chicory, grown either for the large, dense, conical heads with crisp, yellow inner leaves, or for use as a seedling crop. Mainly used in salads.
Reasonably hardy, extremely productive, as at all stages will respond to cut-and-come-again treatment. Headed Sugar Loaf mainly late summer/autumn crop; seedling crop available almost all year round.

Cultivation
Headed crop
1 Sow June/July either *in situ* or in soil blocks, thinning or planting 15–20cm (6–8in) apart each way. Heads normally form autumn. Protection with cloches or low tunnels extends season, but plants may rot in wet winter. Can pull up heads late autumn and store for several weeks in frost-free cellar or shed.

2 Sow end July/August, plant under cover for winter crop. May not form large heads, but leaf can be cut over a long period.

Seedling crop
1 Sow outdoors early spring to mid-summer, either broadcast or in drills 8–10cm (3–4in) apart. Start cutting leaves just above ground level when 5–8cm (2–3in) high, and very tasty and nutritious. Will re-sprout rapidly. After several months can thin plants to 15cm (6in) apart, so remainder will form heads.

2 As above under cover, in January/February for very early crop, or

September to crop in late autumn and again in early spring when growth very fast.

Cultivars
Pain de Sucre, Crystal Head, Gradina – form large heads.
Bianca di Milano, Bionda di Triestino – smaller heads.
All cultivars can also be used for seedling crops.

Witloof chicory (Belgian chicory) (*Fig. 43*)

Parsnip-like roots forced to produce white 'chicons' during winter.

Soil/Site
Open site, average soil, ideally manured previous year (fresh manure leads to fanged roots).

Cultivation
Sow thinly, *in situ* May/June.
Thin when 5cm (2in) high to 23cm (9in) apart. Do not transplant.
Keep weed-free: can be mulched in July.

Forcing Methods (*Fig. 42*)
Can be forced indoors or outside; all light must be excluded.
Roots can be forced twice in succession, though second crop smaller.
Indoor forcing: lift roots in November. Reject very thin or fanged roots; ideal size 2·5–3·5cm (1–1½in) diameter at the top.
Cut off leaves 2·5cm (1in) above root; trim root ends so total length 17 or 20cm (7 or 8in).
Store horizontally in boxes of moist peat or sand in dry shed, or in shallow trenches in open, until required for forcing.
Force a few at a time.
Plant 3 roots close together in 20 or 23cm (8 or 9in) flower pot in any fairly moist soil, cover with inverted pot of similar size, block or cover drainage holes with tinfoil to exclude light.
Put in cupboard or room; temperature needs to be no higher than 13°C (55°F).
Chicons ready within 3 or 4 weeks.
Outside forcing (results in better flavoured chicons): cut down leaves in late autumn.
Cover roots with earth clamp to depth of 17 or 20cm (7 or 8in).
Make sides and tops of clamp firm (forcing can be hastened by covering clamp with cloches).
Chicons ready when showing through, between January and March depending on the weather.

Harvesting
Keep chicons covered until just before use; become bitter rapidly on exposure to light.
Average season for forcing types December to April.
Use raw in salads, braised, in cheese, ham or egg dishes.

Cultivars
Witloof (Brussels Chicory), Normato, F$_1$ Zoom.

VSR*

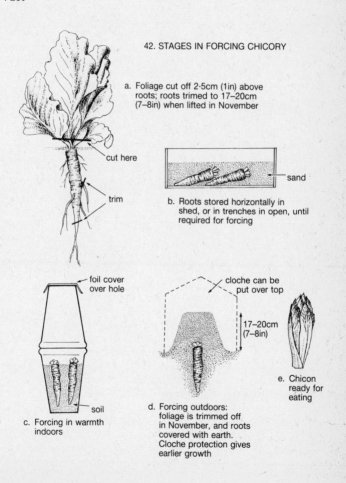

42. STAGES IN FORCING CHICORY

a. Foliage cut off 2·5cm (1in) above roots; roots trimmed to 17–20cm (7–8in) when lifted in November

cut here

trim

sand

b. Roots stored horizontally in shed, or in trenches in open, until required for forcing

foil cover over hole

cloche can be put over top

17–20cm (7–8in)

e. Chicon ready for eating

soil

c. Forcing in warmth indoors

d. Forcing outdoors: foliage is trimmed off in November, and roots covered with earth. Cloche protection gives earlier growth

CHINESE CABBAGE (Chinese leaves) (*Fig. 38*)

Looks like giant cos lettuce; about 37–45cm (15–18in) high; very fast growing; most types form hearts; distinct 'Chinese' flavour; not hardy but withstands some frost under cover, especially as cut-and-come-again crop.

Soil/Site
Fairly open site, though tolerates light shade; do not cramp it.
Very rich, moisture-retentive soil, with plenty of organic matter.

Cultivation
Useful crop to follow peas, early potatoes, broad beans.
Not always easy to grow: if sown too early in the year, subjected to low temperatures, very dry conditions, or transplanted, liable to bolt.
Sow in succession end May to early August *in situ* outdoors, thinning to 30cm (12in) apart each way, or sow in soil blocks and plant out.
Make late sowing late August/September in soil blocks, to plant under cover October. These plants may not form large hearts, but in most years produce very useful tender leaf during winter and spring.
Water drills thoroughly before sowing if weather dry.
Dust seedlings with derris or pyrethrum against flea beetle if small holes appear in leaves. Protect against slugs, particularly in autumn.
Very thirsty plant. Keep well watered and mulched.

Harvesting
Ready to cut 9 to 10 weeks after sowing. Main season September to November.
Cut heads just above ground level, leaving stumps to re-sprout.
Can store heads in frost-free cellar, shed or fridge for several weeks.
Never cook like English cabbage. Excellent raw in salad, or 'stir-fried' in a little oil.

Cultivars
Nagaoka F_1, Tip Top F_1 (most bolt resistant).

VSR**

CHINESE MUSTARD (Pak Choi) (*Fig. 38*)

Many Chinese brassicas, known under umbrella term of 'Pak Choi', are now becoming known in the UK. Those included here are very fast growing, compact, productive, hardy, their main season from late summer to spring, so exceptionally useful for small gardens, grown outdoors or planted under cover in autumn for good quality winter 'greens'. All respond well to cut-and-come-again treatment. Two main types:

Celery mustards

Generally neat, rosette plants up to 25cm (10in) spread. Smooth, rounded leaves, often with prominent white midribs and celery-like leaf stalks. Mild flavour. Excellent raw, or cooked like Chinese cabbage. The flowering shoots are also tender and edible.

Leafy mustards

Larger, somewhat coarser plants, some smooth-leaved, some with finely divided leaves, often extremely hardy. Stronger flavoured than celery mustards (can become very hot just before flowering).
Young leaves edible raw; cook mature leaves like spinach.
Cultivar Mizuna very pretty frilly leaves; can grow in flower bed; useful for intercropping and undercropping (*Fig. 38*).

Soil/Site
Open or lightly shaded site. Fertile soil with plenty of organic matter worked in so it is both moisture retentive and well drained. Chinese vegetables best grown fast under good soil conditions.

Cultivation
Chinese mustard tends to bolt if sown too early. Main sowings:
1 Late June to August for outdoor crop. (Mizuna can be sown in May.)
2 September, planting under cover October for winter and spring. Either sow *in situ* thinning to required spacing, or sow in soil blocks and plant out.
Space celery mustards about 23cm (9in) apart each way; leafy mustards 30cm (12in) apart. Keep well watered.
Cover outdoor plants with cloches or low tunnels in autumn to extend season and improve plant quality.
Pick individual leaves, or cut whole plant inch above ground level, leaving stumps to re-sprout.

Pests/Diseases
See cabbages, though mustards fairly resistant to pests and diseases. Slugs and cabbage root fly can be a problem.

Cultivars
Chinese Pak Choi, Shanghai Pak Choi, Japanese White – celery mustards. Mizuna, Tendergreen, Green in the Snow – leafy mustards.

VSR*** Celery mustards. **** Mizuna leafy mustard.
     ** Other leafy mustards.

CHOP SUEY GREENS (Shungiku)

Form of annual chrysanthemum; 15cm (6in) high as vegetable, 60cm
(2ft) high when grown for flowers.
Decorative, pleasantly aromatic foliage.
Good as edging, or as patch in flower beds.

Soil/Site
Ordinary fairly moist soil; does well on acid soils. Can be grown in
window boxes.

Cultivation
Likes moist cool weather; grows best in spring and autumn.
Summer sowings require light shade or liable to bolt and coarsen.
Fast growing; useful for catch cropping and intercropping.
Sow little and often, fairly thinly, from mid-February (in mild districts)
until September; rows 15cm (6in) apart.
Thin to 7·5–10cm (3–4in) apart; sometimes left unthinned.
Early sowings can be made under cloches or frames in February.
Keep cutting back to a few inches above ground level to encourage
more growth.
Nip off flower buds as they form.

Harvesting
Ready 6 to 7 weeks after sowing.
With successive sowings can be picked from April to November.
Gather leaves when 10–12cm (4–5in) high; eat immediately.
Rich in vitamin C; fairly strong flavour.
Use for enhancing recipes, raw in salads, or cook like spinach in
minimum water, serving with butter or margarine; or cook in Chinese
stir/fry method.

VSR***

CLAYTONIA (Winter purslane, Miner's lettuce, Montia) (*Fig. 38*)

Pretty, dainty little plant. Rarely grows more than 15cm (6in) spread,
and up to 20cm (8in) high when flowering.
Early triangular leaves on short stalks superseded by larger, semi-

circular leaves 'wrapped' around flowering stalks. Leaves, stems and flowers all edible. Mild flavour, succulent texture; use in salads. Can be available all year round, but most useful autumn, spring and early summer. Grows astonishingly fast early in the year.

Soil/Site
Not fussy, but does best on light sandy soil. Tolerates light shade. Be warned: it seeds itself and can become invasive.

Cultivation
Sow: 1 March to May for summer use.
     2 July to mid-August for autumn (plant later sowings under cover).
     3 End August/early September. Plant under cover for spring crop.
Either sow *in situ* thinning to required spacing, or in seed trays or seed blocks for planting out. Seeds are tiny.
Space plants 10–13cm (4–5in) apart each way.
Can also be broadcast in patches for seedling cut-and-come-again crop. Start cutting as soon as leaves large enough to handle.
Reasonably hardy, surviving most winters outdoors if soil well drained, but looks poorly and 'blue' in cold weather. For valuable spring crop have some plants under cover: they will be more luxuriant and ready well ahead of outdoor plants.
Once claytonia is established, seedlings appear all over the garden in autumn and spring. Transplant them carefully to where you want them.

VSR****

CORN SALAD (Lamb's lettuce) (*Fig. 43*)

Low-growing, small-leaved hardy annual.
Very useful salad crop, especially in winter, requiring little space.

Soil/Site
Likes full sun, but grows well in dry or moist situation.
Tolerates ordinary soil; does best in well-dug rich soil.

Cultivation
Sow: 1 In March and April for summer use.
     2 June/July for autumn use.
     3 August and September for winter and spring use outdoors, when most valuable (end of August sowing ready from mid-November until March).

    4 October under cloches, in frame or cold greenhouse border for
       winter use to follow on from crop above.

Sow *in situ* outdoors, or in seed boxes and transplant.

Summer sowings slow to germinate in dry conditions. Water drills well
beforehand, or cover with plastic film until germination.

Space plants 10cm (4in) apart each way.

Can also be broadcast in patches for seedling cut-and-come-again
crop.

Corn salad useful for intercropping and undercropping.

Although very hardy, winter crop better quality if protected with
cloches, etc, or even bracken.

A patch may regenerate itself if a few plants are left to run to seed.

Harvesting
Mature plants ready in 12 weeks; seedlings sooner.

Pick individual leaves or cut head above ground level, leaving roots to
re-sprout.

Pleasant mild flavour. Blends well with lettuce, beet, celery in
salads.

Cultivars
Large-leaved English – long, rather floppy leaves; for any sowing.

Verte de Cambrai, Varella – darker, smaller, hardier for late sowings.

VSR***

COURGETTES, see Marrows

CRESS, see Mustard

CUCUMBER

Types
Indoor or frame: smooth cucumbers, up to 60cm (2ft) long, require
high growing temperatures.

Outdoor: (a) Ridge – usually prickly, broad, 15–25cm (6–10in) long;
may do badly in wet seasons.

        (b) Japanese – recently introduced; cucumbers over 30cm
(1ft) long; climbing plants; crop remarkably well in poor weather
conditions.

Cultivation, indoors
See specialist books for these types, which are grown in greenhouses
and frames.

Cultivation, outdoors
Soil/Site
Sunny sheltered site, tolerate light shade in summer. Reasonably fertile, moisture-retentive, humus-rich soil. Site often prepared by filling 30cm (1ft) deep, 45cm (1½ft) wide hole with rotted manure, compost, etc, and covering with 15cm (6in) soil. In cold districts outdoor cucumbers need cloche protection.

Cultivation
Sow indoors, gentle heat, mid-April.
Sow seeds 1cm (½in) deep on edge, not flat, 2 seeds per 5 or 7·5cm (2 or 3in) pot; remove weakest seedling later.
Harden off; plant out end May/early June, 38–45cm (15–18in) apart (if climbing), 75cm (2½ft) apart (if growing flat).
Stagger planting dates to prolong season as cucumbers only crop for limited period.
Alternatively sow *in situ*, 2 or 3 seeds together under cloches or jam jars early May/June. Thin to 1 per station. This method often very successful as cucumbers dislike being transplanted.
Protect young seedlings against slugs.
Train Japanese cucumbers against trellis, up cane tripods, wire or nylon netting, 23cm (9in) square mesh adequate. Tie with raffia where necessary. Allow for 1 to 2m (4 to 6ft) growth.
Nip out growing point when top of support reached.
Ridge cucumbers climb less vigorously, but cucumbers better quality if grown against support and encouraged to climb a foot or so. Growing point can be nipped out after 6 or 7 leaves formed to encourage fruiting on sideshoots.
Keep weeded, well watered; mulching recommended.
Liquid feeding beneficial mid-July onwards.
Syringing with water in hot weather helps control red spider mite.
Frames: outdoor cultivars crop more reliably in poor seasons and in north in frames or cloches. Keep cucumbers off soil if possible (see *Fig. 30*). Syringe daily with water to discourage red spider mite; give some ventilation. Top dress with soil when roots appear on surface. Removing male flowers unnecessary with outdoor types.

Pests/Diseases
Red spider mite: foliage becomes rust coloured. Burn badly-infected leaves. Regular syringing best preventive. Can spray with derris.
Mosaic virus: yellow-green blotches on leaves. Burn young infected plants. Older plants survive though yields lowered.

Harvesting
Outdoor cucumbers crop mid-July to mid-September.
Keep picking to encourage growth.
Small cucumbers can be pickled.

Cultivars
Perfection (King of the Ridge), Patio Pik (dwarf, suitable for pots) –
ridge types.
F_1 Burpee Hybrid, F_1 Burpless Tasty Green, Chinese Long Green, F_1
Tokyo Slicer – Japanese types.
Crystal Apple (Lemon) – attractive, crisp, well-flavoured round fruit.
Bush Crop – recently introduced, American, non-trailing bush cvs.

VSR**

ENDIVE (*Fig. 43*)

Useful all year round salad plant. Natural flavour somewhat bitter.
Leaves can be blanched to make sweeter – a matter of taste.

Types
Curled – frizzy decorative leaves.
Broad-leaved Batavian – large broad leaves.
On the whole curled endives more suitable for summer, broad-leaved
for winter, but there are exceptions. There are many cvs of varying
hardiness, suited for sowing at different times.

Soil/Site
Rich light soil. Plenty of moisture when growing; dig in manure or
compost if soil very light. Spring-sown best in semi-shade, or may bolt;
open site for summer/autumn sowings.

Cultivation
Sow: 1 March (under cover) to plant outside for early summer crop.
      2 April/May for main summer supply.
      3 June/July for autumn supply.
      4 August, to plant under cover, for winter crop. Use hardy cvs.
Sow *in situ*, or in seed boxes or soil blocks for transplanting. Space
curled endives about 25cm (10in) apart, broad-leaved up to 38cm
(15in) apart each way.
Can be broadcast in patches for use as seedling cut-and-come-again
crop.
Curled types most suitable for seedling crop.
Cover outdoor plants in autumn to improve quality and prolong
season.

43. SOME LESS COMMON SALAD VEGETABLES

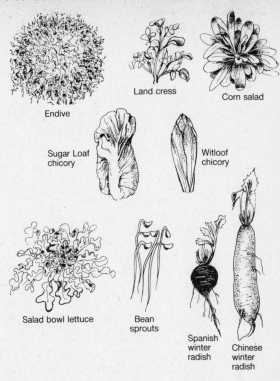

Endive

Land cress

Corn salad

Sugar Loaf chicory

Witloof chicory

Salad bowl lettuce

Bean sprouts

Spanish winter radish

Chinese winter radish

Blanching

Blanch few at a time when full grown (about 12 weeks after sowing).
Plants *must be dry* or may rot (especially curled types).
Tying leaves together with raffia gives partial blanching.
For complete blanching need total darkness. Invert flower pot with
blocked drainage hole over tied plant, or cover with straw held in place
with wire hoops.
Traditionally endives dug up in autumn, transplanted into frames and
blanched by covering with straw.

Harvesting

After cutting leaves, leave stump to re-sprout. Endives naturally
vigorous and productive. Hardy cultivars overwintered under cover
grow very fast in early spring. Excellent value. Much less disease prone
than winter lettuce.

Cultivars
Green Curled, Frisee d'été, Pancaliere (hardy) – curled type.
Batavian, Cornet de Bordeaux (hardy) – broad-leaved type.

VSR***

FLORENCE FENNEL (Sweet fennel) (*Fig. 38*)

Beautiful feathery annual plant, growing about 45 cm (18in) high, grown for swollen 'bulb' at base of stem.

Soil/Site
Must have well-drained, moisture retentive soil, rich in organic matter. Prefers light sandy soil, but tolerates heavier soil.

Cultivation
Risk of fennel bolting rather than hearting if sown too early in the year or checked by dry or cold conditions. Must be grown fast.
Sow: 1 May/early July for outdoor summer crop.
       2 Mid-July/early August to plant under cover for autumn use.
Fennel dislikes root disturbance.
Preferably sow in soil blocks or *in situ*, otherwise in seed trays, pricking out when very small, planting at 3-to-4 leaf stage.
Space plants 30cm (12in) apart each way.
Keep well watered; mulch to retain moisture and keep down weeds.
Can earth up bulb when it starts swelling to blanch it, but not essential.
Tolerates light frost; cloche protection in autumn prolongs season.

Harvesting
Cut just above ground level when bulb formed. Leave stem to re-sprout with tasty smaller shoots. Aniseed flavoured bulb used raw or braised. Use fern (like fern of common perennial herb fennel) for flavouring.

Cultivars
Perfection, Sirio, Sweet Florence, Zefa Fino (most bolt resistant).

VSR*

GARLIC (*Fig. 48*)

Garlic bulbs formed underground; leaves 20–25cm (8–10in) high.

Soil/Site
Open sunny position, not too dry in summer.

Preferably light rich soil, well dug (but not freshly manured). Good drainage essential.

Cultivation
Plant individual cloves split off from bulbs, discarding tiny cloves (garlic from greengrocers can be used).
The longer the growing season the better.
Plant September to November, unless soil very wet. (Garlic is very hardy.)
Alternatively plant February or March.
Plant 10cm (4in) apart with tops just below surface; rows 10cm (4in) apart.
Keep weed-free or apt to be over-run.

Harvesting
Lift when leaves start to turn yellow, mid to late summer. Always handle *very* carefully, as bruised bulbs rot first. Dry thoroughly in sun, raised off ground, for 7 to 10 days. If weather wet, dry under cover in greenhouse or kitchen.
Essential to store somewhere dry, hanging, or on wooden trays.
Well harvested garlic can keep sound for 10 to 11 months.

VSR**

HAMBURG PARSLEY (*Fig. 48*)

Very hardy parsley, with smooth-skinned, edible roots 17–20cm (7–8in) long, up to 7·5cm (3in) diameter, as well as leaves which can be used in cooking. Easily grown. Valuable winter vegetable.

Soil/Site
Will grow in semi-shade; appreciates moist situation. Tolerates poorer soil than most root crops. Soil preferably manured previous autumn.

Cultivation
Requires long growing season to develop large roots.
Sow March to May in drills 25cm (10in) apart. Thin to 13cm (5in) apart.
Germination slow; can mix with radish seeds to mark rows.
Alternatively 'station sow' sowing small lettuce cultivar (eg Tom Thumb, Sugar Cos), radish, etc, between 'stations'.
Can sow late July, to stand winter and give earlier crop following year.
Keep weed-free; mulch and water in dry summer.
Can leave in soil all winter.
Cover with bracken, leaves, etc, to make lifting easier in frost.

Can be lifted October/November and stored in moist sand in shed, but some flavour lost.

Harvesting
Ready August until following April.
Scrub roots before cooking (discolour if peeled).
Roast under joint, mash with swedes and parsnips, grate in salads, fry as chips, etc.
Excellent, sweet flavour. Roots can be dried for flavouring.
Use foliage for flavouring and garnishing; it remains green even in severe winters.

VSR*

ICEPLANT (*Mesembryanthemum crystallinum*) (Fig. *38*)

Fascinating, fleshy-leaved sprawling plant. Leaves covered with bladders that sparkle like dew! Not hardy. Grown in hot climates as spinach substitute, but much better used as salad plant.

Soil/Site
Average soil, sunny site or light shade. Can be grown as undercrop.

Cultivation
Sow indoors April; plant out, after hardening off, after risk of frost. Or sow *in situ* May and thin out.
Space plants 30cm (12in) apart each way.
Requires little attention; remove any flowers that appear.
Mature plants survive light frost; cloche in late summer to extend season and maintain quality.

Harvesting
Young leaves and stems, forming tips of the 'branches', are edible.
Start picking young; pick constantly to encourage more tender growth.
Older leaves and stems become coarse.
Very succulent, so leaves don't wilt like most green vegetables, but keep fresh several days. Refreshing, slightly salty taste.

VSR***

KALE, CURLY (Scotch kale, or Borecole) (*Fig. 38*)

Very crinkled, decorative leaves like giant parsley. Extremely hardy brassica, survives worst winters, valuable in north. Leaves and young shoots are eaten. Dwarf forms, 30–60cm (1–2ft) high, most suitable for small gardens.

Soil/Site
Less fussy than most brassicas, though does best in fairly rich, well cultivated soil, limed if acid, preferably manured previous autumn.
Fairly resistant to clubroot; may succeed where other brassicas fail.

Cultivation
Sow thinly in seed bed April/May, or in seed boxes or soil blocks.
Thin out, so never crowded.
Transplant to permanent position June to August, 37cm (15in) apart.
Keep weed-free; pick off lower dead leaves.
Plants often look grim in winter but recover in spring.
Give general fertiliser in March to encourage production of fresh sideshoots.
For very early greens in cold winters, sow 3 rows thinly under cloches in January. Keep cloched until March. Do not thin or transplant. Cut greens when 15–20cm (6–8in) high.

Harvesting
Leaves ready November onwards; shoots February–April. Very valuable in spring when greens scarce.
Pick off few leaves at a time to encourage fresh growth and prolong season.
Eat young sideshoots when 10–12cm (4–5in) long.
Cook in minimum water, chop and serve with butter or cream sauce.

Cultivars
Frosty – very dwarf; F_1 Fribor, Dwarf Green Curled – dwarf.
Ornamental kale – 45–60cm (1½–2ft) tall. Variegated green, red, white, purple colours in winter. Plant in flower border. Useful for flower arrangement and garnishing. Leaves and shoots just edible!
Ragged Jack – dwarf, pretty, pink-tinged, serrated leaves; less hardy.

VSR*

KOHL RABI (*Fig. 48*)

Very odd-looking, underrated brassica; about 30cm (1ft) high; stem swells into edible ball-like bulb above ground. Leaves also edible.

Soil/Site
Fertile, light sandy soil ideal; limed if acid.

Kohl rabi very tender flavour if grown rapidly in rich soil.

Cultivation
Valuable as catch crop and for intercropping; can mature in 8 weeks.
Withstands drought, heat and clubroot well; often succeeds where
turnip fails.
Can be sown in succession from February (mild districts) until
September, rows 30cm (1ft) apart, though early sowings may bolt.
Sow: 1 Better flavoured green or white cvs March to June for summer
          supplies.
     2 Later purple cvs June to August for winter.
Either sow in seed boxes or in soil blocks, planting at 2–3 leaf stage or
sow thinly *in situ*, thinning early to 10–15cm (4–6in) apart.
Protect from pigeons; keep weed free.
Mulch (after watering) in summer to encourage rapid growth.
Reasonably hardy, so leave winter supplies in soil or store in boxes of
sand in shed, removing outer leaves but leaving central tuft.

Harvesting
From May for early sowings, until December.
Must be eaten small (tennis ball size) or becomes woody though new F_1
hybrids grow larger without becoming coarse.
Cook leaves and bulb separately. Bulb very nutritious. Don't peel as
flavour just below skin. Cook whole, sliced, or in julienne strips.
Can be boiled, stuffed, served with sauces, grated raw in salads.

Cultivars
White or Green Vienna; Purple Vienna, F_1 Lanro, F_1 Rowel.

VSR**

LAMB'S LETTUCE, see Corn salad

LAND CRESS (American cress) (*Fig. 43*)

Hardy, low-growing, fast-maturing plant.
Flavour almost identical to watercress. Very underrated salad crop,
available all year round.

Soil/Site
Plenty of organic matter in soil. Succeeds in damp, semi-shaded
positions most vegetables dislike. Ideal for small city gardens.
North-facing borders quite suitable. Can intercrop between taller or
wide spaced vegetables.

Cultivation

Sow March to June for summer use; July to September for winter and spring use, rows 23cm (9in) apart.

Water soil or drills beforehand if sowing in dry weather.

Thin or transplant to 15 or 20cm (6 or 8in) apart.

Ready 8 weeks after sowing.

Pick individual leaves as required.

Will stand outside all winter, but quality much improved by covering with bracken, straw or cloches from late autumn.

Runs to seed early following summer.

A few plants left undisturbed in dampish soil may seed themselves and save you re-sowing.

VSR***

LEEKS

Very hardy winter vegetable in onion family.

Soil/Site

Open site. Succeeds in most fertile, well-cultivated soil preferably prepared and manured previous autumn; or dig in compost or well-rotted manure before planting. Dislikes compacted soil. Good crop to grow where garden troubled by clubroot.

Cultivation

Long growing season essential for large leeks – but small leeks reputedly taste better!

Sow: 1 Indoors in gentle heat, or outside under cloches February/early March for early start. Prick out and harden off before planting out.

     2 Thinly outdoors March/April, or earlier if soil conditions permit, for main crop.

     3 Early June for late crop.

Planting (*Fig. 44a*): from May (for pre-Christmas leeks) to August.

Main planting end June (in north) July (south).

Preferably plant in showery weather.

Best results by sowing seeds 2·5cm (1in) deep.

Select largest seedlings, plant 10–15cm (4–6in) apart each way. Traditional practice of trimming roots and leaves before planting inadvisable: has been shown to reduce the final yield.

Make 15–20cm (6–8in) hole with dibber. Drop leek into bottom of hole. Water hole gently with fine spout.

No need to fill in hole; earth will fall in gradually, blanching the leek stem.

Can also sow 4 seeds per soil block; plant blocks 23cm (9in) apart.

Water in dry weather; mulching helpful.

Fortnightly feeds with liquid fertiliser beneficial.

Stems can be earthed up gradually to assist blanching.

Trim leaves by several inches when touching ground

Harvesting

Ready September until May or even June. Lift as required.

Lift and 'heel in' in late spring if ground required (*Fig. 44*).

44. PLANTING LEEKS

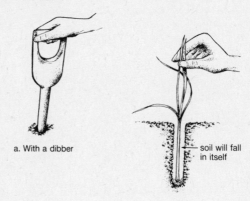

a. With a dibber

soil will fall in itself

b. Heeling-in

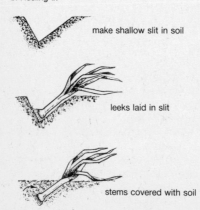

make shallow slit in soil

leeks laid in slit

stems covered with soil

Cultivars
King Richard, Titan, Walton Mammoth, Winterreuzen – early.
Blue Solaise (blue foliage), Giant Winter Catalina, Snowster, Mussel-
burgh – hardier late cvs.

VSR**

LETTUCE

Types
Cabbage type – flat shaped, hearts either soft textured (butterhead) or
crisp (crisphead).
Cos type – upright, longer leaves, hearts crisp.
Non-hearting, eg Salad Bowl (*Fig. 43*) – frilly leaves which are picked
individually so plants continue growing; very decorative.

Soil/Site
Light, well drained, rich soil best; preferably well manured for
previous crop, limed if acid. Plenty of moisture required in summer.
Cabbage type best if soil poor and dry; cos on heavy rich soil. Mid-
summer crops tolerate light shade; dwarf types (e.g. Tom Thumb,
Little Gem) useful for intercropping, inter-station sowing.

General cultivation
Lettuce can be cropped all year round with different sowings.
Matures naturally early summer; new cultivars bred to mature in
autumn/winter. *Must sow correct cultivar for the season* (see under
Principal Sowings).
Sow in seed beds or *in situ*, drills 25–30cm (10–12in) apart, thin or
transplant when 5cm (2in) high to 15–30cm (6–12in) apart according to
cultivar (transplanted seedlings mature 10 days later).
Alternatively sow in seed trays or soil blocks.
Plant shallowly, lower leaves just above surface.

Pests/Diseases/Problems
Bolting: ie running to seed. Common problem in hot summers. Some
cultivars more resistant to bolting than others. Plants more liable to
bolt if transplanted rather than thinned.
Slugs and snails: seedlings and young plants particularly vulnerable.
Take precautionary measures, especially in wet weather.
Birds: protect young seedlings with black cotton.
Aphids: spray with derris and/or pyrethrum as soon as greenfly
noticed.
Mildews and other fungus diseases: autumn and winter lettuce most

susceptible. Choose mildew-resistant cultivars; avoid damp, low-lying sites, thin seedlings early giving maximum space and air. Examine seedlings when planting out and reject any with reddish brown stems.

Harvesting
Always try to pick hearted types at their prime. Bolted lettuce can be cooked like spinach or used in soup.

Principal sowings and cultivars:
1 *Early sowings under glass*
Mid-February (south) to early March (north) in boxes in cold greenhouse, in cold frame or under cloches; thin to few inches apart. Plant out end March/early April preferably under cloches, or in sheltered position in open.
Can be kept cloched until end April.
Ready late May/early June.
Cultivars: Little Gem, Tom Thumb, Unrivalled, Winter Density, Hilde, May Queen, Reskia, Marvel of Four Seasons, Salad Bowl types.
2 *Main sowings in open*
(a) Mid-March to early June for summer crop.
(b) Mid-June to late July (north) early August (south) for September to early winter crop. Late July/early August sowings chancy, but worth trying. In wet autumn mildew is a problem. Lettuces will be leafy rather than hearted.
Sow small quantities at fortnightly intervals for succession, as lettuce may bolt in hot weather.
Thin or transplant March to May sowings.
June or August sowings best made *in situ* or in soil blocks as transplanting often unsuccessful in hot weather.
In late September remaining lettuces in open may be cloched; may then stand into December.
Cultivars: Marvel of Four Seasons (reddish), Reskia, Tom Thumb (dwarf), Unrivalled – butterheads, good for early sowing.
Buttercrunch, Lakeland, Minetto, Pennlake, Saladin, Webbs Wonderful, Windermere – crispheads; Salad Bowl types – all slow bolting.
Barcarolle, Lobjoits, Paris White Cos, Little Gem (very sweet, small 'semi' cos, highly recommended) – cos type.
Continuity – reddish-brown pretty foliage; good on light dry soils, do not transplant.
Avondefiance, Avoncrisp – recommended for mid-June sowings onwards; bred for resistance to mildew.
3 *Outdoor sowing winter-hardy lettuce* (won't succeed in severe winters)
Sow late August (north), early September (south), *in situ*, sheltered position.

Thin to 5–7·5cm (2–3in) apart in autumn. Leave over winter, hoe soil around plants occasionally.

Thin to full distance or transplant late February/early March.

Ready early May/June (this is earliest crop raised without heat or glass).

If cloches used crop better quality, 2 or 3 weeks earlier.

Cultivars: Arctic King, Imperial Winter, Valdor, Unrivalled – butterheads.

Dark Green Cos, Little Gem, Lobjoits, Winter Density – cos.

4 *Protected overwintered lettuce*

Sow mid-October under cloches or in frames.

Thin, transplant as above (3), only under cloches or frames.

Ventilate whenever possible during winter.

Use same cultivars as above. Matures 2 to 3 weeks earlier.

Or sow August/early September in seed boxes or soil blocks. Plant normal spacing in unheated greenhouse, tunnel or frame, for even earlier crop.

Cultivars: Little Gem, Density – cos; Marmer – crisphead; Cynthia, Dandie, Kwiek, Marvel of Four Seasons, Plus, Ravel – butterheads.

Cut-and-come-again seedling or leaf lettuce

Productive way of growing lettuce densely to get leaves rather than hearts. Sow small areas, say 1 sq m (1 sq yd) at a time. Either broadcast, or sow seeds about 2·5cm (1in) apart in rows 10cm (4in) apart.

Make first cut when leaves 7–10cm (3–4in) high and leave to re-sprout for second crop. For continuous supply from mid-May to mid-October sow weekly from mid-April to mid-May and again in first 3 weeks August. Ground must be fertile, weed free, and must be kept well watered.

Cultivars: Any cos or Salad Bowl cultivars, or continental 'cutting lettuce'.

VSR*** Cut-and-come-again.
　　** Summer lettuce.
　　** Winter and spring lettuce (cloched).
　　　* Winter and spring lettuce (in open).

MARROWS/COURGETTES (Vegetable marrow) (*Fig. 38*)

Types
Many types of marrow – green, yellow, white, long, round, flat, etc.

Some suitable for winter storage. Courgettes are immature stage of long marrows. Very productive, each plant producing many fruits. (Use bush F₁ hybrids for courgettes.)
Bush forms – compact growth, about 45cm (1½ft) high, 60–90cm (2–3ft) spread, very suitable for small gardens.
Trailing forms – grow over 1½ or 2m (5 or 6ft) long; can be trained up fences and other supports.

Soil/Site
See cucumbers.

Cultivation
Sowing and planting, see cucumbers.
Bush types: plant 37–60cm (15–24in) apart.
Trailing types: plant 45cm (1½ft) apart if climbing; 120cm (4ft) apart if growing flat.
Tie climbing types to supports with raffia if necessary.
Trailing types can be planted between sweetcorn to trail underneath.
Protect seedlings against slugs.
Very important to water generously throughout summer.
Mulching advisable.
Liquid feeding mid-July onwards beneficial.
Marrow flowers are insect pollinated. In cold dull weather may be necessary to hand pollinate early marrows. Take male flower, remove petals, push 'core' into female flowers (female flowers have tiny marrow-shaped swelling behind petals [*Fig. 45*]). Male flowers often produced long before any females. Be patient!

Pests/Diseases
See cucumbers.

male

female

45. MARROW FLOWERS

Harvesting
Courgettes – ready July to mid-October; pick when 10–15cm (4–6in) long or they develop into large marrows.
Many methods of cooking; peeling unnecessary.
Storage marrows – cut before frost; flavour preserved better if stored in warmish place.
Marrow flowers can be used to make soup.

Cultivars
Bush: Ambassador, F_1 Early Gem, Green Bush, F_1 Zucchini – green. F_1 Gold Rush – yellow.
Yellow and White Custard (Patty Pan) – pretty, flattish, fluted-edged fruits.
Trailing: Long Green Trailing – traditional large storing marrow.
Vegetable Spaghetti – fruits 15–25cm (6–10in) long; after boiling whole for 10 minutes flesh disintegrates into spaghetti-like texture.

VSR**

MUSTARD, SALAD RAPE AND CRESS

Seedlings used in salads and sandwiches all year round. Can grow indoors or in the garden.

Cultivation indoors
Sow in shallow boxes, seed trays, or other shallow containers on thin layer of well-sifted soil, soilless compost, bulb fibre or sifted leafmould, or on dishes on damp flannel or moist blotting paper.
If soil, etc, used seedlings should give a second crop after being cut.
Water sowing medium gently before sowing.
Sow seeds fairly thickly and evenly on surface; press in gently with board, do not cover with soil.
Cover container or put in dark to encourage rapid growth.
After a week move into light for 2 or 3 days to become green.
Cut for eating when $3\frac{1}{2}$–5cm ($1\frac{1}{2}$–2in) high.
Mustard germinates faster than cress, so sow 3 days after cress in same or separate container.
Milder-flavoured salad rape seed can be substituted for mustard.
Sow for succession at weekly or 10-day intervals all year round.

Cultivation outdoors
Light soil; open site spring and autumn; shaded in summer.
Spring and autumn sowings best value; summer sowings run to seed fast. Broadcast seed in small patches, or intersow, eg among brassicas.

If soil moist, as many as four or five cuts can be made in succession. Rape is mildest in flavour, slowest to run to seed, and if allowed to mature, can be used as greens. (Mature cress and mustard become far too hot.)
Useful sowing: September/October in unheated greenhouse, frame, etc. Make one or two cuts before winter, leave in soil for winter, cut again early spring when it grows again rapidly. Early sowings under cover also useful.

VSR****

ONIONS

Large onions used for cooking; green 'spring' onions for salads.

Soil/Site
Open site; rich well-drained, well-dug soil, limed if acid, preferably prepared and manured previous autumn. Never sow or plant on freshly-manured land. Advisable to rotate onions, in spite of 'onion patch' tradition.

Large onions

Cultivation
Grow either from sets (tiny bulbs) or seed. Sets recommended for small gardens.
Advantages of sets: easily grown, tolerate wider range of soils and climate, less disease prone, usually ready earlier, shorter period in soil, generally escape onion fly attacks.
Disadvantages of sets: more expensive, only available for some cvs, tendency to bolt, but good modern sets reliable.

Growing from sets:
Normally planted late February to early April: some new cvs suitable for autumn planting. Plant 5cm (2in) apart, rows 25cm (10in) apart.
Plant so tips just showing above ground, protect with black cotton or birds pull out.
Keep weed-free.
Can mulch in summer; pull mulch away from around bulbs when starting to ripen.
For harvesting, see below.
Cultivars: Sturon, Stuttgarter Giant, Giant Fen Globe (Rijnsburger Wijbo). For autumn planting – Unwins First Early.

Growing from seed:
Firm seed bed with fine tilth essential.
Never sow in cold soil.
General fertiliser can be worked into seed bed before sowing.
Spring sowing:
Sow March and April, drills 23–30cm (9–12in) apart, or February under cloches or in heated propagator.
Thin in stages to 5–10cm (2–4in) apart. Closest spacings give smaller onions which store better. Wide spacing gives larger onions. Eat thinnings as spring onions.
Or sow up to 5 seeds per soil block; plant blocks 25cm (10in) apart.
Keep weed-free, especially in early summer; mulch as for sets.
Cultivars: Allavon, Balstora, Bedfordshire Champion, F_1 Hygro, F_1 Hyduro, Wabasto – all good keepers.
Autumn sowing (traditional autumn cultivars):
(Not advisable in cold wet areas)
Gives larger onions, ready slightly earlier (end July onwards) than spring sown.
Sow thinly August, thin to 2·5cm (1in) apart in autumn.
Transplant or thin to final distance in spring (thinning preferable as transplanted onions more liable to bolt).
Only certain cultivars, eg F_1 Buffalo, Robusta, Solidity, Reliance.
Autumn sowing (Japanese cultivars):
Recently introduced. Mature extremely early in late June when shop prices high, but not recommended for keeping.
Sow first half August (north), second half August (south).
Sow 2·5cm (1in) apart, *in situ*, drills 23cm (9in) apart.
Thin (do not transplant) to 10cm (4in) apart in spring.
Cultivars: Express Yellow, Imai Yellow, Kaizuka Extra Early.

Pests/Diseases
Onion fly: chiefly attacks spring-sown crops. Seedlings go yellow and die. Dress drills with calomel dust before sowing. Burn diseased plants.
Sowing into 'stale' seed bed, prepared 10 days before sowing, helpful, especially with autumn-sown onions.

Harvesting
Onions ready to harvest when foliage starts to die and tops start to bend over, normally August, but earlier if grown from sets.
No point in bending tops over artificially – may cause damage.
Aim to dry quickly.
Handle very gently if storing; tiny cuts and bruises give foothold for rots.
Lift from ground, ideally spread on sacks or trays outdoors to dry, bringing inside if it rains.

In good weather leave outside for about 10 days.

In wet weather do not leave outside for more than 3 days. Better to finish drying in warmth indoors (eg airing cupboard).

Cut off any new roots which sprout.

Store hanging, or on trays in cool dry place, or knotted into suspended nylon stockings.

Spring onions

Cultivation

Very sensitive to soil acidity; lime if acid.

Sow March to June for summer/autumn supplies, at 2- or 3-week intervals for succession.

Drills 20cm (8in) apart, or double rows 5–7·5cm (2–3in) apart.

Sow July to August for winter/early spring use; give cloche protection September onwards in cold areas.

Do not thin spring onions; pull as required.

Cultivar

White Lisbon.

Welsh onion

Useful perennial onion, bulbs swell slightly. Very hardy. Can use tops all year as green onion in salads, bulbs in cooking.

Thrives in ordinary soil, useful edging.

Sow August or April, thin gradually to 20cm (8in) apart.

Plants grow into clumps. Divide clumps every 2 or 3 years in spring or autumn, replanting younger parts.

Everlasting onion – similar hardy, perennial onion. Doesn't form seed, so divide existing clumps as above, planting 20cm (8in) apart.

Pickling onion

Sow fairly thickly on poor dry soil, April; do not thin.

Ripen off early August before pickling.

Cultivar

Paris Silver Skin, The Queen.

VSR** Spring onions.

    * Main crop onions.

PARSNIP

Short and long types grown. Short types best for small gardens and shallow soils.

Soil/Site
Reasonably open site. Grows in most soils (deep soils preferred), provided thoroughly dug. Manure for previous crop. Fresh manure leads to forked roots. Lime if acid.

Cultivation
Long growing season necessary if large roots required.
Sow late February to early May. Good soil tilth essential.
'Station sow', short types 5–10cm (2–4in) apart, drills 20cm (8in) apart; long types 12–20cm (5–8in) apart, drills 30cm (1ft) apart.
Thin in stages to one strong seedling per station.
Germination slow. Can sow radish in rows as 'markers', or dwarf lettuce, etc, between stations, provided stations 17cm (7in) apart.
Hoe carefully, taking care not to damage crowns.
Mulch after final thinning.

Pests/Diseases
Canker: crowns crack, then invaded by fungi. Most likely to occur where there is drought, over-rich soil or crown damage. Small roots less vulnerable. Where canker common, use resistant cultivars, or sow slightly later, ie April/early May.
Celery fly: blisters leaves. Pick off and destroy diseased leaves.

Harvesting
Roots available September to April.
Best left in soil all winter though can be stored in sand, etc, in shed.
Frost improves flavour. Foliage dies down, so mark position of rows.
Can be covered with bracken to assist lifting in frost. Lift and heel in when growth restarts in spring.
Eat boiled, mashed, fried, roasted under joint, baked with brown sugar.

Cultivars
Offenham, Avonresister (some canker resistance) – short.
Hollow Crown Improved (Lisbonnais), Tender and True – long.

VSR*

PEA

Ordinary garden peas

Eaten shelled. Purple podded (with purple flowers), exceptionally pretty grown as hedge. Petit pois – tiny very sweet peas. New semi-leafless cvs almost self-supporting – asset in small gardens.

Sugar or mangetout peas

Whole pod eaten young. With some cvs can also shell mature pods. Superb flavour. Excellent value in small gardens.

Types
'Earlies' mature in 11 or 12 weeks; 'second earlies' in 12 or 13; 'main crop' in 13 or 14.
Height varies from 30cm–2m (1–6ft).
Earlies and second earlies require less space over shorter period, best for small gardens and light soils, though maincrop higher yielding.
Seed types: Round – hardier, used for winter/early spring sowings.
Wrinkled – better flavoured, less hardy.

Soil/Site
Open site, light shade tolerated in summer.
Well-drained, fertile, moisture-retentive, deeply-worked soil essential, preferably manured previous autumn. Or dig a trench and work plenty of manure into lower spit.

Cultivation
General fertiliser can be applied few days before sowing.
Sow in flat drills, 15–20cm (6–8in) wide, 5cm (2in) deep, spacing seeds 5cm (2in) apart, 60cm (2ft) between drills; or in 3 parallel drills 12cm (4in) apart, seeds 12cm (4in) apart, 60cm (2ft) between bands (*Fig. 9*). (Can also sow at this spacing across width of narrow beds, encircling bed with wire support.)
Press peas into soil before covering.
Protect immediately from birds with pea guards or black cotton.
Autumn sowing: see Use of cloches p. 203.
Spring sowings in open:
First sowing possible late February, warm sheltered areas, March/early April elsewhere, according to soil. *Never sow in cold wet conditions*. Where possible, warm soil beforehand with cloches; or draw drill on sunny day in morning, leave open, sow in afternoon. Seed dressings advisable for early sowings. Or give seeds a start by germinating on damp paper towelling indoors, sowing carefully when just germinated.

Summer sowings:
1 Every 3 weeks from April until mid-June for succession.
2 Sow early, mildew-resistant cultivar (preferably) in late June to
  mid-July, for late crop in September. Successful in good autumn.
Support early (even dwarf cultivars) when 7·5cm (3in) high with twigs.
Twine black cotton along twigs against birds.
For support as peas grow higher use twigs, nylon netting, wire netting,
string around canes (*Fig. 46*).
Draw up soil alongside drills in April/May to protect against cold
winds.
Keep weed-free; hoe along drills to aerate soil.
In dry weather heavy watering, about 1cm ($\frac{1}{2}$in) *most* beneficial first
when flowers opening, and then when pods starting to swell.
Apply heavy mulch in spring.
After harvesting dig in roots, which return nitrogen to soil.

Use of cloches for growing peas
1 Sow under cloches in February or March; keep cloched until April.
2 Use cloches to warm soil for March/April sowings.
3 Cloche late June/July sowings in late September/early October.
4 In mild districts, on light soil, sow dwarf hardy cultivars under
  cloches October/November for very early crop. Ventilate when
  possible; keep soil hoed during winter.

Pests/Diseases
Mice: can be devastating. Burrow down for seeds. Set mousetraps.
Birds: protect constantly against birds (*Fig. 19*).
Pea weevils: nibble leaf margins in spring. Dust with derris when
damage seen.
Pea moth: attacks in summer. Maggots found in peas. Control with
derris at flowering time.

Harvesting
Early sowings ready end May, June; others June onwards.
Keep picking full pods to encourage others to swell.
Start picking mangetout peas when swelling peas just visible inside the
pod.
Cook shelled, or in pods and shell after cooking, to retain flavour.

Cultivars (R – round seeded; others are wrinkle seeded)
For spring/autumn sowing under cloches: Beagle, Douce Provence
(R), and dwarf mangetout cvs.
For early sowing in open: above cvs plus second earlies, eg Kelvedon
Wonder, Onward, Progress No. 9.

Maincrop: Bikini (semi-leafless dwarf), Hurst Greenshaft, Titania (petit pois), Victory Freezer.
Sugar peas: Dwarf Sweet Green, Edula, Sugarbon, Sugar Rae – dwarf.
Oregon Sugar Pod, Sugar Snap, Tezieravenir – tall.

VSR** (maincrop)
　　* (early)

46. VARIOUS METHODS OF SUPPORTING PEAS

a. Between rows of twigs

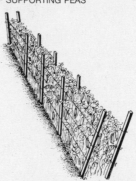

b. By wires or strings attached to
upright posts or canes

c. With wire netting. A
single row of peas can be
planted against the
netting, or the netting can
enclose a band or bed
of peas

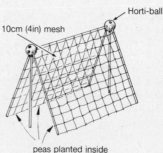

Horti-ball

10cm (4in) mesh

peas planted _inside_

d. On 10cm (4in) square netting,
here attached to canes with
Horti-balls

PEPPERS (Capsicum, Sweet or Green peppers) (*Fig. 38*)

Bushy plants, 30–45cm (1–1½ft) high; peppers up to 7·5–10cm (3–4in) long, 5cm (2in) across, green initially, ripening to red or yellow. Mainly used green; unlikely to ripen completely outdoors.

Soil/Site
Light, medium rich soil. Avoid fresh manure; dig in little mature compost beforehand. In north grow on windowsills, cool greenhouse, cloches or frames. Successful in open in south; choose warm, sunny, sheltered position. Peppers need high light intensity to do well.

Cultivation
Sow indoors February to early April, gentle heat.
Prick out at 3-leaf stage into 5 or 7·5cm (2 or 3in) pots, or into small peat pots, surrounding with extra compost, etc, as they develop.
Keep close to glass so not starved of light.
If growing indoors move finally into 17cm (7in) pots in good potting compost.
Plant out when first flower truss showing.
Harden off well. Plant outdoors under cloches or in frames late May/early June, or in open after danger of frost. Plant 37cm (15in) apart.
Outdoors: If growth spindly, nip out growing point, or first small 'king' fruit to appear centrally, when plants 30cm (1ft) high.
Keep well watered throughout season. Mulching advisable.
Liquid feed can be applied once fruits start swelling.
Indoors: Interplant with French marigolds to discourage white fly.
Syringe with water at least once daily to discourage red spider mite.
Keep well watered and mulched.
Apply liquid feed once peppers swelling.
Will continue growing into late autumn.

Harvesting
Peppers ready August into late autumn. Keep picking green peppers to encourage development. Fruits keep best on plant. Before heavy frost pull up plant by root, hang indoors. Fruit may continue to ripen. Use raw or cooked. Freezes well, whole or sliced.

Cultivars
F₁ Canape, F₁ Ace – excellent outdoors and indoors.

VSR*

POTATOES

Types
Earlies – fast maturing, lower yields; Second Earlies and Maincrop –
longer maturing, higher yields.
In small gardens only earlies worth growing because quickest returns,
require less space, escape most main crop diseases, ready when prices
high, taste delicious.

Soil/Site
Open site; avoid frost pocket. Potatoes tolerate acid conditions, grow
on wide range of soil. Deep, well-drained, medium loam ideal. Manure
previous autumn. Often planted in new gardens to improve and 'clean'
soil.

47. POTATO CHITTING

a. Potatoes chitting in egg tray prior to planting

b. *left:* potato ready for planting;
   right: potato grown in poor light
   which should be rejected
   for planting

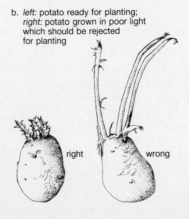

right   wrong

Cultivation (Earlies)

Buy certified seed potatoes February. 3kg (7lb) bag sufficient for 13½m (15yd).

Chitting: (*Fig. 47a*)

Place tubers 'rose' end (end with most 'eyes') upwards in seed trays, shallow drawers, egg trays, etc, in light, in frost-free shed or cool room, to sprout or 'chit'. Chitting takes about 6 weeks; results in earlier, heavier crop.

Sprouts should be sturdy, greenish purple, 2–2·5cm (¾–1in) long before planting (*Fig. 47b*).

Reject unsprouted and diseased tubers.

Plant March/early April. Early planting gives highest yields.

Soil must be moist, but do not plant if wet or sticky.

Make 10–15cm (4–6in) deep drill, or make holes with trowel.

Plant tubers 5cm (2in) below soil surface, rose end upwards. Cover with soil.

Earlies can be 25–30cm (10–12in) apart; rows 37–45cm (15–18in) apart.

After planting, covering with 15cm (6in) compost, straw, or manure beneficial. Or can be top dressed with general fertiliser (note: artificial fertilisers may impair flavour).

Or cover with perforated polythene film for earlier, heavier crops. Remove film 3 to 4 weeks after potatoes have emerged.

Protect young growth from frost with cloches, bracken, twigs or by covering with newspaper at night if frost is forecast or seems likely.

Keep weeds down.

Frequent watering in May and June improves yields.

Earthing up:

When plants 10–15cm (4–6in) high draw soil over foliage until only tops exposed. This prevents greening, checks weeds, and may encourage tuber formation. To avoid earthing-up potatoes can be grown under black polythene film, laid over the bed after planting, edges buried in the soil. When the leaves push up the plastic, cut slits and pull them through. Harvest potatoes by pulling aside the film.

Pests/Diseases

Potato eelworm: causes 'potato sickness' in old gardens and allotments. Plants are stunted; yields lowered. If suspected, lift roots and plunge into bucket of water. Tiny round brown eelworm cysts will rise to surface if present. Remedy: give up potatoes for seven years or be content with lower yields, or try new cultivars (see cultivar list) which are resistant to some strains of eelworm. (Main crop potatoes are prone to many diseases, such as potato blight, which are largely avoided by 'earlies'.)

Harvesting
Open flowers on plants indicate tubers reaching edible size (mid-June/ early July). Dig as required. Do not leave any tiny tubers in soil.

Potatoes in barrels or tubs
Use wooden or plastic barrels about 75cm (30in) deep and 60cm (24in) diameter. Prepare good soil or peat-based potting compost mixed with plenty of garden compost or well-rotted manure. Put 10cm (4in) layer in barrel. Place four sprouted tubers on top, cover with 10cm (4in) mixture. Firm down and water. When stems about 15cm (6in) high, add another 10cm (4in) compost. Repeat until plants about 5cm (2in) below rim of barrel. Add final layer of peat. Harvest when plants flower. Plunge hands into barrel to check if tubers are reasonable size.

Christmas potatoes
Re-plant a few tubers in late July, cover with cloches in September.

Cultivars
Pentland Javelin, Pentland Lustre, Pentland Meteor – resistant to some strains of eelworm.
Arran Pilot, Duke of York, Epicure, Maris Bard, Suttons Foremost.

VSR* Early potatoes.

PURSLANE, SUMMER (*Fig. 38*)

Half hardy, low-growing plant with succulent, rounded leaves and stems, both edible raw. Green and golden forms: former more vigorous, latter more decorative. Refreshing, mild flavour.

Soil/Site
Light, well-drained soil; sheltered, sunny position.

Cultivation
Sow indoors in April, in seed trays or soil blocks, planting out after danger of frost 15cm (6in) apart. Seedlings damp off easily so no point in sowing prematurely. Sow *in situ* outdoors May and June. Or sow broadcast in patch for use as seedling cut-and-come-again crop: March/April sowings in unheated greenhouse or frame very useful.

Harvesting
Pick young growths when large enough to eat. Always leave two leaves at base to allow further growth. Pick continually to keep

growths tender. Remove seedheads that appear. Start cutting seedling crop when about 5cm (2in) high. Grows very rapidly in warm conditions.

VSR**** Indoor seedlings.
     ** Outdoor plants.

RADISH

Types
Ordinary radish small red, white or red and white roots, round or cylindrical shape. Available most of year, must be eaten young.
Winter radish (Chinese and Spanish) round and long forms, can weigh several pounds; keep throughout winter (*Fig. 43*).
The young green seed pods of radishes that have gone to seed are delicious raw. Winter radishes produce the largest, most succulent pods.

Soil/Site
Well-drained, rich, moist soil, plenty of humus but not freshly manured. Open site for spring and autumn sowings; slight shade for summer sowings of ordinary radish or they run to seed.

48. SOME LESS COMMON ROOT AND BULB VEGETABLES

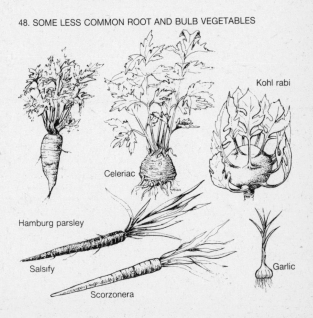

Kohl rabi

Celeriac

Hamburg parsley

Salsify

Scorzonera

Garlic

Cultivation
Ordinary radish
Fast maturing, ready 20 to 30 days after sowing.
Useful for intercropping, marking rows of slow-germinating seeds.
Failures usually caused by sowing in dry position, failing to thin early, or poor tilth on seed bed. Seedlings must never become lanky.
Sow: 1 Outdoors February (provided soil warm and well drained) until September, short rows at 2-week intervals for succession. June to August sowings best in semi-shade, ideally between other crops. Always sow thinly, drills 10–15cm (4–6in) apart, *thin early* to 2–2·5cm ($\frac{3}{4}$–1in) apart. Can also broadcast thinly. Dust with derris if seedlings nibbled by flea beetle. Water if weather dry.

2 Indoors – September and October, February to April in frames, cloches or greenhouse
If sown *very* thinly, thinning unnecessary. Give plenty of ventilation; keep moist.

Winter radish (Chinese and Spanish types)
Sow in open, moist soil, July/August.
Drills 30cm (1ft) apart; thin to 10–15cm (4–6in) apart.
Either leave in soil all winter (can be protected with bracken or straw), or lift and store in sand in dry shed.
Roots can grow over 50cm (20in) long without becoming coarse.
May last until April. (Leave a plant to run to seed for seed pods.)
Good sliced or grated in salads, cooked in stews, in curries or pickled.
Radish tops edible (just). Cook like spinach.

Cultivars
Spring and autumn sowing: Cherry Belle, Helro, Ribella, Rota, Saxa – round red.
Summer: French Breakfast (long red), Prinz Rotin (stands well), Sparkler (red-and-white round), White Icicle (long white), Minowase (very long white).
Winter radish: Mino Early, Chinese Rose, Black Spanish.

VSR**** Ordinary radish.
      *** Winter radish.

SALAD ROCKET (*Fig. 38*)

Dwarf growing, spicy-leaved salad plant; highly productive, especially as cool weather cut-and-come-again seedling crop. Reasonably hardy.

Soil/Site
Tolerant of most soils. Slightly shaded site preferable in summer.

Cultivation
With successive sowings can be available all year round.
Make first sowings in cold greenhouse or frame end January/February.
Sow outdoors early spring until September. (Summer sowings may bolt.)
Sow September/October under cover for winter and spring supplies (see Cress).
Very useful for intercropping and undercropping, eg among brassicas.
For single plants sow *in situ*, thinning to 15cm (6in) apart, or sow in seed boxes or soil blocks planting out when young. For seedlings broadcast in patches, or sow bands between other vegetables.
Keep well watered, especially in summer.
Can also be grown in seed trays or dishes indoors (see Cress).
Start cutting seedlings when 5cm (2in) high. Up to 5 cuts can sometimes be made. Pick leaves from single plants as required.

VSR****

SALSIFY (Oyster plant) (*Fig. 48*)

Long, white root, occupies little space but requires long growing season.
Grown for roots (in winter) and flower buds in spring and summer.

Soil/Site
Open site; rich, light, stone-free sandy soil best; not freshly manured.

Cultivation
Sow April and May.
Sow clusters of few seeds about 7·5cm (3in) apart, thin to 15cm (6in) apart; rows 30cm (1ft) apart.
Water in dry weather; mulch after watering.
Roots can be left in soil in winter, covered with bracken or straw for extra protection; or lift and store in sand in shed.
For flower buds leave in soil for second season.

Harvesting
Roots ready October to following April or May. Very delicate flavour. Scrub roots, cook unpeeled, squeeze skin off afterwards.
Can be boiled; baked; fried; served in sauces; parboiled and finished in pan with margarine and brown sugar.

Pick flower buds when fat, just before opening, with few inches of stalk. Boil lightly, cool, dress with vinaigrette sauce.

Cultivars
Mammoth, Sandwich Island.

VSR*

SCORZONERA (*Fig. 48*)

Similar to salsify; black-skinned, white-fleshed roots.

Soil/Site/Cultivation/Use/VSR
See Salsify.

Cultivar
Russian Giant.

SHALLOTS

Useful substitute for onion in small gardens because more easily grown; shorter growing season, better keeping.

Soil/Site
Open site; deeply worked, well drained, light soils best.
Heavy clays not very suitable. Do not use fresh manure. Soil best manured for previous crop, or dug and manured previous autumn.

Cultivation
Plant bulbs as early as possible – December or January in very mild areas, February or March elsewhere – ½kg (1lb) of shallots sufficient for 4½m (15ft) row.
Firm soil beforehand by light treading or light rolling.
Select firm, medium-sized bulbs; remove loose dry scales.
Plant 15cm (6in) apart, drills 23cm (9in) apart.
Bury bulb to half its depth or plant in shallow drill.
Firm soil around bulb after planting.
Protect against birds with black cotton.
If bulbs get uprooted by birds, dig up, re-plant carefully.
Keep weed-free; can be mulched between rows, but do not cover bulbs.

Pests
Some strains virused. Be suspicious of cheap offers!

Harvesting
Each bulb multiplies into 8 or 10 shallots.
Lift bulbs when foliage starts to yellow, usually July.
Dry outdoors for few days.
Store in airy shed on trays, hung up, or in net bags – never in closed
bags. Will keep sound until following May or June.
Keep some medium-sized bulbs to plant following year.
Use cooked, pickled, or in salads.
Young foliage can be used as green onion.

Cultivars
Giant Yellow (Dutch, Long Keeping) – fastest grower, best keeper.

VSR**

SPINACH AND SWISS CHARD

Several leafy plants are known as spinach: eg ordinary spinach,
spinach beet (perpetual spinach), Swiss chard (seakale beet, silver
chard), New Zealand spinach.
Traditionally ordinary spinach most widely grown, but best returns for
small gardens from spinach beet, Swiss chard and New Zealand
spinach, because heavier yielding, less liable to bolt.
Spinach beet also very successful cut-and-come-again seedling crop.

Spinach beet (Perpetual spinach)

Leaves larger and fleshier than ordinary spinach.

Soil/Site
Well-manured ground, limed if acid, plenty of moisture; but with-
stands drought better than ordinary spinach. Tolerates light shade.
Don't grow near cucumbers: spinach blight caused by cucumber virus.

Cultivation
Station sow 15cm (6in) apart, drills 37cm (15in) apart, thin to 30cm
(1ft) apart.
Sow: 1 Main sowing March/April. Will crop during summer and
autumn, and frequently all through winter until following May
or June.
2 Late July/August. Smaller yielding, but crops through winter
into following summer.
For seedling crop sow in rows 10cm (4in) apart, or wide bands, or

broadcast. Thin to about 5cm (2in) apart. Start cutting when leaves 5–10cm (2–4in) high. Several cuts possible if well watered.
Keep weed-free; water in dry summer; mulching helpful.
Pick off seed heads to prolong cropping.
Cloche or protect with bracken during winter to improve leaf quality.

Swiss chard (Seakale beet) (*Fig. 38*)

Very hardy; thick fleshy leaves, often 45cm (1½ft) high. Thick white leafstalks and midribs edible.

Soil/Site
Succeeds on any soil, but best on heavy well-manured soil.

Cultivation
Sow May. 'Station sow' about 15cm (6in) apart, drills 37cm (15in) apart, thin to 23cm (9in) apart.
Will crop late summer/early winter, and in spring until following July.
Sow again July/August for successional crop following spring and summer. (Can sow in soil blocks; plant under cover autumn for early crop.)
Protection with cloches or bracken beneficial during winter.
Leaves cooked like spinach; stems cooked in bundles like asparagus, served with butter or sauce.

Ruby chard

Beautiful red-stemmed form of Swiss chard with reddish green foliage.
Edible, and very decorative in flower borders and flower arrangements.

New Zealand spinach

Low growing, sprawly, vigorous, half-hardy plant.

Soil/Site
Very drought-resistant, succeeds in dry, sunny corners.

Cultivation
Germination may be tricky. Soak seeds in water overnight before sowing.
Sow outdoors mid-May, sowing few seeds 30cm (1ft) apart. Or start indoors in April, harden off, plant out mid-May.
Space plants 60–90cm (2–3ft) apart.
Tips of shoots and leaves can be eaten. Flavour less strong than ordinary spinach. Keeps growing until frost – very good value.
May self-sow itself and re-appear following year.

Ordinary spinach (Summer)

Best grown as catch crop in shade between peas, beans, brassicas, etc.
Sow in the open March until May in moist rich soil, drills 30cm (1ft)
apart, thin to 15cm (6in) apart.
Ready May to November.

Ordinary spinach (Winter)

Needs well-drained, open site; sow in the open or under cloches late
August/September, drills 30cm (1ft) apart, thinning to 23cm (9in)
apart. May crop from November until spring; top dressing in spring
beneficial; better results if crop cloched from October until spring.

Cultivars for spring or autumn sowing
Jovita, Norvak, Sigmaleaf.

Harvesting
Said to be better to pull rather than cut spinach; never strip any one
plant; wash, and cook only in moisture clinging to leaves.

VSR*** Spinach beet, Swiss chard and New Zealand spinach.
    * Summer and winter spinach.

SWEDES

Very hardy brassica, roots valuable in winter. Usually yellow-fleshed;
milder and sweeter than turnips. Take longer to mature (20–26 weeks)
than turnips. Grown mainly for winter crop.

Soil/Site
See turnips.

Cultivation
For seed bed, thinning, see turnips.
Sow thinly or station sow 10cm (4in) apart mid-May (in north), early
June (in south).
Rows 37–45cm (15–18in) apart; thin to 22–30cm (9–12in) apart.
Can be sown July/August for spring greens (see turnips).
Roots can be left in ground in most areas in winter, but probably best
to lift and store around Christmas (see turnips) or may become coarse.
Forcing: roots can be lifted mid-winter, trimmed, packed into boxes
with soil, and put in semi-darkness. Resulting young, semi-blanched
growths very tasty.

Young leafy growths from roots in soil over winter ready April/May.

Pests/Diseases
See turnips. Where mildew a problem grow cv Marian.

Cultivars
Marian (good resistance to clubroot and mildew).

VSR*

SWISS AND RUBY CHARD, see Spinach

SWEETCORN

Tall growing, half-hardy, sweet form of maize. Gamble in northern England. Early cultivars most suitable for small gardens.

Soil/Site
Sheltered sunny site; soil well drained, fairly fertile, but not too rich. Best manured for previous crop. Moisture essential in growing season; may fail on dry soil.
Save space by planting among brassicas, etc. Grow trailing marrows, courgettes, dwarf beans, land cress or radish under corn.

Cultivation
Corn is grown in blocks or groups rather than single rows, to assist pollination. Short cultivars 30cm (1ft) apart each way; taller cultivars 37–45cm (15–18in) apart.
Sow: 1 For earliest crops, indoors, April, gentle heat, ideally 2 or 3 seeds per peat pot (to minimise transplanting), removing weakest seedlings later. Harden off. Plant outside early May under cloches, late May/early June (*when no danger of frost*) in open.
  2 Outdoors, *in situ*, under cloches or jam jars late April/early May (won't germinate until soil temperature 10°C [50°F]). Harden off gradually. Remove covers when plants touch glass.
  3 Sow outdoors, cover with clear plastic film. Cut slits in film when leaves press against it. Gives earlier, heavier crop.
  4 In open, late May/early June (inadvisable north of Wash/Severn line).
Seed dressing valuable for outdoor sowings; sow 1cm (½in) deep, 7–10cm (3–4in) apart, thinning at 3–4 leaf stage.

Protect seedlings from slugs and birds.
When 30–45cm (3ft) high support stems by earthing up to about 15cm
(6in) depth. In exposed areas support with canes.
Keep weed free. Mulching in July advisable.

Harvesting
Ready July (early districts), August into autumn. Usually one or two
cobs per plant.
Pick when *just* ripe. Test when tassels on cobs well withered, dark
brown, by tearing back sheath and pressing seed with finger nail.
If 'watery' unripe; if 'milky' ripe; if 'doughy' over-ripe.
Cook immediately picked, boiling for 10 minutes at most.
(Ripe cobs deteriorate on plant, but keep in refrigerator up to a week.)

Cultivars
Aztec, Earlibelle, Kelvedon Kandy Cob, Kelvedon Sweetheart,
Northern Belle – early reliable F_1 hybrids.

TEXSEL GREENS (*Fig. 38*)

New leafy brassica that may catch on. Very nutritious. Grows fast – can
be ready within a month. Pleasant spinach/cabbage flavour. Good
cooked or raw. Available most of year; best value spring and autumn.
Useful where clubroot a problem: matures too fast to be affected.

Cultivation
Grow like turnips tops in fertile soil.
Sow under cover (frames, etc) February, and September for winter
crop.
Sow outdoors March to May, again in August.
Sow broadcast, or in rows 15cm (6in) apart, seeds 1cm ($\frac{1}{2}$in) apart.
Cut as seedling; or when 10–15cm (4–6in) high, or use whole plant like
spring greens.

VSR****

TOMATOES

Half-hardy fruit; success outdoors depends on summer weather.
Usually successful in south; cloche protection advisable in north, and
wet, exposed or cold areas.

Tall 'cordon' types require training up canes or strings; can grow 120–150cm (4–5ft) high.

Bush 'self-stopping' types sprawl on ground.

Growing methods

1 Heated greenhouses for earliest crops (ready May onwards).
2 Unheated greenhouses – (crops ready late June onwards).
   In greenhouses can be grown in borders, pots, boxes, bags or bottomless pots (ring culture).
3 Cold frames or cloches, using bush cultivars (crops July onwards).
4 Outside – in borders, pots, boxes or compost bags (crops early August to October).

Consult specialist books for tomato growing in greenhouses.

Outdoor tomatoes (Cordon types)

Soil/Site

Sunny site, sheltered from cold winds or draughts. In north and cold areas grow against wall or fence (not by hedge – too dry).

Well-drained fertile soil essential, limed if acid.

Preferably manured for previous crop, or apply general fertiliser 10 days before planting. Do not dig in fresh manure just before planting.

Plant as far from potatoes as possible; susceptible to potato blight.

Cultivation

Sow in gentle heat mid-March/early April (allow 8 weeks from sowing to planting).

Prick off at 3-leaf stage either 5 or 7cm (2 or 3in) apart into boxes, or singly into 5 or 7·5cm (2 or 3in) peat pots.

Or sow 2 or 3 seeds direct into pots or soil blocks, thinning to 1 seedling later.

Alternatively buy plants late May/early June. Choose short sturdy plants, preferably in individual pots rather than boxes.

Harden off carefully.

Plant in frames or cloches late April/early May.

Plant outside after danger of frost – usually late May/early June.

Plant when about 17–20cm (7–8in) high, first flowers showing.

Plant 45cm (1½ft) apart. Put in 1 or 1½m (4 or 5ft) cane for support.

Make sure roots and soil moist when planting. Can use black polythene film as mulch to suppress weeds and conserve moisture.

Protection from wind with cloches, polythene, beneficial (*Fig. 49c*).

As growth proceeds nip out sideshoots, basal growths, and tie main stem to cane (allowing for stem to thicken) (*Fig. 49a*).

Water in dry weather; mulching beneficial.

Late July/early August 'stop' plants by nipping out growing point, leaving 2 leaves above top truss (*Fig. 49b*). This generally restricts growth to 3 trusses (in north) or 4 or 5 trusses (in south).

In fertile soil additional feeding generally unnecessary.

However, if plants appear starved, give weekly feeding with tomato fertiliser after second truss set.

Remove withered yellow leaves; never pick off healthy leaves.

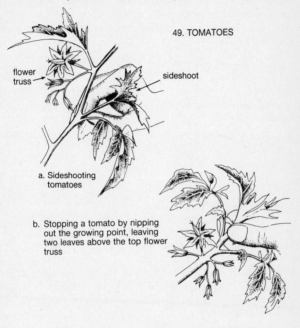

49. TOMATOES

flower truss

sideshoot

a. Sideshooting tomatoes

b. Stopping a tomato by nipping out the growing point, leaving two leaves above the top flower truss

c. Makeshift shelter to give outdoor tomatoes protection when too high for cloches

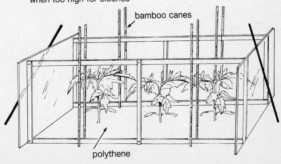

bamboo canes

polythene

In wet humid conditions and 'blight-prone' areas, spray against tomato blight with Bordeaux mixture or other suitable fungicide in late July and again in August.

Harvesting
Ripen off green fruits in late September either by cutting plants off cane on *dry* day, laying them on straw, wire or twig supports, and covering with cloches (protect against slugs); or wrapping or covering with paper and ripening in dark drawers indoors; or hanging whole plants in greenhouse or conservatory. Make green tomatoes into chutney.

Cultivation in pots outside
Where ground limited or soil poor tomatoes can be grown in 25cm (10in) pots or boxes, at least 30cm (1ft) deep, 30cm (1ft) square, using good potting compost, eg John Innes No. 3 (see Chapter 8 for growing in pots). Insert cane. If possible sink pots into soil or ashes to conserve moisture. Must be kept well watered. Feed weekly once second truss set. Add more compost when roots appear on soil surface. Compost-filled bags can also be used outside.

Bush tomatoes

Often ripen earlier than others.
Raise plants as above, plant out 30–45cm (1–1½ft) apart, according to cultivar.
No staking, sideshooting or stopping of growths required.
Put straw under plants in July to keep clean.
Dwarf bush cultivars excellent for cloche or frame cultivation.
Earlier, heavier crops can be obtained by planting through black plastic mulch, and covering plants with *perforated plastic film over low hoops* in the early stages. Slit the film open between the hoops in mid- June when flowers seen beneath, but don't remove it completely as it will give sides of plants some shelter. (Perforated film: see p. 114.)

Cultivars
Enormous choice. Those below suitable for outdoors, but can also be grown under cover. Similarly many 'indoor' cvs can be grown outdoors.
Cordon: Ailsa Craig, Alicante, Curabel, Gardener's Delight, Harbinger, Marmande, M.M. Super, Red Ensign, F_1 Ronaclave, Tigerella.
Bush: Amateur, F_1 Alfresco, Pipo, F_1 Pixie, F_1 Red Alert, F_1 Sleaford Abundance.
Dwarf: (for pots, windowsills) Florida Petit, Minibel, F_1 Pixie, F_1 Small Fry.

VSR**

TURNIPS

Brassica family, edible roots obtainable all year; turnip tops eaten as spring greens.

Soil/Site
Open site. Light, humus-rich soils best. Ground preferably manured for previous crop; limed if acid. Avoid dry ground; need moisture throughout growth or become woody.

Cultivation
Fast-growing crops useful for intercropping, make successional sowings from early February (under cloches) to August.
Prepare seed bed thoroughly. Firm ground, good tilth essential.
Most useful sowings:
1 March/April (February in mild areas) outdoors, for May/June turnips. Rows 23cm (9in) apart. Use early type, maturing in 6–9 weeks. Thin in stages to 10–15cm (4–6in) apart.
2 July/August for winter use. Rows 30cm (1ft) apart. Use better keeping, winter type. Thin to 25–30cm (10–12in) apart.
3 August to September (or even October) for turnip 'top' spring greens. Broadcast or sow in rows 7·5cm (3in) apart. Do not thin. Use winter type.

Turnips germinate rapidly. When grown for roots *start thinning very early*, when 2·5cm (1in) high, or good roots never develop.
Eat thinnings as greens.

Pests/Diseases
Flea beetle: on young seedlings.
Clubroot: yellow cultivars less susceptible.
For symptoms and remedies, see Pests – Cabbage.

Harvesting
Spring/summer turnips; best very small, 2·5–3·5cm (1–1½in) diameter.
Winter turnips: leave in soil all winter if soil well drained.
Can be protected with bracken or straw. Otherwise lift and store in clamps outside or in sand in dry shed.
Turnip tops: best eaten 10–15cm (4–6in) high. With frequent cutting they re-sprout several times. Small patch gives excellent returns in March/April when other greens scarce. Dig in when finished.

Cultivars
Early Snowball, Milan White, F_1 Tokyo Cross – early non-keeping.
Golden Ball, Manchester Market – for winter or spring use.

VSR***

Perennial Vegetables

A few perennial vegetables are covered here briefly. Globe artichokes and asparagus are undoubtedly luxuries in a small garden but, if space is short, are decorative enough to be grown in a flower bed. A small patch of sorrel is excellent value. Perennial broccoli and Good King Henry are worthwhile, old-fashioned stand-bys.

ARTICHOKE, Globe

Handsome plant with beautiful silver leaves; 60cm (2ft) high and 90cm (3ft) spread. Immature flower buds eaten as delicacy. Likes sunny well-drained site, fairly rich soil. Buy good quality plants, plant April in rows or groups of 3, 60cm (2ft) apart each way. Mulch every spring, water in dry weather, apply liquid feed in summer. Protect in winter with bracken. Season July to September; cut buds before scales start to open. Replace plants after three seasons by taking offsets in March.

ASPARAGUS

Lasts many years so grow in permanent bed. Soil must be well drained and completely free of perennial weeds. Work in plenty of organic matter beforehand. Either buy one-year-old crowns and plant 45–75cm (1½–2½ft) apart in April, or raise plants by sowing seed April in small pots or soil blocks and transplanting into permanent position in autumn. Plant crowns 7·5–9cm (3–4in) below surface. Do not cut spears for eating until plants are in third season, then cease cutting annually end June. Keep weed-free by hand weeding or mulching. Applications of general fertiliser 84g per sq m (3oz per sq yd) in spring, or foliar feed in summer beneficial. Cut down foliage to ground level when it turns yellow in autumn. Mulch with well-rotted manure or compost in autumn. Lucullus and F_1 Limbras excellent modern cvs.

GOOD KING HENRY (Mercury, or Poor man's asparagus)

Flourishes in good soil, tolerates poor soil and light shade. Sow outdoors April/May, or start indoors and transplant. Thin to 37cm (15in) apart. Leaves eaten like spinach in summer; flower buds in early spring. Cut back foliage in autumn, cover plants with straw to 'force' flower buds. Old plants can be divided to increase stock.

PERENNIAL BROCCOLI

Nine Star Perennial – type of cauliflower producing good white central head, surrounded by many smaller heads, every spring. Needs very fertile soil. Large plants: allow each 1sq m (1sq yd). Station sow 2 to 3 seeds *in situ* in spring (or transplant 2 to 3 seedlings per station), thinning eventually to strongest. Protect from rabbits in winter. Plants produce for several years if unused heads cut off before running to seed.

SORREL

Low growing, hardy perennial plant, delicious, sharp lemon flavour. Sow *in situ* or transplant, spring or autumn. Either treat as annual and thin to 10cm (4in) apart using whole plant, or grow as perennial, thin to 37cm (15in) apart, pick individual leaves. If cloched in autumn can be used almost all year round. Tolerates light shade and poor dry soil, but lusher in fertile, moist conditions. Cut off seedheads as they appear. Renew plants every three years or so. Use in salads, cook with spinach and chard, or make superb sorrel soup. French Broad Leaved very productive type.

Herbs

Only a few of the commonest culinary herbs are included here. Most of them can be raised from seed or cuttings, (*Fig. 50*) or plants can be bought from garden centres, herb farms, etc.

The evergreen herbs can be used fresh all the year; others can be dried for winter use. This is usually best done by hanging sprigs in an airy place away from direct heat or sun.

A few herbs can be frozen. Fresh sprigs of parsley, basil, marjoram and savory can be frozen in plastic bags; chives are better chopped first. Alternatively chopped herbs can be pressed into ice cube trays, covered with water, put in a refrigerator and transferred to a deep freeze after 24 hours. When required for use put the ice cube in a strainer, so the ice can melt and drain away, leaving the herbs ready for use.

BASIL

Half-hardy annual, 15–30cm (6–12in) high; likes well-drained soil, sunny position; killed by slightest touch of frost.

Cultivation
Sow indoors, preferably in warmth, mid-March onwards for summer crop. Sow again June/July; pot up for early winter crop indoors.
Thin or prick out when 2·5cm (1in) high (or sow direct into small pots or soil blocks or egg shells to avoid pricking out).
Plant outdoors late June, or after risk of frost, 15–20cm (6–8in) apart.
Grows best in frames or under cloches.
Keep watered in dry weather.
Nip off flowering shoots as they appear.
Gather for drying before flowering (but much flavour lost in drying).

If plants wanted indoors for fresh supply in winter, lift plants in September, cut back hard, pot up in rich soil and bring indoors. Keep on warm windowsill. They may last until Christmas. Keep soil moist.

Cultivars
Ordinary or sweet basil – up to 30cm (1ft) high; the form Dark Opal has pretty deep-purple crinkled foliage.

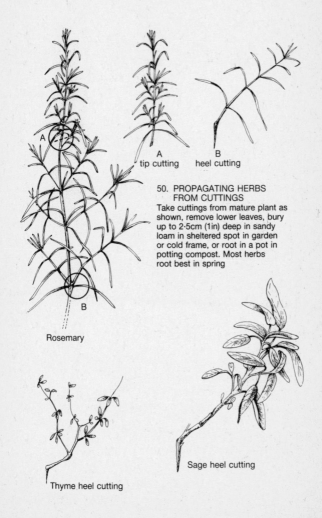

A
tip cutting

B
heel cutting

50. PROPAGATING HERBS
    FROM CUTTINGS
Take cuttings from mature plant as shown, remove lower leaves, bury up to 2·5cm (1in) deep in sandy loam in sheltered spot in garden or cold frame, or root in a pot in potting compost. Most herbs root best in spring

Rosemary

Thyme heel cutting

Sage heel cutting

Bush and Greek basil – smaller-leaved, dwarfer types, 15–20cm (6–8in) high; best for growing in pots or window boxes.

Use
For flavouring eggs, salads, fish, meat, tomato dishes, etc.
Slightly clove-like flavour brought out by cooking.

CHERVIL

Hardy annual or biennial; much the same height and size as parsley. Runs to seed fast in summer, but remains green all winter. Can grow outside in mild areas, but much more productive if grown under cover. Not fussy about soil. Grow in light shade in summer.

Cultivation
Sow February to April *in situ* for summer use; thin to 10cm (4in) apart. Sow August for winter use – outdoors, or in soil blocks to transplant under cover, or into pots for growing indoors. Keep moist.

Use
Delicate aniseed flavour. Use for chervil soup, or chopped, as parsley.

CHIVES

Perennial in onion family; about 23cm (9in) high.
Dies down in winter and reappears following February.
Ideal for edging vegetable or flower beds; very suitable for window boxes if kept moist. Grows in any good soil, in sun or partial shade.
Garlic or Chinese chives – taller type with very pretty white flowers, garlic flavour. Slow growing, so don't cut hard until second season.

Cultivation
Sow seed outside March or April; thin to 20–23cm (8–9in) apart.
Encourage fresh tender growth by cutting leaves back to within 5cm (2in) of ground several times during season.
Although flowers are pretty, best to nip out flower buds.
Keep chives reasonably moist; mulch with compost in summer.
Old clumps should be divided every two or three years and replanted in small clusters in spring or autumn.
Does not dry well.

Use
Very delicate flavour; used in salads, soups, sauces, egg dishes.

CORIANDER

Low growing, fairly hardy annual; looks like broad-leaved parsley.
Grows best in spring and autumn; runs to seed fairly fast in summer.
Prefers light soil. Make summer sowings in light shade. If growing for
leaf (rather than seed) use small seeded European type.

Cultivation
Make successive sowings for continuous supply.
Sow thinly February to June *in situ* outdoors. Sow broadcast, or in
rows 5cm (2in) apart, or in 10cm (4in) wide bands. No thinning is
necessary.
Sow September to October *in situ* in open for autumn/winter supply.
Cover with cloches in late autumn.
Or sow October under cover for winter/spring supply.
Can cut as seedlings, or at any stage up to 15cm (6in) high; often re-
sprouts after cutting. Or can pull up plants by roots and keep fresh in
water indoors.

Use
Distinct musty, curry flavour. Very popular in Indian dishes, chopped
on curries, etc. Can use in salads. Valuable in cold months.

MARJORAM – Sweet or Knotted marjoram

Perennial, but treated as half-hardy annual in Britain.
Makes neat clumps about 20cm (8in) high, 25cm (10in) across.
Likes warm sunny spot, fairly good, well-drained soil.

Cultivation
Sow under glass in March or April: plant out in May or June 15–23cm
(6–9in) apart.
Or sow outside in May and thin to about 23cm (9in) apart.
Keep weed-free.
Gather tops in July to dry for winter use.
Can be grown in window boxes.
Can be used as pot plant indoors in winter.

MARJORAM – Wild and Pot marjoram

Perennial kinds which remain green in winter.
Prefer warm position in light well-drained soil.
Pot marjoram has smaller leaves, more upright habit.
Wild marjoram is a native of chalk downs.

Cultivation

Sow outside in April or May, thinning eventually to about 30cm (1ft) apart.

To increase stock divide plants in spring; or break off a sprig with root attached, or take cuttings in spring.

Keep plants trimmed.

Give light protection such as bracken or cloches in winter.

Can be used in window boxes; trim back before planting in box.

Cultivars

Variegated 15cm (6in) high form of pot marjoram and golden 16cm (6in) form of wild marjoram – decorative and suitable for window boxes or flower borders. Dwarf, hardy *Marjoram compactum* remains green all winter.

Use

Leaves and flowers can be used in salads, vegetables, meat stuffings, etc. Sweet marjoram is allegedly best flavoured.

MINT

Hardy perennial; dies down in winter.
Vigorous growing, inclined to be rampant.

Cultivation

Plant in bottomless buckets, sinks, etc, or put pieces of slate into ground vertically to restrict growth.

Likes moist situations, rich heavyish soil, sun or partial shade.

Plant runners with roots about 23cm (9in) apart in spring.

Pick constantly to keep in check.

Best to renew clumps every 2 or 3 years. Either dig up in March and replant rooted runners about 23cm (9in) apart, or take cuttings of young shoots (pieces broken off stem and dropped into water will produce roots).

Gather leaves for drying before plants flower.

Cut down in autumn, clear debris, and mulch with compost.

A few roots can be boxed up in potting compost or soil in autumn and brought into cool greenhouse to get early growth.

Rust disease is sometimes serious with spearmint. Shoots become thickened, then rust coloured and useless. Difficult to eradicate.

Best to start again in different part of the garden.

Cultivars

Spearmint – most commonly grown. About 30–47cm (12–19in) high. Best kind for window boxes or pots if picked constantly.

Applemint, Bowles's Variety – downy leaves, greyish-green colour,
grows up to 90cm (3ft).
Best for sauces and jellies; less susceptible to rust than spearmint, but
susceptible to mildew in dry weather; variegated form – very attractive
in flower borders.
Variegated pineapple mint – pineapple flavour, very pretty golden and
green leaves, 60cm (2ft) high.
Variegated ginger mint – pretty green and gold colour; ginger flavour;
30–60cm (1–2ft) high.

Use
In sauces, mint jelly, drinks, flavouring peas, potatoes.

PARSLEY

Bright green biennial, 15–45cm (16–18in) high; dies down somewhat in
winter but stays green.
Likes reasonably rich soil, sunny or partially-shaded position.
Good edging; patches can be sown in flower beds.

Cultivation
Best treated as annual.
Sow outside in March for summer supply.
Sow in sheltered position outside June to August for winter and spring
supply.
Or sow in soil blocks and transplant under cover for more vigorous
supplies during winter and spring. Well worth doing.
Germination slow; water bottom of drill before sowing, and cover seed
with dry soil.
Sow thinly; if dry weather follows keep watered until seed germinates.
Thin early to 7·5cm (3in) apart and finally to 15cm (6in) apart.
Young seedlings can be transplanted.
In cold areas protect in winter with cloches or bracken (*Fig. 51*).
Cut back flowering shoots to prolong plant's useful life.

51. PROTECTING PARSLEY WITH BRACKEN
IN WINTER TO IMPROVE ITS QUALITY

wire

bracken

parsley

If allowed to go to seed a patch *may* perpetuate itself, saving you from sowing annually.
Grows in window boxes if soil reasonably good.
Plants can be potted up and brought indoors for winter.
Difficult to dry satisfactorily, but freezes well.

Cultivars
Curled types: Bravour, Curlina, Moss Curled, Paramount – dwarf; best for window boxes and low edgings.
Plain or French Parsley: hardier (therefore best to grow for winter) supposedly better flavoured, not crispy.

Use
Widely used for flavouring and garnishing; rich in vitamins.

ROSEMARY

Evergreen shrub, grows up to 2m (6ft) high, 90cm (3ft) spread, but can be kept small by constant picking. Likes sheltered, sunny site, dryish ordinary or sandy soil, limed if acid.

Cultivation
Sow warm position outdoors April; thin to 15cm (6in) apart before planting in final position.
Or take heel or tip cuttings May to August (*Fig. 50*).
Roots of established plants can be divided every 2 or 3 years to prevent 'legginess'.
To keep bushes small cut off strong growths, trim back young growths.
In cold areas protect during winter with bracken, sacking, etc.
Or trim plants back to 2/3 of size in August, pot up in light soil in September, move indoors for winter.
Shoots ready for use from second year.
Pick for drying in late August.
Small plants suitable for pots and window boxes.

Cultivars
Common rosemary; dwarf rosemary – about 45cm (1½ft) high; prostrate rosemary – 15–20cm (6–8in) high, tender, useful indoors.

Use
With many dishes, particularly lamb, pork, veal, prawns and tomato-based sauces. Strong flavour.

SAGE

Grey-leaved hardy perennial, about 45cm (1½ft) high; retains leaves all winter.
Prefers light dry soil, dry sunny position, but tolerates some shade.

Cultivation
Easily grown.
Sow seeds outside in spring; thin or transplant to 30cm (1ft) apart.
Keep plants stocky by cutting back almost to old wood in late summer.
Gather leaves for drying in August and September.
Old plants tend to get leggy and woody; best to replace every third year.
To do this divide plants in spring and autumn, or take 7·5cm (3in) cuttings of young growths with 'heel' of old wood from April to October (*Fig. 50*) or earth up plants in autumn or spring; pieces of stem will form roots which can be cut off and planted.
Can be grown in window boxes, but keep trimmed.

Cultivars
Common sage; dwarf sage – good for window boxes and small spaces.
Red or purple, golden and silver sages – pretty forms, about 45cm (1½ft) high, suitable for flower beds.

Use
Many culinary uses; best known for stuffings.

SAVORY, Summer

Pretty bushy annual, 15–30cm (6–12in) high.
Likes sunny position but not too dry, fairly good soil (not freshly manured).
Very suitable for rock garden if kept trimmed.

Cultivation
Sow seed outside from April to June, thin to 15cm (6in) apart.
Gather leaves for drying just before flowering; plants will sprout again.
Grows well in window boxes.
Can be potted up in August to grow indoors in winter.

Use
In stuffings, sausages, sauces (especially with beans), lentils, etc.

SAVORY, Winter

Neat compact perennial evergreen shrub, 30–37cm (12–15in) high.
Suitable for edges, rock gardens, window boxes.
Likes full sun and light well-drained chalky or gritty soil; hates to be
damp in winter.

Cultivation
Sow seed late spring or autumn; do not cover seed with soil.
Thin to about 15cm (6in) apart.
Or take cuttings of young growths with 'heel' of old wood in spring,
planting out when rooted in later summer (*Fig. 50*).
Or divide old plants in spring.
Can be potted up in August for winter use indoors.
Does not dry well.

Use
Sage-like flavour, milder than summer savory.
Many uses in stews, salads, bean dishes.

THYME

Perennial evergreen herbs, some creeping, others 15–23cm (6–9in)
high; fairly hardy.
Like well-drained sunny position, fairly rich or chalky soil.
Suitable for rock gardens, crevices in paving stones, edges, window
boxes.

Cultivation
Sow common thyme outside from March onwards; thin or transplant to
30cm (1ft) apart.
Plants best renewed every three or four years.
To do this divide old plants in spring and autumn.
Or take tip or heel cuttings in April or May (*Fig. 50*).
Or earth up plants in spring or autumn and later cut off and plant
rooted stems.
Leaves and stems can be dried; gather before and during flowering
period.
In late autumn trim back almost to previous year's growth, give light
dressing of compost.
In exposed places protect with straw or bracken in winter.
When grown in window boxes restrict roots by planting in a pot; keep
well watered.
Can be grown indoors in pots.

Cultivars

Common thyme (broad leaved or narrow leaved), best culinary thymes.

Lemon thyme – about 25cm (10in) high, lemon flavour, suitable for window boxes, troughs, pots, etc. Not very hardy so protect in winter; take cuttings in April or May or layer sideshoots.

Gold form of lemon thyme – 15cm (6in) high, very pretty, excellent ground cover plant.

Caraway thyme – *herba-barona* – very prostrate, pretty flowers which attract bees. Excellent in window boxes; grow from layered cuttings.

Silver thymes (Silver Posie or Silver Queen).

Use

In cooking fish, meat, soups, stews, vegetables.

Month by Month Guide to Principal Operations (See main text for details)

General Note

The term 'under cover' includes cloches, frames, low and walk-in polythene tunnels and unheated greenhouses. Dates given are 'average'. In cold districts make spring sowings and plantings slightly later and autumn sowings earlier. The reverse applies in milder districts. Perennial vegetables and most herbs are not included in this guide.

JANUARY

Sow under cover (mild areas only): broad beans, lettuce, peas, radish; salad crops, eg cress, salad rape, salad rocket, Sugar Loaf chicory, Texsel greens.
Plant: October-sown lettuce (under cover), garlic (on light soils).
Jobs: digging and manuring when soil not frozen.
Sort through stored crops; remove any rotting vegetables.
Hoe through crops under cover.
Blanche endive and chicory.
Pot up mint roots to force indoors.
Place seed order.

FEBRUARY

Sow in heat: celeriac, celery, leeks, onions.
Sow under cover: beetroot, broad beans, Brussels sprouts, summer and autumn cabbage, carrots, chop suey greens, leeks, lettuce, main crop and spring onions, radish, peas (south only), salad seedlings, eg cress, endive, cutting lettuce, mustard, salad rape, salad rocket, Sugar Loaf chicory, Texsel greens.

Sow outdoors in favourable conditions: broad beans, kohl rabi, onions, parsnip, peas, spinach (summer).
Plant: spring cabbage, garlic, onion sets, shallots.
Jobs: digging and manuring on light soils unless ground frozen.
Start preparing seed beds; apply general fertiliser two weeks before sowing if necessary.
Start chitting seed potatoes.
Blanch chicory and endive.
Lift parsnips and heel in if sprouting.
Thin overwintered onions.

MARCH

Sow in heat: celery, celeriac, peppers, tomatoes.
Sow under cover: dwarf beans (mid-March), beetroot, carrots, cauliflower (mini), celery, celeriac, endive, leeks, lettuce, salad seedlings (see February).
Sow in open: broad beans, sprouting broccoli, Brussels sprouts, summer, autumn and winter cabbage, calabrese, corn salad, chop suey greens, endive (curled), kale, most annual herbs, land cress, lettuce, spring and main crop onions, parsley, parsnip, peas, radish, shallots, spinach beet, summer spinach, sugar peas, turnips.
Plant: Jerusalem artichokes, garlic, perennial herbs, lettuce, autumn-sown onion seedlings, onion sets, early potatoes, shallots.
Prick out: tomatoes, and other seedlings germinated in heat.
Jobs: continue preparing ground for sowing.
Hoe through overwintered crops in open and under cloches.
Top dress spring cabbage and kale with general fertiliser if 'jaded'.
Lift, divide and replant chives and Welsh onions.
Lift and heel in remaining leeks, parsnips and celeriac.

APRIL

Sow in heat: courgettes, cucumbers, iceplant, purslane, New Zealand spinach, tomatoes.
Sow under cover: dwarf beans, celeriac, celery; *towards end month:* runner beans, cucumber, marrows, sweetcorn, tomatoes.
Sow in open: asparagus pea, beetroot, broad beans, Brussels sprouts, sprouting broccoli, autumn and winter cabbage, calabrese, carrots, cauliflower (mini), chicory (forcing), Chinese mustard, chop suey greens, corn salad, endive, Hamburg parsley, annual herbs, kohl rabi,

land cress, leeks, lettuce, mustard, main crop, spring and pickling onions, parsley, parsnip, peas, radish, salad rape, salad rocket, salsify, scorzonera, spinach beet, summer spinach, Texsel greens, turnip.

Prick out: celery, celeriac, peppers, tomatoes.

Plant: Brussels sprouts (sown under cloches), spring cabbage, lettuce, onion sets, potatoes.

Jobs: keep hoeing and weeding, especially among seedlings.

Remove old brassica stumps.

Earth up early potatoes.

Stake peas.

Prepare ground for tomatoes.

Watch out for flea beetle attacks in brassica seedlings.

Harden off seedlings started under glass.

Top dress greens (see March).

Start mulching if soil is warm.

MAY

Sow under cover: cucumber, marrows, sweetcorn.

Sow in open: broad, French and runner beans, beetroot, sprouting broccoli, summer, autumn and winter cabbage, calabrese, carrots, cauliflower (mini), chicories, claytonia, coriander, corn salad, endive, fennel, iceplant, kale, kohl rabi, land cress, lettuce, spring and pickling onions, Hamburg parsley, parsley, peas, purslane, radish, rocket, salsify, scorzonera, spinach beet, summer and New Zealand spinach, swede, Swiss chard, turnip.

Sow in open end May: cucumbers, marrows, sweetcorn.

Prick out or pot up: celery, celeriac, cucumbers, marrows, peppers, tomatoes.

Thin: beet, carrots, lettuce, parsnip, spinach, turnip.

Plant (when ready): Brussels sprouts, French and runner beans (raised under cover), summer, autumn and winter cabbage, celery, celeriac, leeks, lettuce.

Plant out under cloches initially: cucumbers, courgettes, sweetcorn, tomatoes.

Jobs: harden off seedlings under cloches, etc.

Protect seed bed against birds.

Watch out for blackfly, carrot fly, cabbage root fly, flea beetle, onion fly and take protective measures.

Keep hoeing and weeding; start mulching.

Earth up early potatoes; protect with soil if frost threatens.

Stake peas.

Start sideshooting tomatoes.
Mulch all established vegetables.

JUNE

Sow in open: dwarf beans, runner beans, beetroot, calabrese (for late crop), carrots, cauliflower (mini), all chicories, Chinese cabbage and celery mustard, chop suey greens, corn salad, courgettes, cucumber, endive, fennel, iceplant, kohl rabi, land cress (light shade), lettuce, Mizuna mustard, peas, purslane, radish, salad rocket, spinach beet, summer and New Zealand spinach, swede, sweetcorn, turnip.
Thin: beans, beetroot, carrots, lettuce, onion, parsnip, salsify, turnip, etc.
Plant: Brussels sprouts, sprouting broccoli, autumn, summer and winter cabbages, celery, celeriac, fennel, iceplant, kale, leeks, marrows, peppers, tomatoes, sweetcorn.
Jobs: pinch out broad bean tops.
Hoeing, weeding, mulching.
Stake and earth up brassicas when planted out.
Sideshoot, stake and tie tomatoes.
Watch out for pests as in May.

JULY

Sow mid/end July in seed boxes or soil blocks to transplant under cover, mainly for winter: chervil, red and Sugar Loaf chicory, hardy Chinese celery and leaf mustards, claytonia, corn salad, endive, fennel, land cress, lettuce, salad rocket, Swiss chard.
Sow in open: dwarf French beans (to cloche later), beetroot, spring cabbage (in north only), cabbage for spring greens (end July), carrots, chicory (non-forcing), Chinese cabbage, Chinese mustard, claytonia, endive (both types), kohl rabi, land cress (in shade), winter lettuce, spring onion, parsley, peas, radish, salad rape, salad rocket, spinach beet, winter spinach, turnips for storage.
Thin: beetroot, carrots, lettuce, swedes.
Plant: sprouting broccoli, Brussels sprouts, summer, autumn and winter cabbage, calabrese, kale, leeks.
Jobs: keep weeding, hoeing, mulching.
Tie, stake, sideshoot and 'stop' cordon tomatoes.
Tie climbing cucumbers, feed, water if dry, top dress roots with compost if necessary.

Water and feed celeriac, celery, cucumbers, leeks, marrows, runner beans where necessary.

Earth up and stake Brussels sprouts and other greens in exposed sites.

Pinch out runner bean tops when they reach the top of their supports.

Start harvesting shallots.

AUGUST

Sow in seed boxes, etc, to transplant under cover: as July, fennel (early August only).

Sow in open: spring cabbage (first two weeks in August), Chinese cabbage, Chinese mustard, chop suey greens, corn salad, land cress, winter lettuce, spring onions, Japanese and traditional overwintering onions, parsley, summer and winter radish, spinach beet, Swiss chard, winter spinach, Texsel greens, turnips (to eat small and for tops).

Sow to cover later: beetroot, carrots, endive, winter lettuce.

Thin: beetroot, carrot, Chinese cabbage, parsley, spinach, turnip, etc.

Plant: sprouting broccoli, winter cabbage, kale, leeks.

Jobs: 'stop' cordon tomatoes, feed if necessary, spray with Bordeaux mixture against blight in wet conditions.

Earth up and stake winter greens; watch out for caterpillars.

Water and feed as in July.

Harvest onions.

Gather herbs for drying.

SEPTEMBER

Sow under cover: Sugar Loaf chicory, hardy Chinese mustards, corn salad, salad seedlings, eg cress, claytonia, coriander, endive, cutting lettuce, mustard, salad rape, salad rocket, spinach, Texsel greens, winter radish.

Sow outside: spring cabbage, chop suey greens, corn salad, endive, kohl rabi, land cress, winter lettuce, and last sowings ordinary radish, winter spinach, turnips for tops.

Thin: outdoor winter radish, spinach, turnips for storing, etc.

Plant: spring cabbage, garlic, autumn onion sets, winter lettuce, and *under cover*: crops sown July/August for transplanting under cover.

Jobs: ensure greens earthed up, staked; watch out for caterpillars.

Finish harvesting onions.

Cut down tomatoes to ripen off indoors or under cloches.

Bring in storage marrows before frost.

Cut back spring sown parsley so new growth made for winter.

Trim back herbs required indoors for winter supplies.
Continue feeding celeriac and leeks.
Cover late sowings of dwarf beans, carrots, endive, lettuce, radish, salad crops, with cloches or low polythene tunnels in mid-September.

OCTOBER

Sow under cover: corn salad, winter lettuce, salad seedlings such as cress, salad rape, salad rocket, Texsel greens.
Sow outside: broad beans (late October), hardy peas (late October).
Plant: spring cabbage, garlic, autumn onion sets, winter lettuce, and *under cover:* endive, hardy Chinese mustards, and remaining salad plants from August sowing.
Thin: carrots, corn salad, winter lettuce, autumn sown onions, swedes.
Jobs: Lift and store carrots, beetroot end October.
Start blanching endive.
Cut down Jerusalem artichokes.
Earth up leeks.
Lift chicory for indoor forcing; cut back and earth up chicory for outdoor forcing.
Protect parsley and tender herbs from frost.
Clear away pea sticks, etc.
Start digging and manuring on heavy soil.
Mulch celeriac, parsnips, with straw.
Protect red chicories and other salad plants and Chinese mustards with cloches, low tunnels or straw to improve quality.

NOVEMBER AND DECEMBER

Sow: Broad beans, hardy peas.
Jobs: Digging and manuring on heavy soil.
Blanch chicory and endive.
Protect celeriac from frost with bracken.
Occasionally hoe through crops under cloches, and around over-wintering crops.
Check stored vegetables; remove any rotting ones.
Mark positions of overwintering root crops in case of snow.
Remove yellowing leaves from brassicas.
Thin or transplant protected overwintered lettuce to 5cm (2in) apart in November.
Lift and store late-sown beetroot, carrots, turnips, swedes.

APPENDIX II

Economy Tips

With a little ingenuity gardening can often be made cheaper. My thanks to the readers of *Garden News* for many of the ideas below, which were first published in *Garden News*, and to the editor for permission to reproduce them.

Sowing/propagation

For containers use:
2lit (½gal) plastic cans. Cut in half vertically to make two containers (one with handle), or horizontally to make one container and one funnel.
Plastic can be painted for attractive plant holders.
For other improvised containers see Chapter 4, p. 69.
For compost use sifted soil from deciduous woods.
For crocks use:
Polystyrene broken into lumps.
Foam rubber in pieces or sheets.
For labels use:
Ice cream wooden spoons; plastic pots, washing-up liquid containers, etc, cut into narrow strips; write with a chinagraph pencil.
Flat stones from beach placed on ground as row markers; write with Indian ink, or paint.
Write on plastic labels in pencil; erase with rubber or by scrubbing. Can re-use many times.
For sowing larger seeds or pricking out use large nails or metal skewers.
Use metal shoe horn for getting seedlings out of boxes.
To save compost when sowing few seeds only: crock container normally, half-fill with potting compost, finish off with seed compost. Sow seeds very thinly. They germinate in seed compost, and grow on into potting compost. Pricking out will be unnecessary.

Sifting soil for seed compost: use kitchen sieve, or replace bottom of baking tin with perforated zinc.

Seed sowing if you cannot stoop: drop seeds down plastic or metal tubing. Best for peas, beans, pelleted seed.

Heat frame or cold greenhouse with night light or small lamp under inverted flower pot.

If no greenhouse heating, heat cupboard indoors with 40 watt bulb.

Bring seeds and seedlings inside at night in early spring, when night temperatures drop sharply.

Tools

Paint tool handles bright colours so they are not mislaid in long grass.

Paint 10, 20, 30cm (4, 8, 12in) markings, etc, on rake handle for measuring.

Use colander for spreading fertilisers evenly.

Stuff old hot water bottle with foam rubber to make kneeling pad.

Burn bristles off old broom; the remaining flat head on the handle makes a useful tool for breaking clods and levelling a seed bed.

Make a sprayer from washing-up liquid container by sealing original small opening with hot poker, and piercing holes around the seal with sharp or heated pin.

Make holder for small tools, or for seeds such as beans, onion sets (to use while sowing) by cutting top corner (opposite handle) out of 2lit (½gal) plastic can.

Make a spade cleaner from an old spoon. Cut off the top half of the spoon 'bowl' with a hacksaw, flatten the remainder with a hammer. Very handy for cleaning sticky mud from the spade.

Compost containers

Make small quantities of garden compost in plastic bags with holes pierced in bottom and every 25cm (10in) around sides; alternatively use plastic laundry baskets. Use compost activators as containers are too small to generate much heat.

Wind/frost/bird protection

Protect plants from wind with plastic sheeting pegged to canes with clothes pegs.

Use old umbrellas to protect plants from frost. Cut off handles; anchor in soil with handle shaft.

Use nets in which oranges, nuts, etc, sold over seedlings to protect from birds; support them with twigs or wire.

Miscellaneous

Ripen tomatoes by standing on aluminium foil in sunlight; reflection hastens ripening.

Taking cuttings when space is short: wrap cuttings in sphagnum moss, tied securely with wool or raffia; or put cuttings into small pots in potting compost. Drop pot or moss bundle into plastic bag, put teaspoon of water in bag, secure at top, and hang in warm light place indoors.

Watering when on holiday: make wicks about 45–60cm (1½–2ft) long (or longer if necessary) either from glass fibre lagging or by twisting double wool together until the strand is about 1cm (½in) thick. Fill buckets with water, dangle wicks in buckets and trail other end into pots which require watering.

Dry off and harden old chrysanthemums, herbaceous plants and sunflower stalks to make stakes. They last several years.

Cut old nylon stockings or tights (cut in spiral starting from top) to make durable and non-chafing plant ties.

Hang onions, garlic, shallots, in old nylon stockings to store for winter. Can even store Winter White cabbages this way.

Cut plastic gloves into circular strips to use as elastic bands.

Seal pieces of polythene together (to make cloches, etc) by pressing under damp cloth with cool iron. Protect ironing board with old cloth.

APPENDIX III

Sources of Gardening Advice

The following offer free gardening advice on cultural problems, pest, disease and plant identification, etc, to readers and members. *Send stamped addressed envelope* and, where requested, reply coupons from the magazine. Pack specimens carefully (see below).

Gardening magazines

Amateur Gardening, Westover House, West Quay Road, Poole, Dorset BH15 1JG (2 coupons).

Garden News, Bushfield House, Orton Centre, Peterborough PE2 0UW.

Practical Gardening, Bushfield House, Orton Centre, Peterborough PE2 0UW.

Garden Answers, 38/42 Hampton Road, Teddington, Middlesex TW11 0JE. (Specialises in queries. Query Answering coupon in every issue. Free answer to questions published in magazine. Special prompt reply service £2·50.)

Organisations

Henry Doubleday Research Association, Centre for Organic Gardening, Ryton Court, Ryton-on-Dunsmore, Coventry, Warwickshire.

National Vegetable Society, c/o W. R. Hargreaves, 29 Revidge Road, Blackburn, Lancashire BB22 6JB.

National Vegetable Research Station, Liaison Officer, Wellesbourne, Warwick CV35 9EF (members and general public).

Royal Horticultural Society (RHS), RHS Garden, Wisley, Woking, Surrey GU23 6QB. (Members and general public. Soil pH tests members only.)

Public bodies

Gardening advice is sometimes available from local and municipal authorities and educational establishments in your area, either free of charge or for a fee.

County Councils Apply to Parks Department, or general secretary of the Allotments Assocation. A few authorities operate demonstration gardens. Contact your local authority to see what is available.

Agricultural colleges According to a 1947 Act they are bound to 'offer advice to domestic producers'. They will identify specimens if taken to them. Some local education authorities organise adult education classes on gardening.

Local garden clubs

Public libraries normally list those in the areas. Or contact the RHS (address above) for the nearest society affiliated to the RHS.

Soil analysis

Write to the RHS (address above) for current list of soil analysis services. Prices vary according to the depth of the service offered.

Biological control

Contact the RHS (address above) for current list of suppliers.

Sending specimens by post

Seal plants in dry polythene bags.
Wrap leaves and samples liable to rot in wood wool or damp newspaper. Put pests in matchboxes in polythene bags.

Note: This information is accurate at the time of publication, but addresses and prices change frequently, so it is advisable to check. Rising costs force most organisations to reply only if sent stamped, addressed envelopes.

Useful Books and Leaflets

Be Your Own Vegetable Doctor, Dr D. G. Hessayon. Pan Brittanica Industries, 1978

Collingridge Handbook of Greenhouse Gardening, A. J. Macself and Arthur Turner. Collingridge Books, 1982.

Collins Guide to the Pests, Diseases and Disorders of Garden Plants, Stefan Buczacki and Keith Harris. Collins, 1982.

Herb Growing, Claire Loewenfeld. Faber & Faber, 1964.

Know and Grow Vegetables, Vols 1 & 2, J. K. A. Bleasdale, P. J. Salter, and others from NVRS. Oxford University Press, 1979 and 1982.

The Allotment Gardener's Handbook, Alan Titchmarsh. Severn House, 1982.

The Contained Garden, Kenneth A. Beckett, David Carr, David Stevens. Windward, 1982.

The Observer Good Gardening Guide, Joy Larkcom, Arthur Hellyer, Peter Dodd. Webb & Bower, 1982.

The Salad Garden, Joy Larkcom. Frances Lincoln/Windward, 1984.

Worms Eat My Garbage: how to set up and maintain a worm composting system, Mary Appelhof. 1982 (available from HDRA).

Leaflets

NVRS series of practical guides to vegetable growing. Send sae to Liaison Officer, NVRS, Wellesbourne, Warwick CV35 9EF, for current list.

Wisley Handbooks (on wide range of subjects). Send sae to RHS Enterprises Ltd, RHS Garden, Wisley, Woking, Surrey GU23 6QB for list.

Organic gardening

Fertility Gardening, Lawrence D. Hills. HDRA.

Grow Your Own Fruit and Vegetables, Lawrence D. Hills. HDRA.
Raised Bed Gardening the Organic Way, Pauline M. Pears. HDRA.
Leaflets on organic gardening. Send sae to HDRA, Ryton Court, Ryton-on-Dunsmore, Coventry, Warwickshire, for current list.

Wild flowers

The Wild Flower Key, Francis Rose. Frederick Warne, 1981.
Wild Flowers of Britain, Roger Phillips. Pan Books, 1977.

Mail Order Seed Firms

Seeds can be bought from retail outlets such as garden centres, garden shops, supermarkets, DIY multiples, or from mail order seed firms. The last often offer a wider choice of cultivars, with the bonus of much useful information in their seed catalogues, which are almost invariably supplied free. The following mail order firms have a good selection of vegetable seed:

J. W. Boyce, 67 Station Road, Soham, Ely, Cambs CB7 5ED.
D. T. Brown, Station Road, Poulton-le-Fylde, Blackpool FY6 7HX.
Arthur Cole, 17 Victoria Place, Brightlingsea, Essex.
Samuel Dobie, Upper Dee Mills, Llangollen, Clwyd LL20 8SD.
S. E. Marshall, Regal Road, Wisbech, Cambs PE12 2RF.
Suttons Seeds, Hele Road, Torquay, Devon TQ2 7QJ.
Thompson & Morgan, London Road, Ipswich IP2 0BA.
Unwins Seeds, Histon, Cambridge, CB4 4LE.

Specialist suppliers

Chiltern Seeds, Bortree Stile, Ulverston, Cumbria LA12 7PB (oriental vegetables).
HDRA, Ryton Court, Ryton-on-Dunsmore, Coventry, Warwickshire (old 'heirloom' cultivars, salads).
W. Robinson, Sunnybank, Forton, Nr. Preston, Lancs PR3 0BSN (unusual tomatoes; cultivars for showing).
Suffolk Herbs, Sawyers Farm, Little Cornard, Sudbury, Suffolk CO10 0NY (herbs, salads, unusual and foreign vegetables).

Index

Page numbers in **bold** indicate main references